"Paul Maurer's *The Unforgi*... age story about hopes, dreams and the two-way give and take path of mentorship. Running is of course the central thread through the fabric of this endearing story of two men on opposite ends of the age spectrum and their evolving coach/athlete relationship. But the salient theme to me is the ironic nature of how mentors often learn, and mentees often teach. It's also simply a compelling and heart-warming story of a young man chasing his dream. From start to finish, you won't want to close the book. But if you must, it will provide you with something to which you'll be eagerly awaiting to return.

- Jack Fultz, 1976 Boston Marathon Champion

"Whether you are starting your career...or long past your glory days, *The Unforgiving Line* is a book for all runners. Paul Maurer is an author who shares his wisdom."

- Marty Liquori, Legendary Olympian; PR 3:52.2 one mile; 3:59.8 one mile (high school)

"Paul C. Maurer's powerful novel is about middle-distance running on the surface but is really about woundedness and resolve... Maurer clearly understands distance running at a deep, visceral level, and as a writer is able to convey why we run and what we hope to accomplish by running. Recommended reading for sure."

- Tim Tays, PhD, author of WANNA BE DISTANCE GOD

"THE UNFORGIVING LINE needs to be digested just as Parker's, ONCE A RUNNER, as it too will endure. Writing about the struggles each are going through and how their common interest of running a fast 1500 meters, moves the story right to the gun lap. A most enjoyable story, that will inspire many for years to come."

- Roy Pirrung, Ultra Hall of Fame runner and author of *heROYic!*

"Wow, heart rate raised and shaking from excitement. Loved it! One of the best fiction running books I have ever read! What a great story line. The book is on Amazon and now is a great time to read it."
- Reno Stirrat, sub-2:45 marathoner in five separate decades.

"Paul Maurer's "The Unforgiving Line" is more than a book about running and relationships. It is more than a story about a coach and one of his athletes. As a long-standing coach of young runners, I have often found it difficult to describe the complex nature of the synergy between athlete and mentor. Maurer has crafted a narrative that draws the reading in through the eyes, into the mind and then the heart. The Unforgiving Line is an excellent read."
- James Young, Brooks I.D. Coach at <u>Brooks Running</u>

"NEW to the track nerd's overflowing bookshelf...'The Unforgiving Line' is a fresh novel that captures the essence of our sport...it belongs on your reading list yesterday...so, whaddaya' waiting for. Seriously, a total track and field 'page turner'...you're gonna' dig it."

- Mike Fanelli, USA National Track Coach, founder Greater San Francisco Track Club

"Really enjoyed reading The Unforgiving Line. Beautifully written, fair play to you!"

- Shane Healy, Irish Olympian; PR 3:35.29 1500 meters, 3:53 one mile

"This is a great book about an old coach and a young and fast high school miler. Highly recommend for runners, coaches, and those that like a great story of struggle and triumph."

- Dave Montgomery, Head Coach, Highland High School Track and Cross Country

"Gotta love those spikes! On the surface the book is a very cool story about running, the joy, the power, the triumph of it all. But also the heartache it can also bring. If I had Oprah's money I'd buy 100 copies for you. You will enjoy this book even if you have never found the magic in running."

- Jim Blackburn, Catholic University of America Track and Field Hall of Fame

"Kudos on the Paul C Maurer book THE UNFORGIVING LINE! It's an excellent read for runners of all ages!"

- Sam Bair Jr., Running Legend, PR 3:58.7 one mile

"I became so tied to the characters in the book that at one point I was brought to tears. You can tell that the book was written by a runner who has experienced the pain of racing and the agony of defeat, but who also knows the history of the sport. A recommended read."
- Dave Ross, RossRunning

"The Unforgiving Line, by author Paul C Maurer, is one of your requisite tales of good over evil, love over hate and glory over failure. The story transcends running, therefore will be an interesting read for anyone, but is set heavily in the world of high school track and field."
- Christopher Kelsall, Athletics Illustrated

"A compelling story of a miler's journey, for those who have laced up their spikes and those who wonder what makes a runner tick."
- Jim Mosher, UCLA Track and Field, PR 4:16.8 one mile

"Just outstanding! I could not put it down. This book is highly recommended!"
- Keith Hanson, Inducted into Marquette University Hall of Fame; 1986 10,000 meter NCAA champion

"I hooked from the beginning of the story, I kept 'running' until the finish. Highly recommend if you are looking for a sports story for the inner athlete in yourself!"
- Kelly Johnson, Founder of Kelly Johnson Foundation

"I just finished and recommend highly! A great story line about two track runners, generations apart. While from vastly different backgrounds, share the same drive and Love of running and the freedom it brings. The last chapter had me riveted anticipating the outcome. Well done!"

- Shawn Whalen, Veteran runner; PR 2:32:04 marathon

"Within this timeless story, author, Paul Maurer, brings us along as if in-training for our own competitive season. If you've ever laced up a pair of running shoes with the desire to race your best, make sure you order this book, you'll love it."

- Brian Siddons, Veteran runner and author of *This Journey We Call Running - One Runner's Anthology*

"Excellent read and will in some form remind you of many of your experiences as a runner or coach."

- Russell Delap, Head Coach of Cross Country and Track & Field at Concordia University, Decorated Ultra-distance runner

"I could not recommend purchasing/reading this book more highly! Get your copy now, I promise you won't regret reading this wonderfully written novel!"

- Richard Dodd, PR Marathon 2:19:38; Wisconsin 50K record holder

Dedication

For Cecilia Peaschek-Maurer, my biggest fan.

May perpetual light shine upon you.

"It's raining? That doesn't matter. I am tired? That's besides the point. It's simply that I just have to."

Emil Zatopek

Chapter One

Overhead loomed a bloodshot moon. In beauty, there was darkness. Sacrifice required to create art. A price the gods demanded in granting greatness. In pursuit of excellence, he left pieces of his soul on countless roadways and oval tracks. And blood. Most often a combination of the two. He strove for excellence harder than anyone would ever know.

But he fell short.

He knew of pain. Of glory. Of searing lungs and burning legs both craved and avoided. One-hundred mile weeks that summoned cramps in the night and injuries that left him itching to return to the only two places in the world that made sense. The roads. The track. The two settings where he could fulfill his calling. Where he could perform that which seemed impossible. In those years, it was his time. A time to achieve when angel's wings carried him toward a destiny of his own making.

Once he had been on the cusp of greatness. He had made the Olympic trials and wanted more. Expected more. But life parceled out only what fate granted. He took a breath of night air and increased his pace. Now that only meant a crisp walk approaching a vague resemblance to running. He envisioned the days past. When he covered ground with a stride so light it barely kissed the earth. Back then he never realized he was living within a snapshot of youth. He assumed it would last forever and the days of grace would be eternal.

In that he was wrong. Instead his ultimate failure left a film of disenchantment never to be absolved. When his ability faded, both happiness and joy were strangled by that which got in the way: the weakness of his past.

His pace slowed. His invalid wife worried of the evening walks on the darkened lake road but he did as he did. It was a calling that would never end. Movement. Pushing forward. Doing what he could, until he could do it no more. He closed his eyes and took in the scent of the pine. Then he drifted. To a place a thousand times over he tried to hide from his psyche but failed each time.

That day. The day he pawed the track with his spikes. The day he stood with the best the nation had to offer. Jim Ryun. Marty Liquori. Others that had earned the right to represent the nation in the 1968 Olympics. He toed the ground from the fifth lane and stared ahead toward a destiny less than four minutes away. Fifteen-hundred meters. He had earned the right by becoming Baptist Union's first and last sub-four-minute miler. He stood erect and belied the turbulence in his head. Closing his eyes, he released hot breath and willed his heart to slow. Blowing out tension, he waited for the starting gun that would seal his future.

He bolted from the start and settled in behind the favorites. He was a relative unknown and few regarded him as even a dark horse. His recent graduation from Baptist was littered with school and conference records. Primarily an eight-hundred meter runner, he stretched to the mile when his strength improved. It was there he bloomed: conference champion and qualifier for small school nationals. He culminated his collegiate career with a personal best of four minutes and change. It was only the following year while at a dead-end job, he trained non-stop as an antidote for boredom. Self-coached, he begged into the summer circuit and surprised even himself by a fourth-place finish at a major invitational. It was there he latched onto the frontrunners and broke the coveted four- minute mark. He was then surprised again when he was afforded an invitation to compete in the biggest dance of them all – the Olympic trials.

He sought protection in the pack as the energy of the group carried him around the turn. Elbows and knees were the norm and he fought to stay upright. He knew barring catastrophe, Ryun and Liquori were shoe-ins for the Olympics, but third place was up for grabs. He had no right to expect the position but being on the track was all the enticement he needed. Dropping his arms, he relaxed as four laps of hell commenced.

Secure in the pack, he let the blanket of men do the work. He had reached peak fitness, achieving marks in practice that two years ago would have been unattainable. In that, he was confident he could stay with the group. The second lap turned into the third; then the third entered the fourth. As the pack strung out like a resistant coil, he was still in the mix. Remaining in proverbial striking distance, his lungs rasped and legs burned. But his mind was still intact. Engaged. Ready for the slow death that lie moments ahead. He could not beat Ryun and Liquori, their closing speed was beyond his abilities. But third place was all he needed to gain a coveted spot. That was something he believed he could achieve. The other contenders: Von Ruden. Bair. Divine. Patrick. Mason.

Wilbourn. They were fair game. He hung with them and readied for battle. He had steeled for that. He had prepared on the track. In winter blizzards. Through the thick summer heat. He was ready.

Then he felt it.

A slight tweak in his left hamstring. Not pain but discomfort. A foreign sensation at the worst of times. He maintained stride but his mind ramped. With that, so did his breathing. He soldiered on and the years leading to the moment flashed. Miles in the dead of night. Quarter mile repeats in the burning sun. Injuries. Recoveries. Thoughts intensified. In a heartbeat, doubt appeared like a giant headlight in his eyes. Anxiety heightening, he struggled to hang on to the pack. Fighting harder but running as if in quicksand, the battle seemed insurmountable. His breathing reached a crescendo and he feared he would not make it to the finish line. His brain fought to process the input as his legs ground ahead.

He strode on as if in a death march.

He rounded the last turn before the final straightaway. There like a thunderbolt, a stream of sunshine hit his face. His vision flickered. Then focus waned. Enough to cause a break in stride. Von Ruden was moving. Then Divine and Patrick. He tried to respond. But the resolve needed to maintain had weakened. It slowed. Yielded. The moment enveloped him and choked his breathing. Oxygen dwindled. He dizzied and slowed a fraction. Then more. Men ran into his legs and there were hands on his back. He stumbled.

He closed his eyes and stopped the night walk. Leaning forward, he blocked the memory of the race from consciousness. Unstable. Unsure. He nearly fell but placed his hands on his thighs. There he stood frozen.

"Dude! Seriously!" shouted a voice from behind. "Watch out."

He wobbled and fought to stabilize his stance. His lost moment abated and he regained footing on the country road. It was early nightfall and his ritual walk around the lake was nearly complete. But the immersion into the past left him shaken. He had never escaped the seconds that choked his soul. Happiness that others deemed a God-given right had been smothered. The shadowy figure strode past and left him in a lurch. He estimated the runner was at just under six-minute pace. Tall. Lean. A thin reed that covered ground as effortlessly as he once had. He estimated the boy to be a high-schooler for no other reason than he packed on the bare minimum of weight. It was then he admired the stride. Effortless. Graceful. With carved calves that even in the dying light glimmered in the distance.

The boy was a natural. He had been born to run and even if he had no idea of his talent, it was undeniable. He floated as if the ground was a mere inconvenience. The yards multiplied and in seconds he disappeared into the night.

He watched and remembered.

Chapter Two

He didn't sleep that night. The late run had done little to sooth his angst. Even running twice a day, an undefinable anger remained buried in his gut. Anger at a mother that deemed drugs were more important than her own flesh and blood. Anger at a system that placed him with a father he barely knew. They had never even married and ultimately failed to build a life together. As he was loath to discover, a one-night barroom fueled dalliance resulted in his existence. Lucky him. After that he was raised by a mother that worked sporadically as a medical assistant until she quit or moved on by request. He remembered his stomach aching in the night. Longing for food or the comfort of another. Watching a front door he feared would be opened by a stranger well before his mother returned from a graveyard shift. Or even worse, when she disappeared on a drug-induced bender leaving him to fend for himself.

Those were the times he feared the most. The unknown. The hopelessness. The inability to comprehend why he had been granted life. He would lie in a dirty bed and listen to the sounds of the night. Chicago was a hard town; the weak extinguished by predators.

It was then he decided he would be different. He would survive. In doing so he became granite. Impenetrable. Like a streetwise diamond existing hour by hour with no endgame in site. He woke up. Washed his brown face. Boiled an egg. Maybe three if there were enough. If his mother was there, he spent a few moments with her before she went to bed. If not, he simply endured.

Now he was mired in Weston, Wisconsin, with a father he barely knew. His mother had succumbed to her addiction and when authorities realized his plight, he was remanded to his blood relative. A father that was father in name only. They had sporadic contact over the years but now it was real.

He had packed his meager belongings and was now a member of the "up-north" community. A certified city boy transplanted to the northern woods.

He took off his running shoes and set them in the front hall. Despite his upbringing, he had his own style of innate fastidiousness. He placed the laces inside of the shoes as if readying for the next excursion. The shoes were hard to come by. Yet to obtain them, hours as the Sonic fry boy were well worth it. He had always liked to run. At first in the park when he chased butterflies fluttering in the breeze. Then to leading the middle school gym class in laps around the track. And finally, when he tentatively joined the track team as a freshman where he devoured internal demons one stride at a time.

"Lock the front door, boy," rang the gravelly voice from the modest front room. "It's mostly safe here but there are a few meth-heads around looking for quick money."

He complied and stepped toward the voice. The unkempt, bearded man was a semi-stranger, but regarding family, it was all he had. "I got it, Fred." Fred. He had never been asked to call him "Dad". And even if he was, he wasn't sure he could comply. He had never had a dad. Just a shadowy figure that ebbed and flowed in his life like a random storm passing through.

"So, you were running again?" the man asked.

He paused. Considered. Then stepped forward. "Yes."

Silence. Then a question. "Why?"

He knew why. Because it cleared sixteen years of shit from his head. A failed mother. An absent father. A future filled with ragged dreams. But he stayed silent for a moment and bottled his life once more. "Just because."

His father snorted. Then took a hard pull on his beer. "It's a weird-ass thing to do," he said. He examined the boy and scratched a two-day growth. "A job might help with the bills more than running. Just sayin'".

"I'll think about it," he replied. "Maybe once school starts."

Another glance. Then more beer. "There's some mail on the table from the high school. I haven't opened it yet. You better take a look."

He studied the table and the stack of unopened mail. Bills. Mailers. Advertisements. Hidden among them was correspondence controlling the next year of his life.

He nodded. Then blinked. He barely knew the man. A ghostly figure who appeared randomly with a birthday present and a twelve-pack of beer in hand. Now he was dependent on him for a roof over his head. Food in the refrigerator. The barest of essentials. He swallowed, knowing it was far from what he needed: a real father. Committed. Nurturing. Lending even a modicum of guidance to navigate an uncertain world. He accepted that which would never be.

He had been thrown into adulthood as a child: making dinner, cleaning, checking the door was locked. When his mother was home, if sleeping, he covered her. If she was not, he drew his blanket tighter. His early independence had a cost; it formed a hard steel-like shell around a taut exterior. Worse, it sealed a soul that no longer trusted. He had become a family of one.

He sorted through the mail. The school envelope was larger than the rest: *Attention: DuJaun Johnson.* He hated his name and had gone by "D.J." as long as he could remember. He believed it masked who he was, where he had come from. Like a dark cloak, it concealed an uncertain and unstable identity. He tore at the envelope and the contents tumbled on the table. The brochure caught his attention: "Weston High School. Welcome to your future!" The words were ignored. What drew him in was the happy, smiling students on the cover. Filled with bright eyes and radiant teeth. And white faces. As the offspring of a white father and black mother, his caramel-colored skin was inevitable. What was not was his precarious stance perched securely on life's fence: too dark to gain entrance into a white world, yet too light for the other. Now in northern Wisconsin, glances had already come his way. In the grocery store, the post office, even on the roads while running. The runs were the worst. The studied scrutiny from drivers had become the norm as much as the sweat dripping down his face.

It only caused him to run faster.

The start of school was less than a week away. The thought created a tremble down his spine. He had never been an achiever academically. He wasn't incapable, it was more he just didn't care. There was no point. His first year of high school had started well enough but as his home life disintegrated, so did his schoolwork. As spring commenced, his mother was gone more than not. With even less structure than normal, his scholastic effort weakened until there was barely a pulse. At the same time, he had joined the track team for no other reason than a gym teacher thought him gifted. Even a simple nudge and accreditation of talent was enough. He had run casually before and knew he was fast. Fast enough to open the eyes of observers in the know. In track he had ran the four hundred meters solely because he liked the quick, hard effort of the event. Beyond that, any extra distance was deemed unnecessary. He topped out at fifty-three seconds, which was enough to garner a victory against a local school. He crossed the line and breaking the thin filament with an outstretched chest was intoxicating. The feeling was both foreign and addicting at the same time.

He soon graduated to the eight-hundred meters. After two unsteady efforts, he surprised himself and his coaches by recording an unexpected two minutes and six seconds. That victory was immediately overshadowed when simply to fill a spot, he moved up to run the sixteen hundred meters. Instinctively following the leaders for three laps, he gunned the bell lap and won by three steps. He still recalled the stunned look on his coach's face as the loudspeaker announced his time: four minutes and twenty-eight seconds; at that point the top time in the conference. Two meets later, improving on that by three seconds, he was deemed odds-on favorite as conference champion.

That opportunity never happened.

When his grades plummeted, it was the last time he would compete. With academic suspension in tow, he was not allowed to lace up again. But that never stopped him from running. With lack of money for a bus pass, he took to running to school. Measuring nearly four miles, it was longer than he had performed in practice. At first, the coupling of the weight of his backpack and the distance was difficult. But as his body adapted, the effort eased. With a watch on his effort, he took each run as a race against himself. He smiled at best efforts and scowled at weaker performances. He learned new routes in the Chicago streets to add variety as well as more challenging landscapes. Uphills and downhills added stress to the effort but kept monotony at bay. More importantly, they forged a bond with running that was a need more than a simple diversion.

His life had turned in more ways than one.

Chapter Three

He couldn't stop thinking of the boy. His elegance. Grace. And utter dominance of the road. He rarely saw runners in the Northwoods because the pursuit was deemed frivolous. There were fields to tend, fish to catch and animals to kill. And if the skies darkened, maybe a trip to the local tap for a cold one. But running? That was reserved for suburbanites who had nothing better to do.

He wondered where the boy came from. Even more so, who he was. If he was just visiting, it was unlikely he would see him again. But if he was living nearby, he would undoubtedly cross paths on the road. At least he hoped that would be the case.

He fingered the coffee mug and contemplated the gray start of the day. He always arose before dawn no matter how late he stayed up the night before. He spent the evenings reading and listening to sounds of the past. Miles Davis. Charlie Parker. Coltrane. The jazz greats embedded in his soul. They soothed his mind and allowed him to ease into the night. Yet, even after eventually falling asleep, he rustled through the blackness never obtaining the depth desired. It was his dreams that contained a barbed edge in the darkness. The countless jabs into subconsciousness that woke him with a start.

That among other things.

"Thomas?" called the voice. "Are you awake?"

She knew he was. For years he had risen before her and today was no different. She had been declining the last five years of their marriage as her multiple sclerosis worsened. She was diagnosed early in their marriage and fearing the disease, they avoided becoming parents. Him, more than her. When the childbearing years dwindled, the thought of having children faded. They lived productive, albeit quiet lives. Together. Yet alone from both the joys and struggles that a nuclear family brings.

For that they both had a longing that was never fulfilled.

He answered the call. "Yes, Mona. I'm up. Can I get you anything?" He knew the answer before he even asked. Black Earl tea with a twist of lemon. It was their ritual. They both knew it, but the game was always the same. Somehow there was comfort and love in the banter that replayed a thousand times. So, it was again.

"Tea with lemon?" she questioned.

He had it going before she even finished her request. Minutes later, he brought the cup of steaming tea on a silver platter that he teased was fit for a queen. The fact it had been purchased at a neighborhood rummage sale was ignored. As always, it was again. "Tea, m'lady?" he offered with a simple bow.

She accepted with what he always viewed as a curtsey even though it was only a simple nod of her head. "Thank you, kind sir." With that, the day began. He sat in the chair next to the bed and sipped his coffee. He smiled at his wife and absently gazed out the window at the dipping pine trees. She watched him. Then as she had a thousand times before, read his mind. "Thomas," she asked, "what's happened?"

He stiffened. Her ability to sift through his veneer of nonchalance was uncanny. He didn't fight it as it was useless. He had been down this road too many times before. "I saw a boy." He paused, looked out the window, then looked toward her again. "Mona, I saw a memory. On the road. Running." He licked his lips and began. "Young. Free. With the world at his fingertips and greatness in the distance." He closed his eyes, then shook his head slowly. "I saw me from many years ago."

A breeze blew through the open window and the moment settled. She looked to him and smiled. "Tell me, Thomas."

He did. The encounter of the young runner's natural abilities was explained in detail. The movement described down to the last ripple of muscle and sinew flying past. He rambled and barely paused to breath as he described what he viewed as an unearthed work of art. Then breathless, he stopped. Looking toward his wife, he suddenly felt sheepish. Embarrassed. But that was squashed immediately.

"I assume you talked to him and got his name?" she asked.

He swallowed. Fingering his coffee cup, he shook his head. "I forgot to ask."

She sipped at her tea. "Perhaps next time," she said, "you will remember."

He smiled. "Yes, m'lady," he said.

***

He walked in the mid-afternoon. Twice a day rain or shine. Exercise had become the norm since the day he began to run and he never neglected the nearly genetic need for movement. Back then he ran. Most times twice a day. He had done so from seventeen until the time he closed the door on competition.

Still, in his mind he was young and able; fit, fierce, ready to take on all comers and conquer those who dared challenge him.

He laughed aloud. At himself. At his whimsy. But deeper his competitive core growled at the folly that was his current situation. He was old. Never to return to who he used to be. To success achieved on the turn of a dime.

But that was then, this was now.

He strode forward with walking stick in hand. Fingering the coarse grain, he stepped lightly on the faded asphalt. Back in his youth, a fifteen-mile day was average, now a fraction of that was all he could manage. The reality of the decline was both difficult and simple to accept. He was no god-like creation. Not immutable to the simple aging process of earthly creatures. Yet, he wished he could. Dreamed that he might.

In that, he would fail. Still, he strode on, absorbing the thick scent of the woods. He closed his eyes and dreamed. To when running was as easy as breathing. To when he floated like a feather in a buoyant wind. He opened his eyes and he was still there. Fifty years past, when every muscle in his body coiled and rippled. Like an animal built for movement, instincts took precedence when adrenaline summoned. Fight or flight. He believed in both. In fact, he relished them. The battle. The pain. The glory. Or gut-busting failure that left him shattered.

He would do it all again in a single heartbeat. Even less than that. He wished for a fleeting chance to be who he had been. To have one last chance to be on the track and compete with the best the country had to offer. To battle the demons clawing at his thin-soled track spikes. To confront a half-filled life and a heart sodden with regret.

He stepped faster in a vain attempt to outpace that which was impossible.

Chapter Four

He was as nervous as he had ever been. He could not subdue shaking hands and gripped the backpack harder. He had lived through days and nights in Chicago that fused his backbone and thickened his skin. But this was different. Riding on a yellow bus with nameless, faceless people, he was worse than a helpless fish lying on a dock. He was an animal in a zoo; a caramel-colored miscreant whose mere presence garnered looks from those that called the area home.

Home.

Such a simple word. That which meant apple pie and a warm bed at night. But to him it was a dream that never existed. He had been raised in the projects: the government-assisted dwelling providing only the bare necessity of needs. Heat. Power. Water. And the security of a locked door that did little to squelch dangerous sounds in the night.

Now he was in a house with a man he barely knew. He looked at the others on the bus. White. A kid or two that may have Latino or Hmong bloodline running through their veins. Even those looked at him warily. He was a definitive outsider. A piece that did not belong in this Northwoods Caucasian puzzle. His armpits dampened and he wished to be anywhere but where he was right now. He was immutably stuck and there was no way out.

He looked out the window at the cornfields swaying in the early morning light.

***

He had never been in a school like this. Clean. Scrubbed. Like a beacon on a sea, it welcomed its entrants. He was used to faded brick buildings with graffiti threatening ill intent. Now he was amid a bleached schoolhouse curiously lacking threat or harm. Despite its safeness, the hairs on the back of his neck stood in mute alert at the disconnect of the moment.

He made his way to his locker and spun the combination. In a thousand different ways, high school was difficult for all inhabitants. Yet his plate was fuller than most. He was new. From the city. Gangly, almost approaching beanpole proportions. And most decidedly black.

He scanned the hallway. The school was less populated than urban schools attended before. There the hustle and flow were nearly a rumble underfoot. Here, the energy was a thin stream of nervousness emanating like a radio wave through the hallway. He took a tentative step towards his homeroom with three books under his right arm. The silence of the hallways was deafening and blood pounded in his brain.

Like a darkened Dorothy, he was not in Kansas anymore.

Nor Illinois. Nor Chicago. Nor the few blocks that had been his home from as far back as he could remember. Now he was in a small Wisconsin farm town in which he had zero frame of reference. He was the newest curiosity in a place he undoubtedly did not belong. Yet, he had no choice in the matter unless he ran. Not on the roads as he did daily. But fleeing and returning to a city that provided a disquieting comfort. But to whom? To what? To live under a bridge or at best with an acquaintance that was no better off than himself? No, he had no choice but to stay.

He entered his homeroom and avoided looking at any classmates. He had a choice of seats and chose one in the back nearest to the windows. It was there he gazed at the woods beyond the school grounds. The branches swayed in the breeze and the serpentine dance mesmerized him. Called to him. Beckoned for him to join in their freedom. He listened, enraptured by the longing to escape. He was drawn to the branches as if calling him by name. *DuJuan. DuJuan.*

"Du-John Johnson," the voice called from the front.

He stiffened, startled at the proclamation.

"Du-John, are you here?" it sounded again.

"Yes," he replied in a voice softer than intended. "And it's DuJuan," he corrected, "But I go by D.J."

The teacher nodded. "That's fine, DuJuan, or D.J. if you prefer." The teacher rustled a paper and continued. "It appears you have transferred from Chicago." She paused. "That's a long way. How do you like it here so far?"

The eyes of the room were upon him. He saw them. Felt them. Blue. Brown. He tried to speak but the thickness in his throat took over. "Unnk" was all that came out. The class giggled and he reset. "I like it okay. So far." He retreated into his chair. If he could hide, he would. Instead, he did the next best thing.

He looked out the window into the distance.

***

19

The day was uneventful. Traveling from room to room. Listening. Not listening. There but not. When the final bell rang, his shoulders dropped and he made his way to his locker. He avoided eye contact and pretended. Pretended he didn't see them. Pretended they were not looking at him. Measuring him. And worst of all, judging him.

He closed the locker and slipped his backpack over his shoulders. His bus home was waiting but he made a different choice. He stepped through the back door and took a deep breath. He was still getting used to the scent. Of trees. Pine. Clean and pure. He had never known the odor before. He was used to the city. Burning diesel. Exhaust. Oil seeping into asphalt. It provided both comfort and distaste. Yet it was as much a part of him as was the color of his skin.

But that time was over. He was here. In a foreign place that might as well be Siberia. The sun hit his face and oozed into his pores. He always liked the heat. It was as if it melted the permanent discontent rooted in his marrow. The ache of a thousand restless nights. The pain of worrying about a fragmented mother. The absolute and unmistakable difficulty of life.

He hitched up his backpack and walked toward the road. Highway CC was less a highway than a rural road adorned with cornfields and a blaze of countless wildflowers and bull thistle. He stepped on the gravel lining the road and focused on the distance. He had no interest in the bus. What he needed now was freedom. Freedom to do as he needed.

Freedom to run.

He took a step that was more a stab at the gravel. Locking both thumbs around the straps, he secured the backpack.

Running with the weight was unwieldy but he didn't care. The movement erased the day from his head and with each step, his emotionally cluttered blackboard began to clear. He strode faster. Ignoring the stream of cars and school buses, his legs loosed upon the earth. As he gained momentum, the trek became natural. Real. Effortless. And he left himself. His breathing slowed, despite the exertion. It was like he was hovering over his human frame and looking down from above. It was these moments he rejoiced in his abilities. In the simple action of the doing. He ignored the chafe of the backpack and increased his pace. He was gliding over the new terrain and nothing could touch him. The sun was still high in the sky and he squinted overhead. It flashed like a guiding light and he followed its call. He had learned to estimate pace and with each step an unconscious inward count commenced. Seven-thirty. Seven. Six-thirty. Then nearing six. Given the weight he was toting, the effort was a fair test. He envisioned himself a warrior on the open plains. Running like a spirit in the wind, sweat ran down his face and thin rivers poured down his back. He didn't slow down. Wouldn't slow down. That was not in his DNA. He braced as a truck rumbled by and jostled him from his roadside perch.

He grimaced, shored his stride, and ran even faster.

Chapter Five

He woke before dawn. The darkness was both friend and enemy. It shielded the light of day that was identical to the one before. At least the darkness did not hold out promises of hope. That was in short supply these days. Rather, life had taken on a mundane routine that was stark and flat-line.

And so, it began again.

He filled the coffee filter with Maxwell House and waited for the brewing to begin. He had even beaten the paperboy's delivery and there was nothing to occupy his time. There was the television but that rarely interested him anymore. Left-wing talking heads filled with opinions that rubbed against his own. News that was filled with ugliness and violence. In that he was not a taker. He poured a cup and looked out the back window. There the woods covered his property as far as the eye could see. It gave him solace and calmed him. For good or bad, it gave him time to think. To the present and the daily needs of his beloved wife. To those he had loved and lost. Family. Pets. And to what he had done. To what he had failed to do.

He used to amaze his friends at the ability to wake early and go for a run. Even after late nights of countless pitchers of beer, he was compelled to hit the roads. The engrained routine of pulling on shorts and socks. Tightening laces. All was a part of the ritual that transfixed him like an addict awaiting his next high. He craved it. Needed it. Running was a part of him.

He gazed out the back window as a motion-activated spotlight lit his wooded yard. There a young deer meandered from the shadows and sniffed the air. Taking a tentative step, it approached the feeding station installed to nourish wildlife. His wife's bedroom window also garnered a view of the woods and she relished the panorama. Even in the quiet, he could hear her excited voice. *Thomas! Come see the family of deer. There's even a little Bambi today!* He wouldn't wake her today though. This moment was his.

The deer fed methodically. Chewing the grain, the animal enjoyed the feast. The deer's lean haunches twitched in the light and hinted at the explosion held within. He had always admired the aesthetics of natural athleticism; the God-given frame built for movement. His admiration had been admonished by his wife when he studied random lithe female runners. Her scowl at his attentiveness made him feel like a doorway pervert spying with bad intent. But that was far from the case. It was the grace and energy contained in the bodies that buoyed his attraction. The lightness of movement as poetic as a skilled gymnast on a beam. It was the same with the morning deer fidgeting in the early light.

It was only a crackle from the woods that spirited the animal into action. The deer leapt as if spurred and burst from the ground. The animal bound crosswise through the yard and flashed by the window. Each leap was magnified by the thin light and he was mesmerized by the action. He gripped his cup harder and admired the moment. The beauty. Grace.

Power. When the animal disappeared, his grip continued. He stared into the brush until his eyes burned.

***

He took the tray from his wife's lap. As had become the norm, she had eaten only a portion of her lunch. She smiled in appreciation of his act. He then alternated between avoiding and studying her being. She had been losing weight to where she was disappearing into herself. Most days she could still ambulate around the house but her capacity was declining. Simple chores were now filled with effort leading to an increasing necessity for rest afterward. Even her joy of preparing a home-cooked meal left her nearly reeling from the effort.

Today, cooking would not happen. Today was a day she would remain primarily in bed. In that, he would sit in the recliner tucked next to her. He was always impressed by her intellect and they would discuss anything and everything. Trained as a schoolteacher, she read voraciously and could devour a book within a day. In her current condition, he left the local library with an armful of bindings. Fiction. Non-fiction. Periodicals. It hardly mattered. In some respects, her forced inactivity separated their intelligences by her continuous gain in knowledge. She accused him of too often living in the past. He claimed he was a daydreamer. He viewed there was no harm in that. She argued otherwise and, in the end, the subject was viewed as a no-win for either.

It was not that she wouldn't try.

"Thomas," she said, softly, "I read the most interesting article yesterday. I think it might be right up your alley."

He braced, not sure where the conversation was headed. "Why is that, Mona?"

She looked at him with the bluest eyes he had ever known. Despite her physical decline, the energy within had yet to waver. She smiled and began. "It was about the limits of human endurance. The writer was discussing Alpine mountain climbers, bicyclists in the Tour de France and even a few runners."

That got his attention. "I'm listening."

"First they talked about a Greek runner."

"Oh great," he interjected, "the one who keeled over after running. Pheidippides."

She shook her head. "I've heard of him, but no. A man named Yiannis Kouros, he would run as far as one-thousand miles in a race. He claimed he could tell his body it was not tired and it would listen."

He laughed. "Nice trick if you can master it."

"And they talked about that guy you used to like. Emil-,"

"Zatopek."

"Yes. About when he ran three events in the Olympics."

"The 5000 and 10,000 meters and the marathon. Gold medals in all three."

She gave a distasteful glance. "So, you read the article too?"

"No, I'm sorry. He's just one of my all-time favorites. When I was a boy, I had a picture of him on the wall."

She nodded. "The gist of the article was the limitations we put on ourselves are primarily in the mind. That the greatest break the manacles applied internally. It is then that greater heights are reached." She let the information settle. "Do you agree?"

He looked to his wife. She was the smartest woman he ever knew. He recalled their first meeting. Her drinking coffee and reading the *New Yorker*. Him with a dog-eared copy of *Track & Field News*. He was embarrassed by the inequity of the two periodicals despite his appearance in the background of the magazine cover photo. A moment earlier he had been proud of the hint of his face in the pack well behind a frontrunning Jim Ryun. He rolled up the magazine as he summoned the courage to speak to the becoming woman.

"A new *New Yorker*. Anything interesting?" he asked.

She looked up. Bemused. He in turn felt pathetic. "Yes. A story on J.D. Salinger. Such an unusual life."

Salinger. He knew the name. For a past class he had even read a CliffsNotes version of *The Catcher in the Rye*. He doubted that would impress her. "Yes. A great writer," he replied, hoping that would be the end of the topic.

Fortunately, it was. From there they chatted. First of nothing. Then of each other. Then life. He was fascinated by her and her interests in the arts. He knew little of that. What he knew was sweat. Pain. Honing a lonely skill that few cared about and even fewer had the passion toward commitment. In time, he would reveal his quest toward greatness and she would in turn became his biggest fan. Even when education mandated they live separate lives, they never lost touch. Phone calls. Letters. Shared time when and where able. It was clear to both they were destined to be together until death do them part. He waylaid the thought as it was too painful to consider.

"Honey?" she asked. "Do you agree?"

He refocused. "Limitations. Those we place on ourselves."

She appeared puzzled. "Yes, that's what I said."

As a runner, he battled that very dilemma. The clock was always ticking. The distance always daunting. Mocking. Teasing. When competing, he blocked what he could and strove to remove any artificial limits on himself. To put no cap on speed. No restrictions on miles, except what his body could handle. Back then, most runners were self-coached. Post-college there were no endorsement deals to prop a meager lifestyle. Running before the dawn and after dusk were routine. Timing oneself on the track and then scribing the results into a simple notebook was the norm. It seemed like only yesterday.

"I tried not to, but did not always succeed," he began. "Runners have a peculiar pecking order in their head. Like those that have a faster time are endowed with a secret that grants them a god-like ability. That they are somehow special." He took a sip of coffee and went to a place far in the past. A lifetime ago. But somehow, also only moments. "I tried to avoid that trap but didn't always succeed."

"Free the mind and the body will follow, they say." She paused. "Sometimes."

It took him a few breaths before recognizing the irony of the statement. She was nearly bedridden with a declining body and yet she was as positive as ever. The sense of unfairness permanently set on her shoulders had long ago been abandoned. He felt sheepish when reflecting on past missteps on the oval as if they were anything of dire consequence.

"I used to tell myself I could do anything back then," he replied. "I tried to convince myself day after day. Almost like self-hypnosis at times. I came close. I believed I was invincible even in the face of the obvious."

She appeared confused. "Such as?"

He gave a sheepish smile. "Remember when we met?"

"Of course. You had your famous running magazine cover."

"Hardly famous on my part." He paused. "Even so I stared at that cover and knew every millimeter of what occurred before and after that four minutes of my life. I remember lining up with my calves twitching. The pounding of my heart until the starting gun fired and freed me to run. The ease of the first two laps until the race truly began. When the pain started to set in."

She smiled. "You said that was the race you led the greatest runner you ever raced against. That Jim man."

"Ryun." He reflected. "Yes. I passed him on the backstretch of the third lap. I don't know what got into me. Perhaps it was just impulse. Or a belief that I could run away from anyone." He closed his eyes and went back to the moment. "It was beautiful. I was running without touching the earth. A moment as pure as a ray of sunshine on a summer day. I held the lead through the turn and even to when the bell sounded for the last lap." He stopped.

She urged him on. "Tell me the rest, Thomas."

And he did. "Ryun's breath was on my neck. He wasn't that close, of course. But I was being pursued. I was being hunted by a force I could never conquer." He licked his lips and bit down. "We hit the turn with three-hundred yards to go and he exploded. Flew by me like I was on a backyard stroll. I tried to respond but it was hopeless. Not just for me, but all the field. I ran as hard as I could but he disappeared into the distance. I watched him run and for the first time, I wished I was another. Him. A body built from tendon and steel that I would never know." He blinked and looked toward his wife. "It still seems like yesterday."

A smile lit her face. A sweet smile that understood. "You did your best and for that you should be proud."

He was. He had gotten crushed but so had the field. When he crossed the finish line far in arrears, he fell to his knees as the oxygen debt demanded recompense. The crowd cheered Ryun as they hailed the champion. Internally, he did the same. He finally stood and walked with an unsteady gait. Ryun, the graceful champion patted him and the other beaten competitors on their shoulders before taking his victory lap.

"He was a great champion," he said. "Among the best ever."

She reached a hand and beckoned for his touch. "As were you, Thomas," she said. "To those of us in the know."

He held her hand and looked to the only woman he had ever loved.

And in that moment, he loved her even more.

Chapter Six

School had never been a focus in his life. Rather, it was simply a destination to fill the void of hours. He muddled through the mechanics of learning. Algebra. English. History. The basics that the educational establishment deemed essential for his future well-being. He was not as convinced. He was drifting. Rudderless. As a sophomore he was supposed to have an idea as to his future. In one sense he did. He was aiming to survive. To not be swallowed by a world that never gave him a moment's thought. Despite his mother's occasional good intentions, he had always been alone. Now, in the Northwoods, it was the same as it ever was.

He was in the fight by himself.

His father was a shadow that appeared sporadically like a flicker of moonlight. There, then gone again. He drove a truck and was called far and wide to perform his duties. That left the boy to his own devices. To do as he needed. Or wanted. To let his mind wander to places undeniably dark and ugly.

It was those times he was called to the roads.

He laced up his running shoes and stepped out the front door. He was still an absolute outsider in the community but by learning the terrain, he began a kinship with the land itself. He absorbed the overwhelming sensation of being a tiny microbe in an unknown arena. He was deemed irrelevant but in some ways that was the best situation. He would rather be in the background. The border of the picture, rather than front and center. That was easier. People left you alone there.

So did life.

He started into a slow jog and let his body accustom to the effort. It didn't take long before he approached the six-minute mile pace that had become effortless. Striding freely, he covered the lake road as easily as taking a simple breath. Searching for new paths, he slowed as he approached a sign calling out the "Ice Age Trail". Veering right, he head toward a partially trimmed pathway appealing to only the hardiest of local inhabitants.

He was immediately in awe. Having been raised in the city, he was accustomed to brick and mortar. Cement and asphalt. He instantly reveled as if he was a male Alice dropped down the rabbit hole. The trail opened and revealed a pine needle base softer than a pair of slippers. Until now, the bulk of his running had been on pavement as unforgiving as an anvil. This moment was one of wonder approaching joy.

He was free. He was alive. And he was utterly alone. His pace approached the threshold he found comforting. To the place where his heart hammered in his chest, but his legs drifted in a world of their own. Out of body, his mind relaxed and soaked in the moment. Uphill, downhill, it didn't matter. He coasted. Drifted. He ran as if the ground was greased and his feet were simply implements propelling him toward his destination. Climbing a steep hill cut from an ancient glacier, he welcomed the challenge. It was as steep as any in the area and was nearly a quarter mile long. The descent was difficult and he braked to absorb the impact. His quadricep's trembled at the effort and his previously smooth stride eroded into an ungainly effort to maintain the current pace. He gasped at the impediment dead ahead. A man. The same man he had seen on the road days earlier. "Sheeeeettt!" he called as he spun and evaded him. "What the…?"

The old man did the same and twisted a walking stick in his hand. "Jesus Christ Almighty!" he said as he avoided contact.

Both parties stabilized and gained footing. Catching their breaths, they stared each other down.

The old man started first. "You need to lean with the hill. You are fighting the terrain, not using it."

The boy's breathing slowed. He wiped a bead of sweat from his forehead and studied the man. Gray haired, wire-thin with lines creasing his face, the stooped posture gave a tell-tale sign of age. But it was the intensity of the blue eyes that drew the boy's attention. Deep. Penetrating. Probing.

"I don't know what you mean," he finally said.

"You run beautifully. But when you run downhill, you must lean forward and let gravity help. Try to be at almost ninety degrees with the earth. Perpendicular. Frank Shorter was the best I ever saw at it but…" He caught himself. "It is simply the most efficient way."

He nearly laughed at the old codger. But the matter-of-fact demeanor stopped him. "So you are some kind of expert?" he asked. He smirked and nodded toward the cane.

The movement was ignored. "I have experience," was all he said.

"Experience?"

"I ran some back in the day. Way before you were born."

"I would guess that. So now you just give advice to strangers in the woods?" He wasn't worried the man might not like the comment. When he ran, he had a fire inside. Defiance. Anger. A fury used like fuel to propel performance.

The old man spoke. "I see you running day after day. I assume if you spend that much time doing it, one would like to get better." He grasped the walking stick harder. "Am I not right?"

The boy blinked back the sweat in his eyes. The old man was right. But he was not prone to agree with anyone. Not his dad. His teachers. Classmates. And especially some broken-down man in the woods.

"Maybe," was the best he could muster.

"'Maybe' is not an answer. You either want to get better or you do not. Which is it?"

The boy was riveted to the ground. Part of him wanted to move on. To be done with this. But another part was captivated. "I want to get better."

The old man smiled. "Now that is an answer. And it is the right one." He smiled. The gesture lightened the moment and allowed him to extend his right hand. "Thomas McKinley. But most people call me 'Mac'," he said. Out of reflex, the boy softly took the hand. "Lesson number two. When you shake a hand, you grasp it firmly. To let them know you are a man of substance. One to be reckoned with."

Instinctively, he did so. "I didn't know I was getting lessons. Those I don't need."

The attitude had returned. As had the anger. He let the hand go. "I assume you have a name?"

The boy considered remaining anonymous and moving on. Then answered. "Most people call me D.J."

"D.J.," he repeated. "Nice to meet you."

He grunted. "Same."

"I take it you run every day. I see you on the lake road near my house."

"I do. I just moved here. I live with Fred. My…my dad." The word hung on his tongue and tasted foreign. He spit toward the ground and continued. "I go to Weston High School up the road."

"Where did you move from?"

"Chicago." The fact made him proud. Like he was tougher for having come from the city. That he would forever be separated from his counterparts that lived in the sticks.

Mac nodded. "Do you run for the school? Cross country right now, I would guess."

He shook his head. "No. Too busy getting used to this place. I run track. Cross country is for tweaks."

"Tweaks?" he repeated. "I assume that is not a good thing. I also understand that is your choice. But cross country gets one stronger for the track season. And for runners, strength of body only steels the mind." He paused. "What event do you run?"

"The sixteen hundred meters."

He looked amused. "The bastard stepchild of the mile. I forgot they changed it years ago."

The boy nearly laughed aloud. *Who was this old man?* he thought. It was time to move on.

Mac beat him to it. "I walk this hill but most days I do the lake road. Maybe I'll see you here again." With that he propelled the stick forward and moved away from the boy.

Then he called back. "D.J., remember stay perpendicular on the downhills. Your quadriceps will thank you for it."

D.J. watched the man amble away. When he began a slow trot, his thighs trembled at the effort.

***

He returned home to an empty house. His father routinely worked twelve-hour shifts with longer layovers on overnight routes. That he didn't mind. He had grown up alone and was accustomed. He had learned to survive. He would do that again if that is what it came down to. He didn't need anyone.

He had himself.

He linked up his phone to his prize possession: a Bluetooth speaker designated to amplify music. Turning the volume to the level just before distortion, the desired bassline of rap filled the air. He liked rap. Hip-hop. Anything that told the story of life from a dirty, street-level view. To that he could relate. His was not a storyline that touted happiness and contentment. His was of abandonment and confusion. And fear. Fear of the unknown. Fear of lack of control. Fear of never knowing anything about who he was. Or who he would become.

The thump of the beat soothed him. It blocked thoughts from his head and swaddled him in a streetwise blanket. His father hated the music and when home, he was forced to listen through a cheap set of earbuds. But today he embraced the freedom and let the music drive the moment. He sat on the threadbare carpeting and began a series of post-run stretches. Hamstrings. Achilles. Quadriceps. Hip flexors. He did what he had been taught by a disinterested party. His high school coaching had been weak at best. Most attention was given to the sprinters and jumpers. In a city school, distance runners were merely an afterthought. The hurdles coach doubled at distance and often sent the runners on a loop taking the better part of an hour. When it was time for track work, the small group of ten often policed themselves in a series of four-hundred meter loops. It was there he excelled. Once he hardened himself to the grind, he could hit a sixty second lap with ease. Pain accompanied the effort. But to that he paid no mind.

In fact, he relished it.

Pain was part of running. Pain was part of life. But when the physical happened, it negated the other. In that, running became a salve for inflicted wounds. Yet, he felt alone even then. On the track. On the roads. He was solitary without guidance. He did what he could despite the ubiquitous disconnection. Maybe someday he would have a coach. A mentor to guide him. An experienced hand.

Like the old man. Mac. He didn't know what to make of the encounter in the woods. It was strange, yet there was something about his presence. A calming nature. Knowledge. A figure to lead him from the chaos that had become life.

With the music pounding in the background, he reached toward a small coffee table for his wallet. Settling back into the couch, he opened it and retrieved a dog-eared picture. It was of his second birthday party, blowing out the candles on his cake. Surrounding him on both sides was a young version of his mother and father. His father with dark, shoulder length hair and thick sideburns; his mother with a short mass of Jheri curls framing a smiling face. He could not remember the moment but imagined he did. The taste of chocolate cake. The smell of extinguished candles. The feel of his parent's hands as they touched the back of his neck. And the aura of love that existed within the snapshot. As the music pounded, he went back in time. To when he was young. Then younger. To flashes of memory that remained like shards of broken glass; none of which could be reassembled but all leaving a trace of blood in their wake. He wanted to remember. Needed to remember. Yet couldn't.

He turned the music louder.

***

"What the hell? Turn that crap down!"

He jumped from the couch and reached toward the coffee table. Fumbling for his phone, he quickly shut down the music. The silence was immediate but the bassline still hung in the air. "Sorry. I fell asleep."

"How can you sleep with that shit on? It's nothing but noise."

He didn't bother to reply. They had been down the same dead-end road before. He chose another tactic. "So you had a good trip?"

"Yes. Wonderful." He slumped into the far corner of the couch.

"But I'm tired as hell and need to get some sleep. I have to go again in ten hours. Freakin' work," he said. He lay back and his hand gravitated toward the ancient picture that lay on the edge of the table. "I'll be damned. Where did you get this?"

His face warmed. "I keep it in my wallet. Just…just because."

His father studied it harder. "I remember that little place. An apartment in the city. I had just started in construction. Your mom was back in school. Christ, look at us. And look at you."

He craved more. "I can't remember much."

"You were so hyper. We would go to the park and you ran back and forth until you were nearly exhausted. You climbed the slide so much I thought your legs would fall off." He fingered the photo again. "That was a good time."

He was afraid of what he wanted to ask. But after swallowing, he did. "What happened, Fred?"

"What happened," he repeated. "Good question." He set the photo down and crossed his arms. Then he closed his eyes. "Sometimes I'm not sure. I was making okay money and we had enough for a while. But I got laid off and we had trouble with the bills. Then we couldn't afford your mom's school, so she dropped out."

"I never heard of her going to school. For what?"

"She wanted to be a nurse. Always did."

"I…I never heard that. Ever."

He shrugged. "She did. She was smart too. She could have made it."

"So why didn't she? Did she just give up?"

"Yes. No. There was no money and we had to take care of you. Pretty soon it all went to hell."

That he remembered. The loud voices. The shouting matches. The potential for violence hidden around every corner. It was as if he was still there.

"It didn't take long and it was over. She met some guy into drugs and she fell in. I bitched at her but that didn't help." He sat up straighter and looked out the window. "But it wasn't all her fault. I wasn't much better. Whatever I had, I drank up. One of us was usually around for you but it all fell apart."

"I remember you leaving. It was a summer day. I stood by the door and you waved. Said you had to go. I remember."

The man rubbed his eyes and stared straight ahead. Then slumped deeper into the couch. "A friend had a job for me up here and I took it. I gave your mom what money I had and decided it was time to start over. Maybe it was a shit thing to do, but I did it. I can say I'm sorry but that doesn't mean anything now."

He was at a loss. Like waves crashing, his brain was bombarded from all directions. He stayed quiet for a moment and studied the man. He was graying and had a paunch that would never again disappear. Only in his early forties, he appeared well beyond that. A scruffy beard covered his face and the unkempt appearance only added to the illusion. Although he was his dad, he was still just a man. A person who hoped for happiness just like anyone else but had fallen woefully short. Because of his anger, he had never seen him that way. Rather, he blamed him. Blamed him for his own predicament of feeling like an orphan despite possessing breathing blood parents. He softened.

"Fred," he said, "I know you tried. I...I..."

The snore from the couch stopped him short.

He watched the rise and fall of his chest. He listened to the echo of the snore as it filled the small home. He thought of waking him but decided against it. Instead he secured the earbuds and turned the volume to a level that drowned the thoughts in his head.

Chapter Seven

The day was thick and ugly. Mona was not well and her condition was declining. Even with the small air conditioner cooling her room, the stifling heat and humidity of the day exacerbated her multiple sclerosis. He had done all he could: providing cold drinks and laying cool cloths on her forehead. It was days like this she needed space; time to rest and manage the overpowering discomfort. The ranch home was small and when she struggled, he bordered on being overbearing. He couldn't help it, he told her. He just wanted to do something.

"You can help by letting me be. Go outside. Go walk. Anything!"

He did as he was told. Making his way down the road, he swatted at the accompanying horseflies. The heat had drawn them out and hatched any late bloomers. Their annoyance was one of many within the Northwoods but he ignored them as best he could. He knew there were far worse things than insects. Front and center was losing his loved one. Next was losing one's direction. He calculated he had ten, maybe fifteen good years left. His discontent was he had no idea where he fit. Of what he could achieve. Or how he could garner any sense of relevance. He longed to compete again in something. Anything. But as to what that might be, he had no clue.

What he did know was that he needed a drink. He wasn't a heavy drinker as were many in the area. The monotonous routine of the north often called for barstool relief. For that there was always a local watering hole. Each lake had their own tavern and his was no different. The Thirsty Beaver had been there for decades and had seen numerous owners come and go. The latest was a retired postal worker who thought a tavern would fill time while providing supplementary income. Like those before him, he soon found out the road to money was paved with only consternation and bills.

He pushed the door open and entered. It was late morning, so he had the place to himself. A ubiquitous fishing show was playing on the overhead TV screen and the cliché quickly bored him. He sidled up to the rail and slipped onto a cracked, red leather seat. Sliding forward, he raised a finger in acknowledgment.

"Morning, Tony. Just a tap," he said.

A head nod followed. Tony was a good soul, a natural bartender who listened to the ramble of clientele before offering opinion. Stocky, balding and harboring a perpetual five o'clock shadow, as was habit he rubbed his belly. He smiled and followed with a greeting. "Sure thing, Mac. Nice to see you again."

Mac returned the nod. "Yup." And that was it. He had no revelation to expound. Life was as it was. Daily minutia followed by details. He wanted, needed more than that but in his current existence, it was all he had.

"Is Mona okay?"

He sipped the beer slid in front of him. Savoring the taste, he responded in time. "Fair. She does the best she can." He took another draw. "Not as good today, though. We both need some space," he said with a shrug.

Another nod. "Well, you are always welcome here," he said. "And someday if the Missus feels up to it, we'd love to see her."

The thought caught him off guard. Mona. His lifelong love. There had been a time she would have been right there next to him. Sipping at a gin and tonic and illuminating him on topics beyond his horizon. But that time had passed. She was a shell of herself physically and that curtailed her ability to join him at the bar. For that he was sorry. But in guilty self-reflection, it also freed him to be who he was: a loner who stagnated on the past and daydreamed of a future that would never occur.

"Thanks, Tony. I'll let her know."

He nodded and set a basket of pretzels on the bar. In anticipation, he drew a replacement beer into an icy mug and set the drink behind the snack. Begging off, he explained. "The beer guy is out back and I have to meet him. Feel free to use the remote and put on anything you want. I'll be back soon."

Tony ambled away in silence and he had the place to himself. Downing a pretzel, it was followed by a deep swallow of cold beer. He fingered the remote perched on the bar. Fishing held little interest to him. One by one he scanned the channels and grimaced at the selection. Cooking. Ill-tempered divas. Talk shows offering unwanted advice on an ugly political season.

He soldiered on.

He reached sports and that gained his attention. Talking heads and taped football was of no interest. It was only when he reached a random channel, he stopped his search. A track meet. European. An international competition held somewhere in Belgium. At a track he had performed at years ago. Back then it was old school. Cinders. He could hear the noise. Feel the energy of the crowd. In his only foray into the old continent, he would never forget the magnitude. The pomp and circumstance of the brief expedition overseas. He was at best a hanger-on of the top tier. But as the meet promoter warned, warm bodies were needed for sacrifice. His. Given his modicum of success, he was offered a chance to feed his young meat to the lions of the day.

After being granted free plane tickets and housing, he hardly balked at the difficulties of competing in a foreign land. Four events were promised and this was the last. He had struggled to maintain contact with the top echelon in any of the prior three events and was thoroughly humbled. Experiencing borderline exhaustion and recognizing his limitations, he had not even run the past two days. Even with that, he mentally prepared at a starting line he would never see again.

The gun sounded and he vaulted from the line. The butterflies in his stomach dissolved and he fell into his normal position toward the rear of the pack. Surprisingly, for the first time since his journey overseas, he had a spring in his legs. The feeling was comforting and instead of desperately hanging on, he focused on the runners ahead. The New Zealanders, Polhill and Dixon, all in black, were a given, but it was the runner at the front garnering all the attention. Kip Keino; the Kenyan that infused dread into fellow runners.

He was not alone in fearing the man. But given his woeful lack of international success, he no longer cared. Even better, given the unexpected juice in his legs, he was buoyed. His was in a race that no one expected anything but failure. With that he was freed.

Starting near the back of the pack, he methodically increased his pace. Being fifteen meters behind the best runners in the world was not idyllic, but not insurmountable. He pumped his arms and his legs followed the cue. Passing three runners on the third lap, he was well positioned in fourth place as the bell sounded. The two Kiwis in front of him paid no heed. As an unknown, he was the least of their concerns. That only emboldened him as he entered the last lap. On this track, he was a nobody. A ghost in a singlet that had no business being in the position he was. He was undercover. Stealth.

And ready to pounce.

As the last backstretch began, he fell to the impetuousness of youth. He bolted like a skittish colt and passed the pair of New Zealanders. He had been forced to run wide but the freshness in his legs was intoxicating. The second lane was further in distance but approaching Keino he engaged another gear in an attempt to gain the lead before entering the final turn.

Keino was no rube. He had been there before and an upstart was of no consequence. He moved to the outer edge of the first lane and just as the unknown American gathered for a final push, Keino delivered an elbow. Hitting its target, he gasped as his ribs seized. He struggled to take a necessary breath. Following that, when his rhythm disappeared, so did his chances. Breaking stride, he lost any ability to compete. He struggled to maintain pace and drifting around the last corner, the black jerseys of the New Zealanders flew past. He fought to regroup but the moment of glory was extinguished. He lost his stride. His energy. Worst of all, his hope.

His race was over.

Just then the overhead TV blared as the announcer read the lineup for the upcoming one-hundred-meter race. Stirring on the barstool, he debated whether to continue watching. He sipped his beer, then chewed on a pretzel. As he swallowed, the pasty substance stuck in his throat. He tried to breath but for a fleeting moment failed.

Time passed, yet it hadn't.

"What ya watching?" Tony asked.

He flicked the channel forward. "Nothing. Just clicking around trying to find something that matters." He reached for his beer. "No luck in that anymore."

He nodded. "I saw you watching that running meet; that had to have some interest for you." He idled himself with a bar rag and continued. "Mona once told me of your heyday. That you were really something. That way back, you ran like the wind and almost made the Olympics."

Almost.

There it was. The word that haunted both dreams and nightmares. He had been on the cusp. He had a chance. But at the moment of impact, he blew up. Like a horse with no heart, he pulled up lame. Slowed. Then stopped. And he had to live with it ever since. There were days it seemed inconsequential. A simple footrace that went wrong. A blip on a screen that had no relevance to anyone except one man.

Himself.

Tony stopped cleaning and studied him. For a moment it seemed entirely too long. Then he spoke. "At least you were someone once. Some of us never get nowhere in our whole lives." He licked his lips and looked to the bar rag. Then he remained silent before pouring himself a beer. "Hey, Mac, you seen that boy running around here? That darker one? I don't know nothing about running but he looks pretty good to me."

Mac blinked and nodded. "Yes. We have met."

"You met him? How?"

"Him running. Me walking. Simple as that."

"And?"

"And? And what?"

"Well, what's his story? What did you talk about?"

He shrugged. "Well, he's new here. Goes to Weston High." He neared the end of his beer. "Not much more than that."

Tony looked out the front window and into the distant woods. "Sometimes I wish I was young again like him and sometimes I don't. Be nice to do things over. Avoid the same mistakes. Marriage. Bills. Divorce. Then again..." he paused, shrugged, then continued. "Maybe I'm just fine where I am."

He considered the sentiment and couldn't disagree with most of it. Yet if he could, he would go back. To the time he didn't know the outcome. To the time he toed the line. Exploded from it. To the time he met Mona. And right the wrongs he had done. Worked harder. Made more money. Had a family. A hundred thoughts flooded over him and he was spinning. He stared dead-ahead until he was roused by a voice. "What?" he asked at the question.

"I asked, how is Mona really doing."

"Fine. Good. Okay, I guess."

"Goodness. That about covers it."

He explained. "She's the same but she's not. Slowing down like you and me, but at a much faster pace." He took a long draw on his beer and emptied the glass. "I worry there will be a day I can't take care of her. I don't know what I'll do then. Without her, I have nothing." He got up from the stool and slipped a five-dollar bill on the bar. He nodded and smiled at the barkeep. "Tony, it's been a pleasure. But I have to be moving on. Like Frost says, I have miles to go before I sleep."

"Frost? He live around here?"

He smiled. "In a way, Tony. In a way."

Then, giving a half-wave, he moved toward the door.

Chapter Eight

He couldn't sleep again. The quiet was deafening and he awoke in the middle of the night. He was used to the sounds of the city. Buses. Trucks. The honking of horns. Random voices interspersed with the wail of police or rescue vehicles accented by the echo of an occasional gunshot.

Now that was all gone. The white noise of the city had been a troubling blanket his whole life. A cacophony of sounds so pervasive he assumed it was the same everywhere. That was until he moved hundreds of miles north. To a place where the winds whispered to the pine branches, who in turn scratched out a soothing song.

But to him the song of nature was disturbing. Too quiet. Too sedate. Not indicative of the world he knew. As the branches rustled outside his window, he was again wide awake. He lay in his bed and looked outside. The night shadows danced in unison as if gremlins at a nighttime convention. He had been there a month and he was still decidedly an outsider. A person of unknown bloodlines and lineage that made the locals nervous. That he could see. Even worse, he could feel it. The eyes that studied him longer than necessary. The hunch of shoulders protecting them from the threat he embodied. That reaction he did not understand. He was just a boy from a city far away. A city that had been his residence but never a home.

Home. The word meant nothing to him. He knew of apartments and walls that only kept the wind, rain and cold off his back.

Home.

Someday, he thought. *Someday*.

His father was snoring a room away. He chose to stop staring at the walls and crept to the front door. He hitched his shorts, slipped on a sweatshirt and cinched up his shoes. Opening the front door, he closed it silently behind him. He never dared run at night in Chicago. There he would be taking his life into other's hands. Here, there was no threat besides a drunken farmboy behind the wheel of a monster truck. Those he could avoid if the need arose.

He walked to the street and stopped, stretching his arms to the sky to loosen his spine. Windmilling his arms and rotating his neck, he readied for the miles. A midnight run in the black ink of night was like a dream within a dream. He started slowly until the blood warmed in his legs. He hated running slow; to him it was just a prerequisite to what lie ahead – the full-on push toward the exhaustion that was a necessity. His stride lengthened and his breathing ramped accordingly. He followed the road around the lake and eased down the first hill as gravity assisted his journey. Then climbing, his breathing increased as he approached the crest. He didn't mind hills; they were simply challenges to conquer. But it was the smooth terrain he craved. There he could lengthen his stride and hammer the roads as desired. And on this night, he expected to do the same.

He estimated his pace at six minutes per mile. He rarely wore a watch and even if he did, he was not apt to reference it.

The sensation of pace was part of him. Five forty-five. Five-thirty. Five-fifteen. Finally, as he balanced both his breathing and abilities, he reached a five-minute per mile pace. It was there he was flying. The ground was black but the speckle of stars above illuminated the night like a cavalcade of distant spotlights. His breath evened and the rapturous moment took hold. Life had been uneven and smothered him in an uncertainty he could not escape. But on the roads, the past did not matter. What did was soaring down a nameless street with only the heavens above.

He pressed to hold the pace. There were moments in running when his spirit was lifted and watched the flesh below do battle. He was running but he wasn't. There was no effort despite the sweat dripping from his face. He stepped lightly in the night and when the moon appeared, it added to the ethereal glow of the landscape. He wanted to, even needed to, press harder toward his destination. He had no concept of time and space. He just was. He was a man-boy with something ahead. A quest. A hunt for understanding. A race to discover meaning in a world that so far had been cold and forbidding. He pushed to top-end and his chest burned at a fever pitch. Anger and discontent surfaced from a life that had detoured to a madness over which he had no control. He lengthened his stride, pumped his arms as ratcheted breaths escaped his throat. He searched for a point on the road to deem the finish line. Crossing it, holding hands on his knees, his course rasp eventually slowed. Standing tall and looking to the moonlight, he was at one with the world to which he had always done battle.

Sweat blinding his eyes, he walked slowly toward where he had started. He stopped and placed hands on hips. The lights from nearby homes accented the starlight above. Looking to the heavens, a thousand stars danced in the night. He scarcely remembered seeing the stars in Chicago. There his eyes were set squarely on the horizon, focused only on cars, buses and people. He could never escape the threat of being another easy mark or even worse, a statistic.

For the first time since he had moved, he bathed in the independence of his surroundings. Being an unknown, a newcomer, so far had been stress inducing. He was uncomfortable being nearly the only dark face in a primarily white region. That was even more apparent at school. But ignoring that significant difference, he realized being a stranger held advantages. To them he had no history, no past. They knew nothing of his families fractured parts, of his own frailties and weaknesses. Here, he was as fresh as a morning breeze. In this place he could reinvent himself and start anew. There was no ugliness of sleepless nights nor broken dreams of a junkie mother nor absent father. Here he was just "D.J.". The new kid who was as mysterious as an alien dropped from an unknown planet.

He took a deep breath and walked down the street. In the wooded surroundings, he was as cloaked as a young deer blending into the foliage. Closing his eyes one last time, he embraced the darkness of the woods. He was an animal that had no confines. No self-imposed boundaries. No limits.

He was free.

Chapter Nine

Mona was sleeping more each day. He couldn't bring himself to even consider she was fading despite the obvious evidence. From early on she had always been the foundation in the marriage. He admitted to erratic moments. The times his competitive nature clashed with corporate alliances integral to having business success. To when he offended, overstepped or irritated a colleague to the point he feared for his job. It was always Mona who calmed him and assuaged his fears.

What had always worked on the track was a detriment in life. On the oval he competed until there was only one victor. Win or go home. Triumph or be humbled. In the working world, mediocrity was satisfactory. He chafed at what he deemed unacceptable. *If you can't be the best, what is the point!* he railed at co-workers who settled for less. He struggled to fit in but as time went on, he accepted his fate. To do his job, accept the average, and collect a paycheck. It burned but he could not beat the machine he had become part of.

Yet it never stopped him from dreaming of the past.

As Mona slept, he made his way to the basement. It was there he stored the memorabilia of his running career. Hauling out a box from under the stairwell, he pushed it toward a frayed couch that had found a basement home. Opening the corners, he reached for the foot-high stack of aged *Track & Field News* magazines. Setting the assortment on his lap, the blast from the past was a decided jolt. He had not looked at the collection in years, yet knew they were there. Safe. Secure. Having no reason to be saved other than providing evidence of a time he existed in rarified air. He could claim more than most men; he had nearly touched greatness.

He settled into the couch. He was sure the magazines held little value to others but to him they were everything. They reflected a time he coveted. A time, if only for a moment, he was somebody special. It was history written on faded parchment and testimony to the part of his life that mattered.

The top magazine was a grainy black and white photo of Ron Clarke. Perhaps the greatest distance runner of his era, Clarke's face was rawboned and hollowed, earned solely by hard training. But it was the intensity of the eyes that stood out: deep, probing, indomitable. Studying them, he remembered the intoxicating mixture of pain and achievement that competition induced. He held the magazine closer. Smelled the mustiness of a time long since passed. It took him back. To when he was there. Living. Breathing. Waiting to attack the oval at the sound of a gun. His heart pumped as if he was on the starting line. Lowering the magazine, he wished he was there. To have one more chance. Studying Clarke, he wondered if he had ever felt the same.

He sighed. Mona would only shake her head if she saw him reminiscing. *You did wonderfully, Thomas. Not many men could have done what you did,* she would say. He wouldn't argue. At least not aloud. There was no point to try and explain. He could have done better. Should have done better. Maybe most men could not do what he had done. But he could not forget those that did.

He lifted the next item from the pile; so old it was more of a newspaper than a magazine. He studied the images captured. George Young. Michael Jazy. Ron Hill. Men he had run against. Some he had spoken to. They were ghosts of a time that seemed a dream. He read the headlines: *Keino Tops Ryun! Lindgren Tags the Russians!* His chest pounded as he re-lived the past and the wonderment it contained. When in the throes of it, he thirsted for more. Now, fifty years later, he wished he would have enjoyed the moment. Seized it like a shiny penny and held it close to his heart.

Deeper in the box was tangible evidence of his success. Medals of all shapes, sizes and colors. He lifted a handful of ribbons and the metal twinkled in the dim basement light. Raising them to eye level, the assortment of bronze, silver and gold jangled as if calling for attention. From local meets to national competitions, each held their own merit. He read the etchings and tried to recall the specifics of each race. The memory of competitors long since vanquished surfaced and he recalled near death-inducing battles. The pain. The glory. And sometimes bitter defeat.

The medals were a testament to prowess at the peak of his ability. He closed his eyes and remembered his youth. To a time he slipped on a pair of thin spikes and attacked the track like a wild animal. When lap after lap he assessed opponent's weaknesses and vulnerabilities. Masking his own doubts, on days of glory, he beat inner demons and reached the finish line first. On other days, whether displaying weakened will or simply being outrun, he followed another runner across the white line.

Those were the nights he didn't sleep. When alone in his room, he replayed the race step by step, lap by lap. To the time he succumbed to the pace or even worse, his own fear. The fear of losing that was so strong it made his eyes bleed.

Like in the Olympic trials. It was there in the greatest of moments he truly quit. A race where his inner anxiety reached a crescendo and he simply shut down. He had worked his whole youth and young adulthood for a chance at glory and when it came, he buckled. Stepping off the track on the last lap. He later claimed it was "cramps" that arose at the worst possible time. But he knew. It was his own fear and weakness that crippled his pursuit. The failure became a hidden sickness he carried the rest of his life.

A broken dream of his own making.

He set the medals down and reached for the last item in the box. The track spikes he wore in the trials race. Red Adidas. The iconic three stripes still intact. Leather, yet so broken in, the shoes felt like human skin. He traced the stripes. Then the laces. Turning the shoes over, he jabbed an index finger at the spikes on the bottom of the shoe. Despite the years, each had maintained their edge. The spikes were nearly weightless and he was taken by the sturdy design that had survived a lifetime. But they were just footwear. Regardless of the technological sporting advances, when it came to running, it was still simply man versus man. Shoes had little bearing in the result. Rather, it was the training. The hours put in. And the will. The suffering, pain and resolve likened to a savings deposit in a bank. It was only when full withdrawal was taken one could measure the truly deserving. If you paid the price, glory awaited.

He wished to escape. Placing the shoes at the bottom of the box, he covered them with the medals. Then the magazines. Carefully sealing the box, he returned it to its place. In a basement that withheld judgement of victories or defeats. He stood still and tried to clear his mind. Taking a deep breath, he was forced to repeat it again.

When able, he took a small step forward.

Chapter Ten

A month had passed and change of season had taken place.

The woods held a dead hue and fallen leaves cushioned his footstrike. He had never run in the woods prior to moving north. At best, a few dozen steps through a city park that nearly ended as soon as it began. He was beginning to understand the rhythm of the land. It was quiet. Welcoming. Yet unyielding at the same time. His stride lengthened and battled the terrain as the miles and days accumulated. He was not patient in life. But he was beginning to understand that this sport demanded that very attribute. Run. Let his body breathe. Push it. Then repeat when able.

It felt good.

The best of times was when his mind drifted unfettered by past or present. To the pureness of the moment. Of movement that was his own. No interference from anyone. Not a mother, nor father. Or burning anxieties that disturbed his dreams. So, he ran. On an old path that harbored unknown numbers before him. Walkers. Hikers. Those that needed to explore. He had no qualm with that. But he ran for other reasons. To escape. To burn away pain that seemed engrained in his DNA.

He followed the trail as it meandered north. The wind was buffeted by trees and he ran as if in a vacuum. He was as alone as he had ever been before. In his head, he had always been alone. Surviving. But here was different. Here it was physical.

There might have been others nearby but likely from a hundred yards to a mile. More likely it was deer, coyote or even a random bear. In that he felt emancipated. Yet, at the same time still undeniably cloistered.

In school it was the same. He sat in class day after day but said little. Among others but still apart. There but not. He gave a verbal answer when forced but otherwise stayed under the social radar. With little else to do, he began to excel in academics. He had always found school easy but seldom applied himself. For the first time ever, he began to achieve. It was then he found the lessons meaningful; he merely kept his nose down and listened. It was the moments in between that were more troubling. The five minutes between classes. The forty minutes at lunch. Those were the times he could barely breath.

He had made a few acquaintances. Lee, Andy and Jimbo. Good old boys born and bred in the north. Hunters and fishermen. Lee and Andy were twins, who when not involved in outdoor activities, ran on the cross country team. Fair-haired and lean, the two of them were as close to identical as possible except for a small scar on Lee's left cheek. "A fishhook, courtesy of my dipshit brother trying to catch a trout," Lee explained. Andy had no response to the statement except for a helpless raising of his hands. Jimbo was twice their size and an odd compliment to the brothers. He lumbered more than walked and fittingly enough threw the shot put and discus in track. D.J. never revealed his running background to the threesome and chose to keep his skills private. That was personal. Maybe the only thing that he truly controlled in his life.

"What do you do, D.J.?" asked Lee one morning as they moved between classes. "I mean, outside of school?"

He didn't answer as Andy and Jimbo leaned in closer for his reply. "I, uh, I..." he stammered. Then he shrugged. It was painful to reveal himself. Past. Present. Anything at all. Compared to others, he felt less than complete. As if there was a hole in his being only he knew about, that others could not see. It was that void that kept him from letting anyone in. Even three well-intentioned classmates. "I just hang out. Chill," he finally replied.

They nodded. Waiting for more, but nothing came. Then Jimbo's baritone voice: "You ought to roll with us. Shoot the shit." Lee and Andy nodded and with that a commitment was made. He feared the moment at the same time he craved it. Life was safer alone. No one to pierce your flesh and cause a slow bleed. Yet, he was bone marrow lonely more than he cared to admit. The irony that a solo run on an abandoned wooded trail eased his isolation was not lost on him. But sometimes he tired of his own thoughts. Of trying to figure it all out. Why life had led him to this singular place in the world. It was at those moments he ramped the pace to shut down his mind.

It was far easier to just run.

***

He estimated he had covered eight miles in under an hour. Dusk was setting in and he walked the last few hundred yards as a cooldown. He lowered the volume of the music blaring through his earbuds. As the thump of the rhythm lessened, he squinted ahead. The road was darkening as a shadowy figure approached from the opposite direction. He braced as he had been warned of a seedy local element that lived hand-to-mouth. He had done the same in Chicago but there he was part of the fabric. The culture. Here he was a newcomer to the northern world. He balled his fists and approached the figure. It may be nothing but he would still rather be ready. Coming closer, he studied the outline. The hunched shoulders. The thinning hair. The walking stick.

"It's you. D.J." stated the shadow.

He struggled to remember the man's name. As he pulled out his earbuds, it came. "Mac. Hey."

The old man looked to the devices. "Not a fan. A runner needs to listen to the rhythm in his head. Not avoid it."

"What?"

"Never mind."

He shrugged. "Taking a late walk?"

"I might ask you the same."

He shook his head. "Just cooling off. Ran the trails for an hour."

Mac nodded. "Good base work. Just like Lydiard used to say."

He wiped sweat from his brow. "Never heard of him."

"I'm not surprised. From way before your time." He laughed. "Hell, mostly before my time. Anyways, Lydiard was a coach from New Zealand in the 50's. Taught that runners need to get a good endurance base before they work on becoming faster." He paused. "You've never heard of anything like that?"

He chafed at appearing ignorant. "No, last year our coach would just have us run. Sometimes in the park and other times on the track. I just did what he told me to do."

He smiled and twirled the walking stick between his fingers. "That's okay. A successful runner should listen to others in the know. But also be independent. It is the line a champion has to straddle very carefully."

He couldn't help himself. He pushed back. "You make it sound like you know something. Like you were a champion." A near sneer appeared. "Ever win the Olympics?" He licked sweat from his lips and waited for the old man to answer.

The tone of his voice sharpened. "No, I did not. But I raced against men that did. Maybe someday you will be lucky enough to do the same."

The reply caught him off guard. He paused. Swallowed. "You ran? What event?"

"The mile. Just like you."

He was startled the old man knew. Then he remembered their past discussion. "Yes. I mostly run the mile. Usually they call it the sixteen hundred. It depends on the meet."

"That's right. The sixteen hundred." He shook his head. "The 'new' mile." He shrugged.

He didn't debate. "I like it. Each lap harder than the one before. Each one sucking more from you. Making you hurt." He looked at the old man. "I don't mind the pain."

"Embrace pain. Love suffering," he said.

"What?"

"Nothing, D.J. Just something an old coach used to say."

"That Lanyard guy?"

"Lanyard?" he asked, chuckling. "You mean Lydiard. No, Cerutty. But that is for another day." He studied the young runner. "I have an idea."

"An idea?"

"Yes. I hope this doesn't sound too strange, but I'd like to have you over for dinner. Me and my wife, Mona. She cooks a mean spaghetti sauce from scratch. Then I'd like to teach you some things from the past. About running. There is a history that many young runners never know about. And we learn from the past." He ground the end of the stick into the road. "There is no need to repeat the mistakes made before. Let others teach you." He looked him in the eye. "I wish someone had been there for me."

The sincerity caught him off guard. He wasn't used to adults advising him. They usually preached submission or demanded obedience. This was different. Warmer. Somehow more real. He barely knew the man but sensed no ulterior motive other than a shared interest in a lonely sport. In that he was intrigued by the offer.

"Dinner would be fine," he said.

Mac smiled. "Mona will be happy to have a visitor. So will I. How about 6 o'clock tomorrow? We live in the last house on the right at the end of Elm Street." He looked to the sky. "It's getting dark. You better finish your cooldown and get home before you get chilled. See you tomorrow, D.J.?"

"Sounds good. I'll be there, Mac."

Without a word the old man strode forward. Then as he faded into the dark, there was one final comment. "Do a bit of stretching when you get home. Warm muscles respond better." Then he disappeared into the night.

***

His father was on the road again. That by itself made dinner an easy proposition. Anything was better than eating alone. He had no idea what to wear but settled on faded jeans and a button-down black shirt. Part of him worried he was being summoned by some pervert and he was an idiot for accepting the invitation. The rest of him was intrigued. The old man had knowledge about the sport that had him firmly in his grasp. He thirsted for a teacher that could show him the way. Running was the only thing that gave him direction. Satisfaction. The rest of the day was just time filling the moments before he could run again.

He walked in the dark and measured the fatigue in his legs. He had pounded another hour run after school and the burn remained. The trace of weariness was becoming the norm. He relished the knowledge he was accomplishing his daily goal; cleansing his soul and carrying on.

He approached the house and the single burning bulb lighting the doorway. He was hesitant and almost turned back. Then, stepping onto the simple porch, he had nothing to lose. He pressed the doorbell and a listened to the chime. Nervous, as if at a starting line, he coiled. His mind played tricks; telling him that he was a fool and that no one was home. He nearly pivoted and backtracked until the door opened.

A face appeared. "D.J. Thanks for coming!" The door swung wider and light from the house was cast. "C'mon in." He hesitated, then accepted the invitation.

"No problem, Mac." He wanted to say more but was unsure of the protocol. He entered slowly. Nervously, he sipped from the bottle in his hand.

Mac raised his eyebrows. "Thirsty? We have water."

He shook his head. "Just Gatorade. Hydrating after a short run."

He smiled. "I liked Gookinaid back in my day. Same-same as far as I know."

"Sounds gross."

"Yes, it was a little. But it's all we had."

He nodded, agreeing for agreement sake. He tentatively stepped forward into the home. He had rarely been at other residences for dinner. Maybe an occasional distant relative in Chicago but for the most part he had been isolated from festivity. He was uncomfortable and felt woefully out of place. That was until the sweet smell of a homecooked meal caught his attention.

"This way. Mona has a nice pot of spaghetti brewing that I think you'll like." He paused and looked concerned. "I never even asked if you liked spaghetti. I just assumed."

He smiled at the attention. He usually ate whatever was there. Peanut butter and jelly. Bologna. Hot dogs. Nutrition was the furthest thing from his mind. What was important was filling the hole in his stomach with something tangible. Anything. It had been that way as long as he could remember. This was a special treat; a homemade meal that nearly called him by name.

"I like spaghetti just fine. It smells wonderful," he added.

Mac lowered his voice. "Mona struggles these days. She has a condition that is wearing her out. But she was thrilled to have a visitor and did all she could. We work together, my Mona and me. Always have." His eyes moistened but he collected himself. "Ahh, enough simpering. So pathetic, hey?"

Then a voice from another corner of the house. "What's all the commotion out there? Am I missing the party?"

Mac smiled. "She likes to be part of things. More of a party person than me." He waved his right hand towards the kitchen. "Follow me."

He did as instructed. They passed through the small front room. A head-high curio cabinet filled with Amish sculptures. An old piano bracketed by matching armchairs. Three walls covered with paintings of birds, deer and other natural wildlife. But it was above the fireplace mantle that garnered his interest. In the center, a framed picture of a young couple, hand-in-hand, wearing wedding clothes. A young Mac. Lean, angular and eyes burning with the vigor of youth. With him was a young woman. Mona. A brunette with a haughty and irrepressible smile. Together they stood and committed themselves to each other. To the future, wherever that may lead. His eyes then gathered on the framed pictures bordering the centerpiece. A runner on a track. Straining to break a finish line with his chest. On the other side was a photo of the same runner on a victory stand accepting a medal validating his achievement. Mac. He was in his twenties. White thighs so rippled it was like he was standing on a pair of albino beef jerky sticks. The body clad in a white singlet and shorts that barely reached his upper legs. The boy was riveted to the captured time and nearly walked into the ottoman in front of one of the chairs.

"Careful, D.J. I don't want to be the cause of injury." Then he followed his gaze. "Yes, that was me. Mona insists I display my past. As repulsive as it sounds, she says I was 'sexy' back in the day." He laughed. "Be that as it may, I had my moments." He caught the boy's eye. "Someday we will talk about those times. I don't know everything about running but I know enough to be dangerous."

The boy didn't respond. He looked to the pictures. Then back to the man in front of him. He couldn't rectify the two. The present incarnation was old. Nearly feeble. The pictures represented power and grace. As confusion set in, the third voice again.

"Anytime soon, Thomas?"

Mac whispered. "She calls me Thomas. But I like Mac better." In a matter of steps, they were in the humble kitchen. "Mona, this is D.J. D.J., Mona."

He studied her. She barely crested five feet and her stooped spine appeared painful. Her lined face was creased but the vibrancy of her eyes made up for her otherwise aged appearance. She used a walker to support herself as she extended her right hand.

"So nice of you to spare some time on a Friday night, D.J. I've heard so much about you from Thomas. He says you are a special runner." She squeezed his hand before letting go. "Even more than that, he said you are a respectful young man." He was caught off guard but luckily, she continued. "It's so nice to have a visitor. One of these days we're going to wake up dead and the world will not even notice."

"Mona!" shouted Mac. "That's terrible!"

She chuckled and turned to the boy. "He doesn't like me talking about us croaking," she whispered. "But I think God has a plan for all of us. Don't you think, D.J.?"

God's plan? He had no idea. He had rarely been in a church much less thought of life and death. And even less of the afterlife. "Umm, I don't really know. I guess," he mumbled.

Mac took control. "I think the boy came to eat, Mona. Not to discuss where to spread our remains when the time comes." He turned to D.J. "Ain't that right, young man."

He nodded. "Yes. Sure. It smells awesome."

Mona smiled. "Looks like you could use a little spreckle on your bones, D.J. Tell you what, why don't you two put a little music on and I'll get dinner on the table. Okay?"

"Sounds fine, ma'am," he replied.

"I'll lead the way," said Mac. "To the front room."

He ambled to a small box that D.J. had only seen in movies. Mac explained as he noticed the puzzled look on the boy's face. "It's a record player. Looks old, still works." He smiled. "A lot like me and Mona."

"I guess. I've seen them before but only on T.V. It looks funny."

"I suppose. And it only plays albums. Ever hear of those?"

"Yes," he lied. "Sort of."

Mac reached for a stack of records and set them in the boy's hands. "Pick your poison."

D.J. widened his eyes and studied the first album. *Dizzy Gillespie*. Then the next. *Herb Alpert*. He stiffened. "I don't think I've ever heard of these, these guys before."

With that Mac let out a hearty laugh. "I expected as much. Not quite from your era."

"I think these are from about five eras ago."

He laughed again. "Maybe. But I suppose you're right." He took the stack from his hands. "Let me help you or we'll be here all day." He flipped through the records. "Perfect," he said when his search stopped. "A little Coltrane to soothe the soul." He slid out the album, opened the player and placed it within the spindle. Turning a nob and placing the record needle within the grooves, a subtle crackle of sound became audible. "Coltrane is complicated jazz but good. Sort of like life and death amplified through an instrument." D.J. stayed silent. "You ever hear much jazz?"

The simple truth was he had not. Then when a single note from a saxophone filled the room he responded. "I like rap and hip-hop. But sometimes there might be stuff like this mixed in."

He nodded. "Give it a chance. Like a lot of things, it takes time to cultivate appreciation."

D.J. shrugged as the music continued.

"Suppertime!" came a call from the kitchen.

"Coming," Mac called. "Let's go, D.J. It's not nice to keep a lady waiting."

That he did not know. But he didn't disagree. "Sure, Mac."

They made their way to the small kitchen and sat down. The boy followed the man's lead and set the cloth napkin on his lap. He had no idea why; he had never done that before. Then when Mona set a salad in front of him, he waited again. He watched as Mac poured dressing over the greens and then did the same. The ritual was foreign. He was uncomfortable but unafraid. He smiled at the strangeness of the moment.

"Something funny, D.J.?" asked Mona. "Fill me in."

He poked at the salad and came clean. "I don't get salad much," he admitted. "Sometimes I eat a carrot. That's about it."

The couple looked to each other. Then Mac spoke. "Why is that? As an athlete, you owe your body. Gasoline for the engine. Otherwise it is all a waste of time and effort."

"Thomas! Shush," said Mona. "Stop preaching."

He feared getting between the two but responded. "It's just the way I was raised. Sometimes I cut up a potato and fry it on the stove. That's a vegetable, right?"

"Yes, D.J., it is," she replied. Then she poked at her salad. "D.J., do you mind if I get personal? I'm not nosy, but rather I care. And if Thomas took a liking to you, it's because he sees something special. Inside and out." She set down her fork. "Are you comfortable telling us about your background?"

The boy blushed as he contemplated the response. Thoughts flooded his brain. Days and years of images barraged him as if an internal tsunami arrived full force. He had no idea where to start. But with aged, trusting faces surrounding him, he didn't hesitate. "I live with my dad up here. I barely knew him as a boy. My mom is long gone. She…she does drugs. I haven't seen her in a while."

She nodded slowly as if to measure her words. "We are all born with shackles. Be it genetics, poverty or sheer happenstance, each of us must work to escape our bonds. It may be hard but it is mandatory." She looked to Mac. Then back to the boy. "I suggest today is a good day to start."

He stayed silent and studied the old face. Blinking, he let the words bathe him. He then nodded back at her and replied. "Yes." Stabbing at the salad, he took a forkful into his mouth, chewed carefully, and swallowed. "I like this. I don't think my mom ever made a salad. At least not that I can remember."

Silence hit. It was uncomfortable but after a few seconds, Mona spoke. "Well then D.J., today is a good day for you."

She said it so succinctly, it was as if it were a given. He nodded and plowed into the salad like a meal for a starving man. Then he finished two heaping mounds of spaghetti and barely inhaled. It was delicious and topped anything he had eaten in weeks. As he scraped up the remnants of the second helping, he finally took time to look up. His belly was full but it was the warmth of the gathering that mattered. He felt right. He felt welcome. And he told them so.

"That was incredible," he said. "I mean it, really."

Mona spoke first. "I'm glad you think so. I used to love to cook but..." Her voice trailed into silence.

"Mona has M.S.," Mac explained. "Multiple sclerosis. Do you know what that is?" He admitted he didn't and Mac explained. When he was done, the boy was at a loss. "There are a lot of shitty things in the world," Mac said after taking a deep breath, "M.S. is one of them."

Silence hit the room. Mona looked at D.J. and nearly reached across the table to hold his hand. She stopped short, then spoke. "The world is not always a happy place. But if one tries, they can find happiness wherever they are. My mother taught me that in life, we should never get tired of living. No matter how bad the circumstances. No matter how tough the situation." She stopped talking as her eyes moistened. "I've had a good life, D.J. I had a good job. A good husband. I've met wonderful people. And now I've met you." She looked him in the eye. "Don't let the moments of brilliance escape. When you get old like me, it's all you have left to remember."

She smiled as the sound of a distant saxophone filled the room.

***

Mona insisted on clearing the dishes and let the two of them spend time together. "Men need to talk," she said waving them away. Neither objected as they moved to the front room.

They sat in the upright chairs as the music ended. Without asking, Mac flipped the album and settled the needle. He looked to the boy as the music regained momentum. "So, what do you think?"

He blinked and rubbed his belly. "The spaghetti was awesome," he said. "Amazing."

Mac smiled. "Good. But I meant the music."

The saxophone drifted from the antiquated speakers. As it filled the room, the boy spoke. "I like it. It is different than I'm used to, but I feel it."

"Feel it? How?"

"Emotion. The hurt." He looked away. "I understand."

Mac leaned forward and studied him. D.J. tried to appear nonchalant but was uncomfortable. The old man stared at him as if looking at an oracle. D.J. had no idea, but the man had been him once. He may have been a different color but they were the same. Bold. Impetuous. Independent. Mac stirred, then straightened in his chair before speaking. "I want to show you something."

The boy followed his lead and stood up. "Sure. But first tell me about these pictures," he said, motioning toward the fireplace mantle.

Mac pursed his lips. He clearly didn't like the pictures placed in full view but there they were. He carefully chose his words. "In nearly fifty years of marriage, I have learned to pick my battles and this one I have lost. Mona likes them there. She says it reminds her of youth. Of vitality. Of dreams that everyone should have."

The boy nodded. "Tell me, Mac. What are they all about?"

He struggled to get started. He was clearly uncomfortable and took a deep breath. "We all have a past. Mine is as complicated as some, but simple at the same time." He paused. "I've told you I used to be a runner," he said. "I realize that seems impossible looking at me now, but we all had our day in the sun. Back then God touched my hand and we ran as one." He walked towards the largest of the photos and fingered the glass. Beneath it was a dark-haired athlete straining to break the beckoning tape. "I ran for Baptist Union then. And on my own after I graduated. It was different then. We were all pretty much independent. No real help. Even the best of us. No sponsorships. No money. Just for the love of the sport."

"But you ran."

He thumbed the picture. "I ran. It consumed me. I lived my life around it. Most times twice a day, like an alarm clock." He smiled. "Most of my friends thought I was nuts. Skipping beer parties. Women. All so I was rested for the next day's run." He laughed. "Maybe I *was* nuts. Who knows?"

"You were good?"

"Depends who you ask. To some I was. To others I was just roadkill."

"What does that mean?"

He paused and collected himself. "I won conference championships. I ran at Nationals. Small schools. Won that once also."

"You won a national title? Seriously?" he asked.

"Yes. I ran the fifteen-hundred meters. The mile." He stared at the picture. "Right here. That was the moment. I can still feel the tape on my chest and the burn in my lungs. It was painful yet glorious. Both the hardest and best thing that I ever did. Even had a shot at the Olympics."

The boy swallowed. He had no idea the stooped man had such a history. A glorious past. One that was hidden behind wrinkles, with eyes carrying both darkness and light. "Tell me more."

"I was in the 1968 Olympic Trials against some of the best in the world. It was all there for the taking. I was with the leaders and the top three would go to Mexico City. It was the last lap and I was on the backstretch with the pack. It had thinned. There were only a few of us left. I had a chance." Then his voice drifted.

"What happened?"

He took a breath. Coltrane held a mournful note longer than seemed humanly possible. When it ended, the old man nearly wilted in front of him.

"I failed. Not an easy thing to admit but I failed." He struggled to breathe and collected himself. "I'll tell you the rest another time. But not tonight. Right now, I want you to show you something in the basement. Something you need to see."

The boy stood silently but didn't protest. He hesitantly followed the man toward the basement door. Then he raised a hand toward the boy. "Don't worry, D.J., it's okay. I'm no weirdo. And it's not like you couldn't kick the crap out of me if I was. Actually, I think you'll like what I have to show you."

The boy trusted. He rarely did but the old man was different. Generations separated them but that didn't matter. He followed without a sound. The basement smelled of moisture and years. The light of the room was muted and Mac motioned for him to take a seat on the frayed couch. After he complied, a moment later a weathered cardboard box was set at his side.

"What is this?" he asked.

"History," came the succinct response.

"Of what?"

"Of a time before you. But of a time that runs through you."

He shook his head. "What are you, Yoda? I have no idea what you are talking about."

"I understand." He motioned to the box. "Open it."

He shrugged and did as requested. The moment was strange and intriguing at the same time. He lifted the lid and studied the contents. Magazines of years past. The top one broadcasting a picture of a name he never knew. "Ron Clarke. Never heard of him."

He looked into the boy's eyes. "No, I suppose you haven't. But those that have gone before you can show you the way. To greatness. To victory. And for some, immortality."

"Immortality? Sounds like you're talking about Greek Gods."

He laughed. "In a way, yes. Their accomplishments have stood the test of time. And young runners like you can learn from them. Build on it." He paused, then swallowed. "And avoid their mistakes."

"Mistakes?"

"Never mind." He put his hand on the boy's shoulders. "I want you to take the box home. I think there are things within that will help you. To realize where you are going is a journey that has been undertaken before. And that yours can be as important as anyone has ever dreamed." He took a breath and then smiled. "That may sound a bit deep but, well...if my guess is right you will appreciate the contents."

"Mac," he said, "I don't know what to say. I'll be glad to take the box home and look." He replaced the magazine and sealed the box. He smiled. "I feel like maybe you invented running or something." His smile widened. "Did you?"

That brought a hearty laugh. "No, I did not. But given how old I am, sometimes I feel like it. But I can tell you it meant the world to me. Even though it only covered fifteen years of my life, it became engrained in my core. My spirit. My being. I think of running everyday even though those days are long gone. I wish I could go back. To compete again. To the moments that defined me." He paused. "And now consume me." He swallowed slowly before continuing. "The rambling of an old man. How pathetic."

The boy studied him in silence.

Chapter Eleven

He sat back in the chair and let the music bathe him. He loved jazz. It was the one form of music that touched him; found the sweet spot to his soul and calmed his anxiety. The shifting notes and freeform intuition of the players encompassed him. No matter how many times he listened to each album, he still discovered nuances of rhythm, beat and style that played new. *New*. A foreign word to him. Nothing much was.

Except for the boy.

He was fresh. Full of piss and vinegar in generous amounts. He liked that. He didn't even mind the belligerence that reared its head from time to time. It was a necessary ingredient to survive in the world. And even more so, on the track. There it was a prerequisite for success as essential as a strong heart and indefatigable legs. From what he could discern, the boy had the whole package. He had seen it. Felt it. And knowing with a better mindset, the triumvirate would be complete.

He had provided the box of collectables to the boy freely. It served no use to be gathering dust and spiders in the basement. Rather, it provided a glimpse into the past not available any other way. A verbal description would not suffice. Words and recollections meandered and swirled like puffs of smoke to the ears. Some might enter but others would drift into neverland destined to be forgotten. But pictures were irrefutable. Print on a page was calculating. Finishing times even more. They were facts. Cold, hard facts of achievement that could not be dismissed by opinion. There were winners and losers. Champions and those that only competed. He wanted to give the boy a choice to make.

With Coltrane reaching a peak, Mac hoped it would be one he could live with.

Chapter Twelve

The second Friday night dinner had been as enjoyable as the first and when it neared the end, he was reluctant to leave. Mona had been a hoot and they bonded easily. Ailment and all, she created a lightness to the proceedings well beyond expectation. He gratefully accepted her offering of leftovers and promised to return. Mac was a different matter. Morphing from entertaining to distant, his complexity was harder to understand. The evening was filled with stories of the past. Of work, accomplishments and tidbits that filled their years. All were entertaining but when Mona attempted to cast a light on Mac's past running years, consternation crossed his face.

"Not now, Mona," he had said. "Some other day."

The boy watched the interaction between the two. Childless, their communication was nearly telepathic. Each had their roles and responsibilities. It had been that way for nearly fifty years and would continue until one of them passed. He measured Mona's health. Frail yet with a strong backbone, she ambled about methodically and completed the necessary tasks. Physically the work was an effort but she didn't complain. D.J. admired her for that.

Now, back with his father, he listened to him snore in the next room. He would undoubtedly be leaving for another route the next morning. They had reached an uneasy peace and each stayed out of the other's way. It wasn't a perfect union, but for the time being it worked. Putting in his earbuds, the music pulsated as he reflected on the evening. The dinner. The conversation. And ultimately, the cardboard box.

The box sat at the side of his bed. He reached down and dug into the contents. The magazine title was clear as to what lie inside: *Track & Field News.* Names of the past sprang forth, none of whom he recognized. Mills. Roelants. Gammoudi. Ghosts from long ago. Of a time which he had no knowledge or understanding. Each item held mystery of a distant era. He sifted through the stack and vowed to digest their contents. The next layer was more fragile. Newspaper clippings. He picked up the first and studied the picture. Mac. Or in full print, Thomas McKinley.

He raised one to the light. The thin paper was crepe-like and he was careful not to damage the document. The picture was nearly transparent but the image of the runner was clear. A lean, slim hipped youth with mouth agape bursting past a finish line. Above the photo was a streamer: *McKinley Cracks Four Minutes!*

His mouth dropped. The old man had run 3:58.2 in a mile race. It seemed impossible. The bowlegged man with a walking stick had achieved what once seemed unachievable. A four-minute mile. He moved to the next article. Another photo. Another victory. And then the next. He went through twenty clippings before he reached the end. Each documented a superior athlete at the height of his glory. And then the last: *McKinley's Olympic Bid Falls Short.* There lay a picture of a crestfallen runner with hands on his hips looking toward the ground. The brief article documented the result: a runner failing to complete the race for unknown reasons.

He set the article down and lifted a thick, faded red notebook. In black ink, it was simply labeled: *Thomas McKinley – Workouts.* Underlined twice. Opening it, it was an unabridged look at the past. The first entry was dated, March 1, 1964. Then in painstaking handwriting, the day's effort was recorded. *Eight miles. 55 minutes. Felt pretty good for a windy day. Need to get more rest for tomorrow.* And that was it. He thumbed through page after page. Five or six workouts per page. Never more than the bare bones of what transpired. Mac was measured and meticulous, superfluous words eliminated. One year, then another. The thick notebook held the guts of his running career. D.J. hesitantly went to the last page. The last entry was dated, April 1, 1974. He read it slowly. *Four miles. Terrible. Achilles bad again. Can't do this anymore.* And that was it. A career over. A flash of cherished time ended. Sensing he had violated the man's privacy, he felt dirtied, like an uninvited peeper into Mac's private life. He set the notebook down. The next layer was more uplifting. He lifted a string of medals from the box. Ten, twenty, then well beyond that. Each with inscription marking a significant achievement. Now, just dusty remnants of youthful exuberance.

Then below them lie a hidden jewel. He reached gently and lifted it from the bottom of the box. Delicate, as if an oracle from the past, he held the gift in his hands. He had never seen such a beautiful thing. Track spikes. Red. Leather. They were weightless in his hands and he raised them to eye level. Rubbing a forefinger over the laces, then the tongue, lastly tracing three lines on the outside of the shoes. He touched the inside wall of the shoe and admired the construction of the dinosaur from yesteryear. Turning them over, he poked at the spikes nearly bonded to the sole of the shoes. Less than a fingernail in length, they only hinted at the power and drive once propelled. He had raced opponents wearing spikes but he justified they were a frivolous commodity. He reasoned he was fine in his flats and that spikes were just something others wore. More than that, he could never afford the cost and that made the whole exposition pointless. When he beat those wearing expensive spikes, the endeavor was even more satisfying than it had any right to be.

He lifted the shoes and took in their scent. Although well-traveled, they still bore the pureness of a quality leather. Like a classic car, they carried an exaggerated ambiance well beyond reality. He closed his eyes and drifted. The track spikes were a symbol of the past. Of events and competitions which had gone before him. Men that he had little knowledge of. It made him dream about the future. His future.

He set the spikes on the floor and returned to the magazines chronicling bygone years.

***

His cell phone buzzed on the dresser. He had fallen asleep looking at the magazines and the alert startled him. His interest was piqued because he rarely received calls or texts from anyone except his father and a few friends from Chicago. It was a text from a number he didn't recognize but the message was clear.

Dude! Comin to get ya. With Lee and Andy. Outside in 5 mins!

He remembered giving his cell number to Jimbo. His classmate had seen him running on the roads and they discovered they lived only a short distance apart. He asserted he could even give him a ride to school if he wanted: *Don't take the bus, bro. Only shit-brains do that!* He didn't commit but that didn't stop Jimbo's insistence. Now, on a late Friday night they were nearing his place. He was tired but excited at the same time. This was a chance to do something. Anything. Aside from school and running, he had done little else. Video surfing had gotten numbing and he had even fantasized about returning to Chicago. But to what? Friends who were no better off than he was? At least here he had a roof over his head with food and heat readily available.

Then a set of headlights from the street. They were already here. He texted back and the vehicle waited patiently. It was nearly eleven; too late to wake his father so he left him a note. He doubted he would even care but thought it best to short-circuit any potential issue. Grabbing his jacket, he slipped out the front door and into the night.

He spied three heads in the truck windows bobbing to the beat of music. Approaching the car door, it sprung open before he even got there.

"D.J. man, good deal bro!" said Jimbo from behind the wheel of the truck. "Did we get your ass out of bed?"

"Yeah," he said with a laugh. "Actually, you did."

"It's eleven on a Friday night," said Lee as he offered a fist-bump. "You can't be crashing yet."

"Totally," seconded Andy from the front passenger seat. "Ain't much going on here but *anything* is better than doing nothing."

He didn't disagree. "I was reading and I fell asleep," he admitted.

"Reading?" asked Jimbo. "On a Friday night? What are you? Some kind of honor student?" He laughed. "Seriously, bro. Please don't tell us you're a genius or we'll have to kick you out. You'll give Andy an inferiority complex, even though he's too stupid to know what that means."

"Look who's talking!" replied Andy. "Jimbo big. He lift weight. Kill deer. Eat meat."

"F-you," said Jimbo. "Keep it up and I'll take you shit-stains home right now." D.J. was uncomfortable and wondered what he had gotten into. That moment quickly passed when Jimbo farted and sighed. "On second thought you d-bags can stay and enjoy my sweetness," he said with a booming laugh.

"D.J.," said Lee as he rolled down the window, "you may want to reconsider your choice of friends."

As cool air filled the truck, he was surer than ever he was in the right place.

***

The music pulsated as the three others trash-talked. He had heard it before but previously it was with black friends. Before moving to Wisconsin, people of color were nearly all he knew. Despite his white father, his past neighborhood was primarily black. But there his mixed heritage was typically treated with suspicion. Too black for whites and too white for the blacks. He lived in a land of racial drift; of surviving day by day on his own accord. He calculated he was accepted by blacks more than whites. He never questioned why, it was just the way it was.

He was happy to have anyone at all.

These three were different. The talk wasn't about city life. Basketball. Thugs. Surviving. It was about fishing. Hunting. Dairy Queen. And girls. He feigned interest. Knowledge. Of those topics he knew little. Nodding his head to the commentary, he was drawn into the dialog.

"What do you think, D.J.," asked Jimbo. "You want to have a few brews?"

The other two watched his reaction. The hairs on the back of his neck prickled. He had never been a drinker aside from a few sips from a bottle here and there. He had coughed at cigarettes and the one time he got stoned he didn't like it. It only made him feel lost and confused. His friends laughed at him and told him it had been laced with chemicals. He immediately exploded into boiling fury. That was the sensation that bothered him most.

Control over himself was all he had left.

But for the time being that was forgotten. Now he was with a set of friends he hardly knew. The pressure to fit in was palpable and he responded accordingly. With a simple nod of his head, a decision was made. "Sure," he said. "Why not."

Smiles of approval reigned as the night had officially begun. Beers were distributed and three cans were raised in the air. Tops were popped and a toast was made. "To D.J.!" said Jimbo. "May he happily enter into the world of rednecks and musky fishing. And don't mind me children, I'll catch up soon enough."

Lee and Andy seconded the toast and for the first time D.J. felt as if he belonged. He had exchanged a gangster's paradise for one of backwoods buddies. He may forever be a misfit but for an instant that was suspended. As the beer disappeared and country music intensified, the moment was increasingly surreal. Like abstract performance art, flashes of color darted past his window. The headlights of passing cars illuminated the night shadows and streams of light danced inside the vehicle. The truck cruised with dips and swerves through the countryside and he imagined himself running. Gliding in the night with darkness as his bodyguard. Running within a dream. Effortless. Endless. Away from the past he wished to leave behind. To a present that was fresh and unvarnished.

"D.J., yo, D.J.! You okay?" asked Lee. "You look like you're freakin' hypnotized."

Finishing his beer, he crushed the can in his hand. "Naw, dude," he replied, "I was just looking out the window and catching the sights."

"Sights?" chimed Andy. "It's dark and there is nothing to see." He smiled. "I think you need more beer," he said, tossing him a fresh can.

"Damn straight!" shouted Jimbo from the driver's seat. "It's the Law of the Northwoods. A new day is a day meant for beer. Or hunting. Take your pick."

From the back seat he popped the beer and opened a floodgate. "What else do you guys do at night but drive around? Anything?"

As usual, Jimbo was the first to speak. "Well, Wautoma has a McDonalds but most times there are house parties or bonfires in the woods."

"And today is your lucky day, D.J.," said Lee. "There is a bash on Rock Ridge. We'll be there in a few minutes."

"Rock Ridge?"

"A great view of the bluffs," said Jimbo. "A bring-your-own and usually a lot of girls come too. Up here it's pretty much make your own party. There ain't much else to do."

He nodded. "Sounds good to me." But he lied. He was nervous. He had a fledgling relationship with the three in the car but even less with others in the area. In that he was anxious. But he never let on. Rather, he watched the flash of roadside roll by.

***

The light from the bonfire lit the distance. They approached first with D.J. hanging in arrears. Like a first-timer in a race pack, he was out of his element. Tentative. There were fifteen, maybe twenty others seated around the fire and loud voices dominated. D.J. expected most were regulars and he second-guessed his decision to come. Life was nothing if not safer in your own room. But it was too late now. He was here and there was no way out. The crackle of fire was threatening yet enticing. Chicago fires were of a different nature. Rusted steel barrels housing lit garbage. Abandoned buildings aflame. Random electrical fires engulfing dilapidated storefronts. That he could relate to. This new fire had him petrified.

"Jimbo!" shouted a voice from the crowd.

This was followed by another.

"Andy! Lee! C'mon over, man!"

The three rushed forward and D.J. momentarily froze. Part of him wanted to retreat but he fought the impulse. He stepped forward. Even from ten feet, the heat of the flames warmed his face. He braced and reached out to do the same to his hands. Fall had set in and the night air was cool. He breathed slowly and considered the crowd. He recognized a few faces from school and nodded. Others he did not. To those he just played hard.

That came easily.

"D.J.," called Andy. "Over here. You gotta meet a few of the regulars."

His shoulders stiffened. He was aware of being the "new" guy in town. Just as much, he was of mixed race. Besides a small number of Hispanics, Asians and Hmong, he was a decided minority. In fact, so far he had not even seen a black man or woman in town. Real or imagined, he felt judged.

So far, he had found it easier to run.

He headed toward Andy and the others. With them he felt almost normal. Not the new guy and even more so, not the new, *black* guy. He was just another person traveling through the requisite years of high school. What would happen along the way was like a race on the track. Meandering, full of elbows and entangled moments. He was grateful so far, he hadn't fallen. *But maybe tonight*, he thought.

Andy laid a hand on his shoulder and recited the names of the closest partygoers. Jeremy. Adam. Rachael. Jenna. Luke. All of them were shadows in the dark and he squinted to see the faces.

"Nice to meet you guys," he said with a nod. "Thanks for letting me come." The words escaped his lips and he wished he had them back. *So lame.*

Lee rescued him. "It's an open party, dude. The place changes so the cops don't bust us but most weekends there's something, somewhere. It only takes a text from someone and a party gets legs." He took a swallow of beer from the bottom of his can. "Even people from other schools. Most times it's cool." He paused. "Unless they are a-holes."

"Never in short supply," added Andy.

"What, beer? In short supply?" interrupted Jimbo as he rejoined the group.

"No, a-holes," explained Andy.

"That's twisted," said Jimbo. "I don't even want to know."

"I was just saying---"

"Nooooo!" Jimbo howled. "Keep your love life to yourself." That got a laugh from the crowd. He turned his attention to D.J. "Hey, some of you know this guy, but to those who don't, this is D.J. He's from Chicago. Smart as shit and he runs like ten miles a day." This gained an admiring look from the crowd. "Seriously," he said louder, "this dude flies down the roads like he's on a four-wheeler. Gonna kick ass in track this spring, mark my words." He finished his beer and continued. "'Course, he ain't going to go to state in the shot and discus like me. But not many can do what I do." That brought a series of empty beer cans at his head. He swatted them and took the assault in stride. "Jealous bitches!" he shouted.

The crowd laughed until a new face stepped forward. Tall and lean, his presence burned as if generated from the fire itself. He had been at the gatherings before and was well known to the group. Dalton Scarie. He went to nearby Mission High School and was their prize possession. He had made the place-winners podium at state his junior season in cross country and expected even more this year. But his domain was even more pronounced on the track. It was there he was the defending sixteen-hundred meter state champion who had made his future intentions clear. He was going to repeat and attack the state record of 4:04. No one doubted he could get it and college suitors were drooling over his talent. It was Andy who spoke first. "Dalton," he asked, "what's up?"

Dalton nodded slowly as if measuring his words. He brushed back the blonde, wavy hair resting near his eyes. The effect provided a mysterious look cloaking his thoughts. This time, however, he was less transparent. He nodded to the crowd and then focused on D.J. But this was no specimen to be examined, he was worse. He was competition.

"Not much," he finally replied. "Running. Chilling. The usual."

"You win today?" Andy asked. "We had off this weekend."

He nodded and looked D.J. in the eye. "Yeah, I won. Set a course record but I had a lot left. Not much competition today." He then spoke directly to the newest member of the group. "So Jimbo says you run? But no cross country?"

D.J. looked at his feet before looking up. He had been challenged before in more difficult arenas than this. But engaging in the stare down, the hairs on his neck prickled. He struggled to find the words. "I…I got here too late. I just moved in."

Dalton considered the statement. "But you'll do track in spring? Any particular event?"

90

The heat of the fire burned his face. He nearly stepped back but held his ground. "Sometimes the half. But mainly the sixteen-hundred," he said directly.

Dalton smiled before responding. "Interesting," he said. "Can't wait to see you on the track." Then with a nod he pushed his hair back one final time. "Enjoy your beer," he said as he raised a can of Coke in the air. Then he addressed the crowd. "See you all later."

A muffled goodbye sounded before the crackle of the fire escalated. D.J. watched him disappear into the darkness and fought the churn in his gut. His heartrate elevated and sweat dampened his armpits. He looked at the fire and then to the wisps of clouds that blocked the stars.

He raised the beer to his lips but couldn't swallow.

Chapter Thirteen

He always enjoyed when the boy came by. Mona did as well. Even the simple visits broke up the monotony of life: coffee and the morning newspaper, a simple breakfast, then a *Matlock* rerun on TV. Later a cleanup and running errands if any were deemed necessary. If not, he sat and stirred.

Most days he walked early. If not, he tended to pace through the small house. It was then Mona nearly pushed him out the door. She used to join him on walks when she was able. But over the last five years, her abilities waned to the point that only basic daily tasks were obtainable. He nearly shielded his eyes from her decline as she methodically pushed through the most uncomplicated activity. Washing herself. Emptying the dishwasher. When he attempted to help, it was met by rebuke. "I can manage quite well," she would say. "Mind your own business!"

There-in lie the rub: he had no business; he was simply existing. There was always puttering around the house and yard but after the early days of retirement, the appeal soon vanished. Now when weeds appeared in the flower bed, he simply shrugged and justified he would get to them tomorrow. His life degenerated into a void filled with nothingness.

It was then he walked to suppress the demons residing in his head. He had always battled anxiety and borderline depression. Although never formally diagnosed, he knew. As far back as high school, he recalled the unsettling stirring of thoughts that ping-ponged nonstop. Thinking. Overthinking. Backtracking on decisions made and then regretting the self-imposed change in plans. The cycle was endless and in the worst of times caused him to curl up in bed. His parents thought he was just "going through something". He was too young to know otherwise and the shadows haunting him became the norm. Day to day survival was all he could manage until he found his salvation - donning running shoes and losing himself on the roads. It was only there he was bathed in contentment. Only there did the anxiety dissipate like smoke wafting into nothingness. He had no understanding as to why running helped and he did not question.

He just ran.

He was an outlier then. In 1961 there was no running boom and those that did were deemed "odd ducks" and worse. Wearing skimpy shorts and leather shoes with rock-like rubber soles was almost an affront to society. Traversing over hill and dale was an irregular activity and the resulting catcalls were the norm. But those were ignored. Running was real. Tangible. The log book recording the daily numbers became an obsession. As the length of his runs extended, a curious thing happened.

His mind calmed.

Not completely, but he was able to function. To manage the day long before "endorphins" became a buzzword for runners. To him, the sport simply felt good. When running hooked him deeper, the days he didn't hit the roads he felt woefully off balance. Even worse, when a nuisance injury occurred and time from running was mandated, he became lost. Confused.

Like a portion of his being was slagging through mud. He had no knowledge of a "positive addiction", he just knew he needed to run. To sweat. To cover the ground like a primitive being. No mechanical vehicle to roar through Main Street, no bicycle, nor horse. But only two feet propelling him effortlessly mile after mile.

It was then he became alive. Purposeful. Free from the minutia of life. He lived to run. Then compete. To test himself against others that had the same mentality. First, he competed in high school track meets. Then in the off-season, non-descript warriors collecting at races spread only by word of mouth. No internet or blasts of social media.

Just runners meeting on a roadside because they could.

His anxiety quelled but never disappeared. It would arise at the most inopportune of times. A biology exam. A family gathering. Even prior to competition. And on one disastrous occasion, during the biggest race of his life. He had no explanation for the waxing and waning. It was a cross he bore in silence. His doctor once said he had a case of "nerves". He nodded in agreement and accepted the pills given. When they only dulled his desire to run, he soon tossed them aside.

Mona knew of his affliction. She recognized it in his face by the consternation and actions displayed. Fidgety, short-tempered, and ill at ease, sometimes she was able to quell it by simple interaction. The right dialog. A simple look. Other times it needed more.

Those were the times she simply pointed to his running shoes. And on more than one occasion she picked them up and dropped them onto his lap. He took the less than subtle hint and would soon be off. Grinding miles. Pumping blood through every cell in his body. Creating and circulating hormones to help balance the precarious chemical cliff on which he was perched. It was the therapy that saved their relationship.

This day was no different. "Please go, Thomas," she said. "Take a walk. You need it."

He nodded. He didn't take affront to her urging him out the door. More so, he knew she was guiding more than pushing. He slipped on shoes and bundled in layers before grabbing his walking stick. "I'll be back soon, Mona. Don't miss me too much."

"I always do, Thomas. You know that."

When she blew a kiss, he was on his way.

Chapter Fourteen

A month passed since the bonfire and morning frost had appeared. The change of seasons was nothing new to him as Chicago fall winds blew cold and angry. But he had never seen the ground frozen as early as this. The leaves had fallen and those that stubbornly remained held no purpose but to paint a picture of bleakness. At times he missed the city with its lights and sounds. The perpetual white noise of traffic and voices where he was part of a living organism pulsing an unpredictable lifeblood.

Here in the Northwoods, he was decidedly alone.

But the woods had a rhythm. Nearly imperceptible, there was a heartbeat at its core. The land had been here forever and swatches cut by man were merely flesh wounds. The roads winding through the fields and woods were like a network of arteries. He had become merely a thread among a greater mosaic of an undeniable Wisconsin fabric.

He kept mostly to himself. Simple interactions with his small group of friends was relegated primarily to lunch. There he was happy to have a place where he was accepted. Given his background, he would never be one of them completely. He was more the stepchild granted entrance to the household but still tiptoeing down the hallways at night.

But at the very least, he was enduring.

He had seen Mac and his wife on a nearly weekly basis since their first dinner. He began to look forward to the outings more for the interaction than even the food. In an unexpected way, they were becoming family. Family was a term he rarely used. It was just a word on television. His blood family was merely a collection of individuals each with their own cross to bear. His mother was gone. To where he had no clear idea. His father was there at the same time he was not; he appeared after a long day on the road and vanished the next morning. Even when he returned for more than a day, it was only to recover for his next expedition. They rarely talked. Surface level at best.

But with Mac and Mona it was different.

The Friday night gatherings were comforting. He nearly inhaled the food Mona cooked. When he devoured oversized portions and dug in for more, he ignored the amused eyes of the couple. They were happy to provide for him and he was happy to be there. Then, after a hearty dinner, he and Mac sat in the living room as Mona cleaned up the meal. It gave them time to connect. Jazz music filled the air and conversation drifted. About school. Family. Life. About the complications they all held. For that he was grateful. But best of all were the stories Mac told.

Especially about the running.

Of an era of time Mac embraced. Well before corporate sponsorship and six-figure contracts. To when men toed it up with only pride at stake. Mac revealed his successes; a collegiate scholarship, conference victories and invitation to championships. The prior visit he brought up the Olympic trials but cut himself short. Silence ruled the room as if he had bared too much of his soul. It was then apropos when Miles

Davis filled the air with a mournful wail exuding the bleeding of a wounded man.

Mac's mood suddenly darkened and uncharacteristically ended the night ahead of schedule. After an ungainly exchange, D.J. walked the short distance home under a starlit sky. He had yet to figure out the dynamics of the old man and the darkness he carried.

In the black of night, he vowed to find the answer.

***

With his bedroom lit from the screen of his laptop, he began the search. A simple hunt of "Thomas McKinley" turned up a variety of false leads regarding different men. Adding "runner" after the name provided little else. There were a few notations where his name was listed as a team member but nothing beyond. It was only when he added the postscript of "1968 U.S. Olympic Track and Field Trials" that he discovered more. An archive of track and field results summarized the race and centered on the heroic deeds of Jim Ryun winning the fifteen-hundred meter race going away. The gushing over his accomplishments was prone to hyperbole as it expounded on the accompanying grainy picture of him crossing the line. The text then drifted to the other competitors and the battle of the trailing runners racing to make the team. Outlining the backgrounds of the next two crossing the finishing line, Marty Liquori and Tom Von Ruden, the coverage concluded. The storyline was thin but captured the essence of a smaller picture of the pack on the final backstretch.

Then he saw it.

Within the pack was a thin youth with sunken cheeks and an unmistakable burning in his eyes. It was Mac. No more than two hundred yards from the finish line and in the thick of the battle.

The article ended without a notation of his performance. D.J. scrolled down to the conclusion. At the bottom were results with one name that stood out: Thomas McKinley – DNF

Mac had not completed the race. The ugly letters were attached to his name forever. But there was no explanation why. D.J. stared at the screen and wondered. Questioned. As far as he could find, there was no further information available in the cyberworld. After an hour, he gave up the quest.

Until it struck him. YouTube. He searched and nearly instantly the race was viewable. It was a step back into time. The results yielded a grainy black and white film uploaded for anyone to review. In front of him were recorded images of runners he had read about in the magazines. He could barely breathe. Then with a tap of a single finger on his laptop, a recasting of the live race unfolded.

He watched, spellbound. When the race ended, he watched it again. Then again and again. When he had seen enough, he shut the laptop down. Even upon multiple viewings, he still could not answer the questions that arose. He decided when the time was right, he would ask the source.

Chapter Fifteen

When the doorbell rang, he grimaced. *Damn!* he thought. *D.J. is coming over.* The boy was always welcome but this time he had forgotten the invitation. Their Friday evening dinner had become the norm and as usual the boy was right on time. He headed to the door and his greeting revealed his reticent sentiment.

"Mac? Are you okay?" the boy asked.

He opened the door and motioned for him to come in. Raising a finger to his lips, he explained. "I'm fine," he said in a hushed tone. "It's just that Mona is sleeping. She hasn't been well." When D.J. sat down, he continued. "Her M.S. has been hitting her hard. She not getting around well this week. She has been sleeping a lot."

He replied. "I'm so sorry. I can go. I didn't mean to cause a problem."

He quieted the boy. "There is no problem. We invited you. It's just that...it's just that I don't have any dinner made. I totally forgot." He raised his hands helplessly. "I feel like a schmuck."

"Mac, no problem. The food is nice but I just like to hang with you guys." He sensed the doubt. "Seriously. For old dudes, you guys are pretty cool!"

Mac chuckled. "Thanks, I guess. I'll take that as sort of a compliment."

D.J. shrugged. Then turned serious. "So tell me about Mona."

He was reluctant to complain but began. The weakness. The fatigue. The inability to finish things she started because her body simply would not perform. He did not go into detail about how she was beginning to struggle with even the most basic personal needs. He had promised he would take care of her forever and she would never have to leave their home.

Now he doubted whether he could fulfill the vow.

D.J. stared straight ahead. In the short time he had known them, Mac and Mona filled a void. Without saying it, it was clear he didn't want that taken away. "Is there anything I can do?" he asked.

Mac smiled at the offer. "No D.J. Your visits are enough. But tonight, I think we should just let her rest."

"Okay, Mac. Just let me know if you want me to leave. I understand."

He nodded. He admired the maturity of the boy given he had been forced to fend for himself. *If it doesn't kill you*, he thought. "I'm going to rustle up some grub and you can't say no. It'll be men's night out so don't expect much."

"I have low expectations."

"Me too."

D.J. smiled and stayed silent.

***

D.J. slouched in a weathered Victorian chair. The home was silent. The music, the ambient jazz usually filling the room was missing. Tonight, there was no joy in the house. No warmth.

He studied the walls and his eyes were drawn to scattered pictures. Of marriage. Random vacations. The two of them always smiling.

Except in the pictures of the runner in flight.

Those images were filled with intensity. Of concentration. Of effort. Of pain. He studied them from the chair.

"Deep in thought, D.J.?" he asked as gnarled hands set down a small tray of crackers, sliced sausage and cheese.

A forced smile appeared on the boy's face. "Just daydreaming. Nothing really."

"Okay," he replied as he settled onto the couch. "Nothing fancy tonight. Sorry, son."

"Mac, stop. I don't come just to eat." He paused. "Well, maybe I do a little."

Mac laughed. "Mona may be up and at 'em soon. Then we'll get back on track." The mention of her name quieted the room. "She's a tough bird, tougher than me."

D.J. nibbled at a cracker and could hardly swallow. The effort was noticed.

"You need something to drink?"

He shook his head. He swallowed and grimaced. "No, Mac, nothing like that." He almost continued but stopped.

"What is it, D.J.?"

He sat upright. "Mac, have you ever heard of YouTube? Like on a computer?"

"I've heard of it. They talk about it on the news sometimes." He centered a piece of sausage on a cracker and took a small bite. "Why do you ask?"

He looked to the man. "Because I saw you on it. Running in the Olympic Trials in California."

The cords on his neck tightened. He set his cracker back on the plate. "Say that again?"

He explained how the site contained videos past and present. Of how he had searched for old track and field highlights. And of his discovery that brought history to the screen. When he finished, he took a deep breath. "Do you want to see it?"

Mac looked at him. Then to the floor before his eyes searched the running pictures in the room. He answered in a word. "Yes."

D.J. pulled out his phone and tapped at the screen. When he was ready, he sat next to Mac on the couch. "It's a bit grainy but you can see the race pretty well. It's from 1968 and technology back then---." He stopped when he recognized the uselessness of his words. "I'll start the video."

Mac was mesmerized. The screen was small but after adjusting his glasses, he started to speak. "My God in heaven." He leaned in closer. It had been over fifty years but his youth was right in front of him. He pointed a finger at figures on the screen as they gathered at the starting line. "Good Lord. Look at Von Ruden. Liquori." He paused. "And look at Jim Ryun. Holy Christ. What a stallion."

D.J. moved closer. "As were you."

He shook his head. Then wiped at his eyes and replaced his glasses. "I can't believe this. This...this is amazing."

A young Mac was crouched on the line. Not hidden but not in the limelight. Right where he preferred to be. In a place he expected to shock the nation. The gun sounded and his eyes followed the race. His heartbeat accelerated and it was like he was on the track again. Hearing the breaths of his competitors.

Feeling the nick of track spikes at his heels. Elbows grazing his chest as each jockeyed for position. He pointed at the pack of runners. "You couldn't wedge a piece of paper between us. We were that close."

"I think I watched it ten times. It's like a classic race."

He didn't disagree. "To some of us it was everything." The first lap continued and in a hushed voice, he dissected the race. "I didn't have the speed of Ryun but no one did. He ran the eight-hundred way faster than any of us. He was out of this world." He licked his lips. "I wanted to run the last six-hundred hard. To use my strength." He pointed at the screen. "I was content to hide in the pack and bide my time. I was in the best shape of my life."

D.J. looked into his eyes. Eyes so energized they nearly popped from his skull. His own excitement ramped. "I've never seen a track with trees. It's weird."

"The location was new. Built just for the trials in Echo Summit, California. Supposedly they wanted to mimic the altitude of Mexico City where the Olympics were at. It was strange for all of us." As they watched the second lap start, the pack was still intact. The jockeying continued while the smooth amoeba-like group of runners devoured the track. "I'm not sure any of us felt we could beat Ryun. Maybe Liquori did."

"He thought he was the shit?"

"No, just the opposite. He was a cocky kid who thought he was really good."

D.J. chuckled. "That's what I meant."

"Oh." He started again. "Anyways, the rest of us just wanted a spot on the team." He pointed to the screen as the group finished the second lap. "I was still feeling pretty good there. Waiting. Being patient. I remember thinking I should push the pace but held back." He blew out a soft breath. "Ego is something to be kept in check. On the track it is better to be calm. Calculating. Those that give in to impulse will die a painful death."

D.J. watched the old man absorb the moment. Fifty years. A lifetime. A moment recorded that had been rerun in his mind a thousand times. But memories faded. Changed. Distorted. Now in front of him was the cold, hard truth. Four minutes of time that would follow him forever. Mac was mesmerized. They had opened Pandora's box and there was no way back. The past was no longer buried. No longer in a secure place. It was wide open for all to see.

The race played on.

Mac nearly whispered. "There are moments in a race that only the runner knows. When the pain starts. When it gets beyond your comfort. When you must decide how much it means to you. How one will respond."

"And in this race?"

He watched himself on the backstretch of the third lap. "Right here I was still good. Not fresh but confident. Ryun had a presence that was hard to describe. Poised and almost from another planet. He was a special talent. But the others I could run with. And beat." The runners strung out and Mac pointed to himself. "I was ready to go. Right there. Six-hundred meters left and in just the position I had planned." The lap ended and he watched the runners hit the near turn of the last lap. As they entered the backstretch, his shoulders suddenly drooped. "Then it happened."

"What, Mac?"

He shook his head. Closed his eyes in a forced attempt to erase memories. Then opened them to view the small screen. "I felt a tweak in my right hamstring. Just a small twinge that I tried to ignore. It wasn't pain but enough to get my attention. Attention that should have been elsewhere." He bit his lower lip and continued. "I wanted to accelerate but doubt crept in. Maybe I was hurt. Maybe I wasn't. But it was more than that." He closed his eyes. "For the first time, I began to think that maybe I wasn't good enough."

"But you were!" D.J. urged. "You were right there!"

He opened his eyes. "I started to panic. Get anxious. I have always battled self-doubt and at the top level that just can't be. You have to master it. You can't see it, but it happened. In races before I had been able to contain it, but the stakes were higher here. Magnified tenfold. It was like gears suddenly locked in my brain and I could hardly think." He blew out a slim stream of air. "I had felt that way in life before but never in a race. I...I didn't know how to handle it. I was breathing faster. More than the effort called for. Ryun started to move and I wanted to counter. Like every runner worth his salt, I had dreamed of the moment a thousand times. Practiced it. I was prepared." He watched the screen as the runners pounded down the backstretch. "But I was broken inside."

D.J. worried. "Mac, I can stop the race. Seriously. It's no big deal."

"No big deal," he repeated. A race that had defined his life. A race brought to life every time he encountered a jogger on the street. The time he was on the cusp of greatness but failed. He shook his head. "No, D.J. Let it run." The race announcer droned on. Extorting the exploits of the race leader. It was when the runners approached the last turn that Mac spoke again. "I was one-hundred and fifty yards from the finish when I stepped off the track. I had never done that before, not even in grade school. My hamstring was funny but not enough to make me stop." His breathing labored. "I couldn't bear to be a failure. To not make the team. So I gave up. The fact is, I simply quit." He gave the device back to the boy and didn't watch the end of the race. "I know how it ends. He wins. I did not." He sat back in the couch and stared straight ahead.

D.J. held the phone in silence.

***

The boy stayed only half an hour more. They nibbled at crackers and exchanged minimal words. The discomfort from both parties was evident.

At the door, D.J. looked into the old man's eyes. "Mac, I'm sorry. I never should have played the video."

He shook his head. "It is what it is. Isn't that what you young kids say?"

"Yes. Maybe. Still…" He trailed off.

"It was a long time ago, D.J. I have more important things to worry about," he said, signaling behind him.

"I understand. I'll stop by and see Mona in a day or two." He nodded. "Night, Mac."

"Goodnight, D.J.," He said. "Oh, I almost forgot. I have something for you. I found it in the basement." He handed him a small brown paper bag. "You might find it interesting."

With that he closed the door. Before returning to his chair, he set the needle on the record at the top of the stack. Soft strains of Chet Baker pulsed through the room. The sounds were both soothing and caustic. Melodic yet jarring. The music took him back. To a time he savored, yet wished to forget. His eyes burned and he closed them. He wandered. Drifted. As the music pierced his subconscious, he found himself again on the last lap. Losing contact with the leaders. Desperate to hang on to their heels, he strained. Fighting, flailing his arms while trying to maintain a semblance of form. Yet, the leaders separated with each stride. His neck stiffened. His hands clenched. Thighs burned as overburdened lungs struggled to draw in oxygen. With two-hundred yards to go, he knew his dream was over. He hung on to the turn and looked to the trees.

With that he took his final step.

He stepped off the track and grabbed his hamstring as he searched for an excuse. Walking through the infield, he sat down. From there he watched the top three runners celebrating their run to the Olympics. He envied them. Maybe even hated. They had done what he could not. He put his forehead on his knees and shielded the remaining light with his arms. He blocked the moment as if he could erase it from time.

Then, just as now, he failed in the attempt.

Chapter Sixteen

Christmas break arrived without fanfare. With school closed, his days took on a predictable rhythm. Sleep until mid-morning, eat some cereal, then prep for the upcoming run. He had a new routine since his solo dinner with Mac. The gift he received at night's end was unexpected and a curiosity. He opened it that evening and plowed through the contents. It was a book that bordered on antique. *Run to the Top* by Arthur Lydiard. At first glance it was archaic. Written in 1962, it was a faded hardcover from a bygone era but inside was information approaching a hidden jewel. Advice that made nothing but sense to a hungry runner. In essence, it was how to build the running engine one step at a time. Endurance base. Hill springing. Steady state. Aerobic and anaerobic. Terms that previously meant nothing to him.

For the first time he was beginning to understand a new language. One that both excited and made sense. He had read the book three times since acquiring it and ascribed to the basics. Instead of pounding the roads until exhausted, he began to embrace a science previously hidden. Increase his capacity gradually. Build a base that could carry him to greater heights.

For the first time ever, he had a plan.

Track season was not far off. Less than three months. When he thought of it, sharpened probes prickled his gut as if searching for an exit. He couldn't wait to toe it up on the track. To compete on the oval and be freed from life's shackles. To run hellbent with lungs on fire, crossing the finish line before all others. It was then he was most complete.

It was then he would be relevant.

He glanced at the book as it rested on the dining room table. His father had thumbed through it on one of the rare moments they had spent together. *What the hell is this?* he asked. *It looks like it's from the Stone Age!*

In that, maybe it was. He tried to explain its significance but when his father's phone rang, it was clear the book was already forgotten. To that D.J. didn't care. It was a private treasure given to him by Mac. It would stay private because no one else would understand. Least of all, his father.

The knock at his door jarred him from reminiscence. He had completely forgotten his commitment to running with Lee and Andy. He had bonded with the classmates and along with Jimbo, their friendship had been growing. When running, he preferred to train alone but the twins had gradually worn him down. Unnecessarily, he felt an itch as if readying himself for competition.

He opened the door as two reddened faces greeted him. They had accumulated two miles before meeting him and were ready for more. "D.J., get your shit together!" said Lee. "We said we would be here at eleven. What's your problem?"

"Dude, you're still in your shorts?" Andy asked as he examined him. "Let's roll, man!"

D.J. flushed at his forgetfulness and tried to cover. "Damn, I was just getting to it. I thought I had ten minutes yet. Just give me a second." Retreating to his bedroom, then returning moments later, he was ready for the excursion. "Let's move!" he half-shouted.

He stopped when he saw them gazing at the old running book. The twins looked at each other before Lee spoke. "This looks like the Dead Sea Scrolls of running." He paused and put his hand on his brother's shoulder. "That means it's really, really, old shit, Andy. Like biblical."

Andy blustered. "I get that, Lee. Don't be a tool."

D.J. stepped in. "Chill, guys. It's a book from a friend," he explained. "An old guy who ran a four-minute mile a long time ago. He lives near here."

Lee looked confused. "Under four minutes? A guy from this shit-town?"

D.J. nodded. "Yes," he said. "And that ain't the half of it. You guys have no idea." When they looked at each other, D.J. laughed. "Let's get on the road and I'll fill you in."

When they moved toward the door, the workout had officially begun.

***

They caught their breath the first mile and waited until a rhythm arrived. To an outsider it was remarkable; how can one run and talk at the same time? But to a fit runner it was a pedestrian achievement. To them it was the norm and nothing more than a simple act. When the runners turned a corner, they accelerated with a spring in their step.

Andy spoke first. "Ok, D.J. Tell us about that old book in your house. That thing looked like an ancient bible my Busia used to keep."

D.J. shook his head in bewilderment. "Busia? What's that?"

"I think it's Polish for grandma. Either that or it means 'free sausage'."

"Nice," replied D.J. "I'll remember that." Then he got serious. "I met this old guy named Mac. His first name is Thomas," he explained, "but only his wife calls him that." He shook out his hands to let blood flow. Then a breath before speaking again. "He has a history that is whacked." He explained the beginning of their relationship. How they met on the roads. Then, how he had been making regular visits to his home. His failing wife. The old track and field magazines along with the track spikes. How he had discovered Mac's accomplishments and his rare achievement of participating in the Olympic Trials. Lastly, his deadening failure in the event itself. It was then he stopped talking. Almost as if he had revealed too much about a man they did not even know. He had no right to pass judgement on a runner that had reached heights he could only dream about. When it was clear he had finished, they responded.

"D.J.," said Andy, "that's crazy stuff. How can a guy that good be stuck here in Skidmark, Wisconsin? No one famous lives here."

"For real," seconded Lee. "The only other guy here that has ever done anything like that is Jackson Jones when he won some bullshit world lumberjack contest a few years ago. But this Mac guy is for *real*."

D.J. ramped the pace of the run and absorbed the thoughts. Mac *was* real. He had knowledge of the sport far beyond the three of them combined. But he was an unsettled soul who avoided the sun for fearing it would reveal the truth: he had failed in the biggest moment of his life. Because of that he had eternally restless days and sleepless nights. D.J. knew the drill himself. About never feeling right. Settled. Of never being on solid ground even when others around him were. And even worse, the fear of never getting to a place where contentment was achieved.

This he didn't tell his friends. He kept his pain to himself. When he again increased the pace, he didn't explain. He just ran in silence as the others tailed behind. He had no intention in breaking their spirit; there was no glory in that. It was only that the speed drove his angst deeper.

That by itself was a victory.

**

He slowed soon thereafter. The gap had widened to fifty yards when he broke from the zone. He barely even remembered pushing the pace. That was the way it was for him. His body hovered over the ground and he ate up the distance in elongated strides. He had no explanation for the way running made him feel. But only that it was right, true and pure. Even more, he needed it.

He was sheepish and apologized for the burst but they were having none of it. Running was mano a mano; the meek were vanquished with no questions asked. Nor were apologies accepted.

"Don't be stupid, D.J.," said Andy. "If we could keep up, we would. This may sound weird, but I like watching you run." He explained. "You make it look easy. The way most of us wish it was."

Lee nodded. "I have to work my ass off to keep up but I'm good with that. I know it will make me better. But more than that, like Andy says, you have something different." He looked to D.J. and gave a tiny shrug. "Like God made you for this."

Andy continued. "We can't wait to see you on the track. We've talked---,"

Lee interrupted. "Andy, not now."

"What?" asked D.J. "Talked about what?"

Andy looked at Lee and got the go ahead. "That we want to see you run against Dalton. He's such a cocky a-hole sometimes."

Lee laughed. "But he's a *fast* a-hole. Last year in the sixteen-hundred he beat most of us by nearly half a lap."

"We saw him win state," Andy said. "He won by fifteen yards and it might have been more but he screwed around by waving to the crowd. It was freaking annoying."

"He says he wants to break the state record this year," Lee added. "I think he might."

D.J. let that sink in. "And that is?"

"I think it's around 4:04. The talk is he can run at any college he chooses." He sighed. "And he thinks he can even win nationals. At the bonfire he told me that no high school runner can beat him."

They both looked at D.J. and his shoulders tightened. When his heartbeat elevated, the inbred impulse to accelerate had to be restrained. There was plenty of time for that. He held back. Today he was with friends.

On the track there was no such thing.

.

Chapter Seventeen

Blackness covered the room like a shroud. He tossed and wished for sleep that despite consumed whisky was hard in coming. He was not a drinker but it was necessary given D.J.'s unexpected video replaying endlessly in his head. His own version had done so a thousand times but to see it in black and white made it harsher and more brutal in honesty. He tossed uncomfortably until he was able to drift into the darkness.

But there was no escape.

The fog thickened as if a cloud had reached the earth. He ran through it. Driving his legs. Pumping his arms. He never avoided the effort. In fact, he relished it. The harder the better. The more pain, the greater the reward. The cloud thinned. Faces. Childhood friends. A high school coach. Then lightness. Mona! A youthful face that years had not yet altered. He smiled and increased his pace. Then another visage. His father. Stern. Taciturn. Glowering at him from the fog. Harsh. Critical of his endeavors. Seeing only frivolity in a footrace. To win would prove the man wrong. To lose was unacceptable. Teeth clenched, he drove on. Chasing the men in front of him. Yet they separated. Losing him despite his effort. He panicked. Felt a tug in his hamstring. The fog condensed and the effort to proceed became unbearable. The pack ahead disappeared and he was lost. Out of balance. Out of hope. His father was right.

He stopped running and stepped further into the darkness.

He awoke gripping the blanket. A thin trickle of sweat ran down his back. He was disoriented and his eyes darted around the room. The dream was not new. It recurred on lonely nights when images of running were regurgitated. Spurred by television commercials where a jogger was used to sell a product. Or when a neighborhood plodder chugged along on a quiet roadside.

The worst was when he remembered.

Despite all his successes, he boiled his career down to a singular failure. He buried it deep. Never talked about it anymore. Only Mona knew the weight he carried. They dissected it in the early years. After that it was rarely mentioned again. But she knew. It was the distant look. The faraway eyes that looked back fifty years. He knew it was ultimately insignificant. It was only a footrace. But to him it was more. It was his chance at greatness. At immortality. A chance that only came along once.

A chance he would never have again.

He sat up in bed and gripped the edge of the mattress. Mona slept peacefully on the other side and for that he was grateful. He worried of the future and of her precarious health. She never complained but the vibrancy was slowly draining from her eyes. It was as if a small spigot dripped incessantly until her reservoir of life was nearing empty. They never talked about that either. That was too painful, too hard to comprehend. It had always been the two of them and no one else. But that time was nearing an end.

"Thomas? Are you okay?" asked a soft voice from the other side. "Can't you sleep?"

He paused. His concerns were microscopic compared to hers. So, he did what he had done before. He lied. "I'm fine. Just a little upset stomach." Then he revealed a portion of the truth. "I had a little nip of whisky and even that didn't help."

"You know it usually doesn't," she admonished. But she knew him better than that. "Is there something else?"

"Yes. No." he replied.

She sighed. "Are you going to make me ask again? After all these years?"

He wanted to feign ignorance but knew its futility. Given her present physical state. he felt small. Petty. But he knew she would not let it go.

"Remember I told you D.J. had been over?" She nodded. "Well, he found a video of the 1968 Olympic Trials. It was on YouTube. On his phone."

"I've heard of that YouTube thing. And?"

He had no response. Instead he looked into the darkness. Searching. Wishing he could avoid the words. Then he released his grip. "It was like when I was watching it, I was someone else. A ghost from the past. Like I was in a dream. A horrible, cruel nightmare I could not escape." He took a breath and her hand met his. "I watched and my heart almost burst from my chest. It was me, yet it wasn't. It was a thin boy I used to know. I willed him on, as if I could change the outcome. But of course, it was the same. I rounded that last corner and stepped off the track. In the biggest moment of my life, I failed." He stopped. Slumped. Then closed his eyes. When he opened them, he looked toward his wife. She was lying back on her pillow and even in the dark, her eyes glistened. He held her hand and wondered what she thought. Did she feel for him? Understand his pain? Or worse, pity him? Maybe even embarrassed at his self-loathing that in the face of her own ailments was incredibly pathetic?

The answer never came. Instead she gently ran her thumb over the back of his hand.

He didn't have the strength to ask.

Chapter Eighteen

The long winter plodded ahead. He had survived the season before but this was a different species. In the city there were snowplows and buses incessantly pushing through the snowfall. There he walked to school no matter the accumulation. Here, in the Northwoods, he was at the mercy of the weather gods. There were chest-high drifts, frozen snow crackling underfoot, and worst of all, black ice. Eventually the roads would be tended to, but given the convoluted network of country roads, they were cleared on a random schedule. But in spite of the obstacles, he ran through the general petulance of the season. He never missed a day; like simple needs, running was just one more.

Mac had talked to him about the importance of running becoming as routine as brushing one's teeth. Do it every day, even better, twice. In that it would become part of your pulse - engrained in the core of who you were. Ultimately, leading to what it took to be a champion. Those words struck a resounding chord. A champion. Someone who mattered. And the weather? Mac clucked at his concerns: *Why don't you get a treadmill?* he taunted. *So you can go to where the weak get weaker. Or maybe you can decide to be a man and beat the elements? Challenge yourself that you will not accept defeat*, he railed. *Ron Hill ran every day for fifty-two years. Ted Corbitt ran hours a day through the streets of New York. Ron Daws wore extra layers in the summer to make running more miserable. To harden himself like a diamond in order to crush the pretty boys running to get a suntan.* In Mac's mind, this was the time to harden. D.J. accepted the advice because he had nothing else. Without running, he simply existed. But when he took flight, he was alive. When he strode on the roads, he was part of something bigger than himself. Something he could not explain. With each run he did not change the world. He simply covered ground that barely noticed his imprint. It was then he was pure. And even if no one else understood, he was arriving toward his own destiny.

On a Saturday morning, he sat on the couch and prepared for a run. While securing laces, he braced at the sound of movement from his father's room. He had returned late the previous evening with heavy footstrikes echoing in the dark. D.J. had not greeted him and feigned he was sleeping. His stomach still knotted when they interacted but admitted the discourse was slowly lessening. He barely knew the man; only yellowed memories from the early years. What was in their place were only faded snapshots of time.

What was new was a small package sitting on the coffee table. A shoebox. He read the note softly:

D.J.,

I stopped in an outlet mall on the way home. I thought if you're going to run your ass off, you might as well do it in good shoes. Hope they fit.

Fred

He opened the box and examined the pair of Nikes. Dark blue. Sleek but built for running. Even the size was correct:

11.5. His current two pairs were nearing the end. Uppers frayed and soles worn down to the midsole. He had worried of their state but was leery to ask for replacements. He palmed the new shoes in his hand. Smelled their newness. Then he set them on his lap and looked to his father's bedroom. Hearing a droning snore, he decided against waking the man.

Instead, he slipped the shoes on. The right, then the left. Both cradling his feet like slippers. He stood and wiggled his toes. *Perfect*, he thought. He decided to leave a note:

The shoes fit great. Trying them out. Thanks!

He headed out the door and cinched his jacket to cover his neck. His clothing was still a hodgepodge of rummage sale purchases collected over the years. Layered to protect from the cold, they were less than fashionable but provided adequate defense. He moved north and tested the shoes. Feeling an unaccustomed spring in his step, the sensation buoyed him. *Like pillows on my feet,* he thought. The adrenaline bursting forth was akin to a spring day of penetrating sunshine. He eschewed a proper warm-up and let his body flow. The roads were white from melted salt distributed to combat ice but the footing was secure. He stretched out his stride and picked up the pace. The roads, bordered by snow-filled pine trees, wove ahead endlessly. Winding. Smooth. And imminently intoxicating. Moments like this he was utterly alone. No present or past. No mother or father. No teammates or competitors. Just the beating of his heart. Confusion and anxiety extinguished like a candle in the wind.

He ramped the pace and ignored the whispers to slow down. Flying recklessly down the road, he let the news shoes provide lift. The jarring of the asphalt was muted and his legs nearly murmured in acknowledgment. *Go for it*, they said. He accelerated as brisk air cooled his flushed cheeks. Although he preferred summer running, the temperature was conducive to maximum performance. In no danger of overheating, he just let himself go.

At six-minute pace he pushed harder. Five-thirty per mile was just as easy and he continued to explode. Getting on the balls of his feet, he soon eclipsed the five-minute mark. His fitness had improved and it was a delicious sensation to cover ground like a wild-eyed cheetah. His breathing accelerated in accordance with the pace. Feeling omnipotent, it was the closest he had ever felt to God, as if a single index finger escaped thin clouds overhead and touched his forehead. The sensation was both powerful and mystifying. He had never been spiritual. Had barely set foot in a church. Yet, here in the Northwoods, running at top speed, there was something bigger than himself. He suddenly dizzied and the edge accumulated in the last thirty minutes was lost. He looked ahead and chose a knotted oak tree as his final destination before turning back. He repeated his mantra of "never give in" nearly aloud. Holding top-end speed, he strode on as his breathing reached crescendo. Imagining a bare branch a finish line tape, he leaned and broke the barrier. With hands on his knees, he enjoyed the artificial moment for what it was – a good effort that would reside only in memory.

When ready, he turned to retrace the course already covered. He immediately felt a chill trickle through moist clothing. The wind. He hadn't noticed the stiff breeze at his back that undoubtedly aided the effort. He steadied against the wind and leaned into the effort. The moisture on his uncovered face began a slow freeze and for the first time since being transplanted to Wisconsin, he worried about the elements. He knew of frostbite and hypothermia from school. They were a real threat and not to be taken lightly. Yet, alone in the woods, there was no option but to fight against the natural hazards. He grimaced at what lie ahead.

He steadied his run and simply wanted to get home to warmth and comfort. He vowed to check the wind next time and avoid the rookie mistake of starting with the wind. But that was in the future. This was now. He calculated he still had nearly four miles before completion. This distance was not daunting but his discomfort crested. The luxury of his new shoes was forgotten. What became front and center was the sweat freezing against his skin as inferior clothing failed the test. Continuing to stride, he rubbed his gloves over his chest to ward off the chill. His fingers were becoming numb but those he could wiggle to fight the affliction. Then a new region got his attention.

He touched his privates and was alarmed at the lack of sensation. He was immediately fearing the worst and wondered if frostbite could affect *every* area. Even there. He decided not to take a chance and slipped a glove into his pants to shield the wind. Then he pulled his exposed hand deep into the sleeve of his jacket to protect it as best he could.

"This sucks so bad," he said aloud.

The remainder of the run all but obliterated the glorious nature of the first half. Survival mode was summoned and he increased the pace to minimize the time outside. Fatigue set in but he ignored the call. He would handle this and dreams of a warm soak in the bathtub drove him forward. Heading around the last bend, he spied his house in the distance. The ranch home appeared luxurious as he slowed his cadence to a trot. Closing his frozen lashes, he rejoiced silently at his successful return.

Opening the front door, he trembled from the depth of the winter effort. Stomping the grit from his shoes, he peeled off his ice-covered hat and wiped away the film of frozen spit from his chin. It was only then his eyes met his fathers.

Sizing up the boy, he spoke. "Wind up here cuts cold, D.J." Then after further study. "You look like shit."

He didn't disagree.

Chapter Nineteen

Early spring crested and a trickle of thaw filled the streets. For Mac it was not a minute too soon. He was tired of the monotony. The gray. The darkness. And the insufferable cold. By mid-March he was not out of the proverbial woods, but at least there was a slim beacon of light arising. He had long ago run out of simple chores and his days were filled with longing. For what he couldn't quantify. But he knew it was something just out of his grasp.

Mona was puttering in the kitchen as she prepared a homemade chicken noodle soup for D.J.'s imminent visit. It was the one thing they both looked forward to on Friday nights. Mona's energy waxed and waned but revitalized at the prospect of a visitor gracing their home. The evening's visit was simplified even more than usual given unexpected car trouble. Tonight, the meal would contain only that which was already in their possession. A hearty broth was something Mona could make in her sleep and with that, she was hard at work.

He had sliced the vegetables for the soup and boiled the chicken. Dicing the meat was his job too. Mona no longer had the strength to wield the knife and without prodding, he performed the preparation. He worried about her and how long he could provide what she needed. He was strong in relative terms, but with aging, his decline was also gradual. He could help her from bed and perform simple physical acts but if needs progressed, an assisted-living center loomed on the horizon. Mona had brought up the possibility but he downplayed the eventuality. But as she sat on a stool methodically preparing the soup, her frail countenance revealed the obvious.

She was declining week by week.

"It smells good, honey," he said, breaking the trance. "D.J. should be here shortly. And I doubt he has had homemade chicken soup anytime recently."

She clucked back at him. "I would have made dumplings too, but I just didn't have the time."

He nodded. Time. In one sense she had all the time in the world. The hours of each day were filled with books, game shows and reruns. But time was dwindling. A day was twenty-four hours closer to the afterlife. His anguish was relieved when the lilt of the doorbell filled the room. "I got it," he called, needlessly.

D.J.'s broad smile met him. He looked thinner in the face. Angular. Like an animal after a lean winter. Mac welcomed the visitor. "C'mon in, son." Son. He wished for a better choice of words. but it was too late. "Not too bad out there, D.J.?"

"It's been worse," he replied. "Spring sometime soon, I hope."

Mac shook his head. "Up here the weather is a cruel playmate. T-shirt weather one day and snowshoes the next. Just wait and see."

D.J. slipped off his jacket. "I hope you are wrong." Handing it to Mac, he continued. "But track starts next week. I can't wait."

An unfamiliar rustle appeared in Mac's gut. It had been nearly fifty years since he last competed and still an uncharacteristic itch arose when competition was mentioned. Sweating palms. An increase in heartrate. He took a deep breath and quelled the uprising. "That's great, D.J. I bet you're excited."

He nodded. "Absolutely. I've run a lot and for the most part followed the Lydiard book you gave me."

"For the most part?"

He shrugged. "I'm an independent man, Mac. Can't no one pen me in." When he smiled, his intent was obvious.

"That so, D.J?" he asked as he smiled back. "A little bluster goes a long way."

"You know that for a fact?"

He did. On the track there was always bravado. A sideways glance while warming up. A cocky smile indicating uber confidence. Or complete disdain for an anxious opponent. The mental game existed and always would. But as Mac knew, some did it better than others. "I remember Jim Ryun at the '68 trials. He didn't talk to any of us. It was like we were children in the race and he was royalty. In fact, he was," he said with a laugh, "but he didn't have to make it so obvious."

"He was that good?"

Mac rejected the inference. "Yes. In a race your job is to destroy the opponent and that starts by planting seeds of doubt in their mind. Like you are more fit. Faster. Stronger. And that you can take anything they dish out and retaliate. Make them hurt. And in the end, crush them."

D.J. studied him. Mac wondered what he saw. The gray hair. The wrinkles. But did he see the passion that bubbled just below the surface? Many runners never considered the mental gamesmanship of running. Most just lined up on the starting line and ran as hard as they could and hoped for the best.

Then D.J. spoke. "So, the race starts before the gun goes off."

Mac smiled. The boy got it. "Yes. The moment you hit the venue, the game is on. Don't kid yourself. Races can be won in the warmup." He raised a crooked finger in the air. "Not all, mind you, but some. Some psyches are more fragile than others. There are those you can break. But the great ones are made of tougher stock." Saying this, his own failure reared its head. Back then as often as not, he had it all. Ability. Speed. Toughness. It was only a crack in his shell that appeared at the worst of times.

"I get it, Mac. And I'll keep all this in mind when the time comes." He licked his lips and narrowed his eyes. "You should have been a coach, Mac. No one last year ever talked about this stuff. They just told me to run faster."

Coach. Him? Mac nearly laughed aloud. "Sure, D.J. I'll get my walker and bullhorn and be right on that. I'm sure your new coach will know what's up. Just you wait and see."

Yet, deep down, he was unconvinced.

***

"Mona, that was awesome," D.J. said as he finished his third bowl of soup. "I'm used to the canned stuff. You know, Campbells."

She wrinkled her nose. "Dreadful," she said. "Full of salt and poisons and God knows what else."

"Tell us how you really feel, Mona," said Mac.

She shooed his statement and continued. "Kids these days have no idea. All fast food and chemicals coursing through their veins. Parents should have their heads examined. Some should be brought up on child abuse for giving them chicken butt-nuggets and French fries, like they're some kind of delicacy."

D.J. reddened at the dialogue. "I grew up on fast food, Mona. It's all I knew. It sucked, but it's the way it was."

The pall over the kitchen table could nearly be touched. But Mac was grateful the boy felt he could speak honestly. That here was a place he would be listened to.

Mona broke the silence. "That's not your fault, D.J. You were just a child doing all you could to survive. You were in a difficult situation and had to keep your head above water." She reached across the table and touched his hand. "What is remarkable is that you are doing so well." She squeezed the hand. "You are a good young man, D.J. If you weren't, Mac would not have invited you here. He saw something in you. Something good. Maybe even great." Moisture lit her eyes and she let go. "Life isn't always fair, but to those that rise above, happiness and achievement is." She paused. "But just to be safe, avoid those goldarn buttnuggets whenever possible."

When she winked, all was right again.

Chapter Twenty

He was nervous all day. The first day of track practice had finally arrived. He had lived in the Northwoods nearly six months and time dripped like sap from a tree. The school day was uneventful and making his way to the locker room, his heartbeat ramped. Blowing out a soft breath, he tried to calm the moment.

"Deej!" called Jimbo from behind. "Finally, time to kick ass and take names. We got this, big boy!"

His sheer size was imposing. Over six feet tall with tree trunks for thighs, he would never be mistaken as a whippet-thin distance runner, nor would he want to be. But the flow of passion he exuded was an adrenaline rush. He was a natural leader and captain material from the moment he set foot on campus.

"Hey, Jimbo, what up?" he asked.

"Only the dog shit on the bottom of my shoes when I stand on the victory podium," he replied. "This is going to be a great year. Me throwin' and you rollin'. We got this 'bro."

He was at a loss for words as he was just hoping to get through the stress of the first practice. Anything more than that would be a victory in itself. "I guess we'll see, Jimbo." He didn't admit his uneasiness. In this venue he was still new. A transfer. Different. Decidedly an unknown.

Time would tell.

***

He estimated the count at fifty athletes, both male and female. The school was markedly smaller than his last urban setting as was the turnout of competitors. Like the rest of the gathering, he sat in the gym stands and awaited the coach's entrance. He had heard good things about the man as well as the rest of the small staff. Tough but fair was the general feedback. Sitting near Lee and Andy made the waiting more bearable.

"Coach Heck is the head coach," Andy explained. "He also teaches math. He'll be around and gives us workouts but doesn't really get involved with the distance guys."

"Unless we really suck," interjected Lee. "Then he'll get in our faces."

"True," said Andy. "Mostly he tells us to work hard but that we are on the honor system."

"Honor system?" asked D.J.

Andy extended his arms with palms down as if waiting to be handcuffed. "We police ourselves. The route. How many miles. The pace." He pointed out the windows toward the track. "On the track sometimes, he'll time us. That is, when he's not too busy with the sprinters."

D.J. followed their gaze. "So, there's no distance coach?"

Lee shook his head. "Not specifically. Last year there were only about ten of us running distance. Some of the guys come and go, anyways." He shrugged. "Jobs, hunting. You know, the usual."

That he did not know. He once briefly had a part-time job and had never hunted. "I guess. But how do you get better if you don't run?"

Lee and Andy looked at each other. Then Lee smiled. "To some guys on the team, track is just something to do."

Something to do? He blanched at the thought. To him it was *all* he wanted to do. Needed to do. To think otherwise was blasphemy. He didn't understand a weak mindset and was prepared to tell them. Then a voice boomed from the floor of the gym.

"Quiet down, ladies and gentlemen!" the voice said. The crowd's attention focused on the thin man dressed in a blue tracksuit. Buzzcut salt and pepper hair framed a craggy face and jutted chin. D.J. estimated he was pushing sixty but had energy well beyond that.

Andy almost read his mind as he whispered. "He's been teaching here thirty years. Coaching track for ten. The team does okay and we usually end up somewhere in the middle of the pack."

D.J. nodded as Heck continued. "Today starts a new season for us. I trust you have all trained this winter and are ready to ramp it up today?" The muffled laughter echoed the truth. "Just as I thought," he said. "Then I guess it is my responsibility to bring out the best in you. I want to start the new season with a confession." He paused narrowing his eyes. "Just like you, I look in the mirror each day. In doing so, sometimes it is just a mundane activity. The usual process that we don't give much thought to. But today it was different." He paused. "Today I looked into my eyes. Beyond the obvious. And I asked myself if I was doing all I could to bring out the best in myself. Then I thought about all of you. It became clear to me that I had failed the both of us. Too many times I settled for mediocrity when I could have reached for greatness. This year things will change." He strode forward and looked to the stands. There he returned the looks of the athletes. "I absolutely believe that today, right now, if we commit to the same goal, that for the first time ever we can win the conference championship. I believe that with all my heart and soul. Beyond that, I believe we can send athletes to state where they can compete on the greatest stage. But our commitment must start now. No longer will I accept excuses of jobs getting in the way. Or choir practice. Or a sniffle that leaves you less than your best. No more!" he said with emphasis. "We are either in this to win, or I will be glad to step down." The gym was silent as he quieted. He looked them over and waited. Then nodded. "So, what shall it be, Weston High? Are you committed, or should an old man hand in his resignation right here and now?"

The room was silent. D.J. looked straight ahead as his shoulders clenched. He was new to the team but was aware what the man craved. To succeed. To bring out the best in them. Even more than that, he wanted to win.

Then a body stood from the middle of the bleachers. A single voice spoke. "Coach Heck, do you mind if I answer for all of us?"

He smiled. "Please do," he replied.

The crowd looked to Jimbo. "Hey y'all," he said. "Most of you know who I am and the ones that don't will soon. Anyways, I agree with Coach Heck. I'm tired of getting beat by the peckerwoods from Wautoma and Montello and other shit-towns. We can do what we always do and just show up." Then he took a deep breath. "Or we can decide we are better that that. That we are special. Champions." He whistled. "Damn, that's a sweet word. But that ain't up to coach. That's up to us." He looked to the crowd and narrowed his eyes. "I know what we can do. So do you. And now's the time."

The gym was silent as he sat down. A single clap. Then another. A rhythm generated as more joined in. D.J. shivered as his hands automatically followed along. As the cadence continued, an energy reverberated from the stands.

Coach Heck only smiled.

***

The first workout was prescribed and D.J. was itching to begin. It was a simple distance run of eight miles. He was told the early season runs would often be in the roundabout hallways of the school or in the gym, but today the weather had cooperated. It was mid 30's and the ground was dry. Compared to some of the winter, the day was a stroll in the park. Along with the other distance runners, he met towards back door of the gym.

"Coach told me to get us started," said Lee, with a slight beam on his face. "That we should stay together and get a nice effort going. Medium pace, he said." He looked over the group of six runners. Himself. Andy. And three non-descript runners swaddled in bargain basement togs. "I'm Lee. This is my brother, Andy, as if you couldn't tell," he said, pointing to his sibling. Then he nodded to each of three freshmen. "I've just met them, but this is Bill, Eddie, and Till." He paused and nodded to one final runner. "And this is D.J." The runners mumbled greetings and he continued. "We are going four miles out to Indian Point and then turn back. Coach said to stay in a pack if we can but work the last part as each see fit. But to remember, that today, it's not a race."

D.J. stirred and studied the others. He wanted nothing more than to start the workout. To blast the roads and prove his worth. Lee's words barely registered.

He needed to run.

They exited the gym doors and a cool wind slapped their faces. Aside from the distance runners, the rest of the team would stay in the bowels of the school and perform what they could. Jogging. Short sprints. Throwing implements as safety enabled. It was only the distance runners freed to the elements.

"You okay, D.J.?" asked Andy. "You seem so quiet."

He was. But true or not, he couldn't help but feel he was being tested by all. The new teammates. The coach. Most of all himself. He needed to find out if he could pass muster on the first day of practice. "I'm fine," he replied. "I just want to get going."

With that they took off. At first, a simple jog for the first mile. Then a subtle increase in pace that was nearly imperceptible. Strides lengthened. Breathing sharpened. Chatter disappeared as the effort became real. Lee, Andy and D.J. took the lead as the others dropped. The threesome clung together as they gobbled the roadside stride by stride. There was strength in the pack, albeit small, but a power nonetheless. The three veterans traded leading and talk subsided. The three became one as they flew down the isolated road. The breathing ramped then stabilized. Frozen breaths puffed in the late winter air as they ran step after step. Minutes, then miles, disappeared until they reached the turnaround point.

Andy wiped a sliver of sweat from his forehead before speaking. "D.J., don't let us hold you back. You heard what coach said. This is our year."

Lee chimed in. "It starts now D.J. I'll stay with Andy so he doesn't get lost." He laughed and a tiny cloud of frozen air followed. "Go, D.J. Now."

With that he was freed. Allowed to enter his own realm, he almost said, "thank you", but held the words. He didn't need their okay to run hard. That was undeniable. He increased his cadence and within seconds they were yards behind. His adrenaline coursed and his journey began. To where it would take him, he was unsure. But he vowed he would approach the task with reckless abandon. Running was a passion no one could take away from him. He grasped the moment harder and galvanized it into his subconscious. It was then he became something more than he had been minutes earlier.

A contender.

He ran harder. He was alone on the roads but that did not bother him. In fact, he preferred it. It was then he was in control of his own destiny. He increased the pace. Striding harder, he did not bother to look back. His friends had their own internal struggle and that was their business. His immersion was his own. The streams of frozen air intensified as he maximized pace. He reached top limit and focused on the hardened gravel lining the roadway. Ignoring the occasional vehicle speeding past, he fixated on the moment. Each step was a tiny victory. One stride closer to his goal that at that moment solidified.

He vowed to win state and be damned if he did not.

The run continued until the school came within site. The low-lying winter sun glared as he strode on. Cars exited and random students dotted the landscape but he ignored their existence. He had a mission to complete and did so. Entering the school's parking lot, he slowed to a jog until finishing with a recovery walk. Hands on his knees, he caught his breath and looked behind. He was alone. Ahead of the rest.

It was exactly where he wanted to be.

Chapter Twenty-One

Purpose. Seven letters. It was a simple word yet complex at the same time. But it was what he lacked. A simple reason for being. The three-mile walk had done little to calm the tempest in his head. He was a husband that was needed, that much was sure. But he desired more in a world that had forgotten he existed.

He closed the front door and placed his shoes on the floormat. As was ritual, he double checked the lock. He stood and considered the habit. There was nothing of consequence in the home to entice a burglar. Knick-knacks, figurines, and a stack of worn jazz albums well past their prime. Yet, he still sealed the home like it was Fort Knox.

The very thought depressed him even more.

"Is that you, honey?" Mona called.

Who else would it be? he thought, frustration overflowing. But he withheld the impulse to lash out. "Yes, Mona. I'm back."

"Did you have a nice walk?"

Walk. He despised the word. "Yes, it was fine."

The discontent was broken by a ringing of the phone. Phone calls were rare and often only a misdial or a salesperson fulfilling their quota. He hated calls and would ignore them whenever possible.

Mona was the opposite. She could chat for an hour and beyond about the day's events. Not him. Get to the point and move on. He wanted to let it ring until Mona called. "Can you get that?"

He sighed. "Yes. Okay, Mona." He walked to the front room and picked up the receiver. Expecting the worst, his voice displayed apathy. "Hello," he said slowly.

When the other voice spoke, he sat down. He grunted. Said yes. Said no. Told the caller it was something he had never thought about. Then mumbling a semblance of a final greeting, he said goodbye. He stayed in the chair another minute and looked out the window toward the front yard. It was only when Mona called, he roused from his trance.

"Who was that, Thomas? Anything important?"

He moved to the bedroom. There she was nestled under covers, propped up by an oversized pillow. Book in hand, she slid down her reading glasses to gain a better look.

"Thomas?" she questioned.

He sat down next to the bed. Tapping the arm of the chair, he calculated how to continue. "It was Dan Heck from Weston High School. He is the head track coach there." he said. "He had a question for me."

"A question? What was it?"

He stopped tapping. "He said he talked to D.J. after practice today. It appears they have no one to coach the distance runners and D.J. told him about me. He told Coach Heck I would do great." He paused. "Apparently Heck thought it was a great idea too." He paused. "D.J. told him what I had done when I was younger and Heck wants to meet with me. To see if I have interest."

Mona smiled and her eyes widened. For a moment the wrinkles disappeared as if fifty years were erased. To a time of contentment. Of satisfaction. To when they were young. Then she spoke. "Well, I'll be goldanged knackerd and tied on the side. That is about the most exciting thing I have heard since I don't know when. Thomas McKinley, you will absolutely look into the opportunity, correct?"

The idea both excited and terrified. He had never thought specifically of coaching. Daydreamed, maybe, but years ago life had extinguished the possibility. But now here it was, at his doorstep.

"I can't do that, Mona. I mean…you…we have things to take care of. Appointments. Shopping. You know how it is."

She lowered her eyes. He rarely saw the look and prepared for the ballast. "Thomas McKinley, don't you dare use me as a means to reject this opportunity. I see you day after day with a hang-dog look on your face. Bored. Discontented. And even just plain lost." She pulled herself up in the bed. "I can manage just fine for the small number of hours it would take." Then she swung her legs to the side of the bed and stood in front of him. "Thomas, you need this. The boys on that team, and more than that, D.J. needs you." Then she reached and held his face in her hands. "And I want this for you. Live before it is too late."

He sat, stunned. He moved his hands to meet hers. "Mona, I don't know what to say. There is so much to consider. It's not so easy."

"Thomas, it absolutely is."

Looking into her eyes, the fierceness of her conviction erased any remaining doubts.

He was in.

Chapter Twenty-Two

The first race was on Tuesday of the second week. Acting as more of a hard workout, Coach Heck called it a glorified scrimmage. Located in the Weston gym, it was an attempt at mimicking an outdoor meet until weather permitted a true race. The periphery of the gym was lined by red cones as a rudimentary track was carved out on the hardwood floor. D.J. had run a few indoor meets in Chicago but there the track surface was congruent with the sport. This was decidedly Hicksville but he was eager to get the season under his belt. At twenty-two laps per mile, the sharp turns prohibited a time of consequence. Coach Heck explained that wasn't the point of the endeavor. Competition was.

D.J. sat with the other distance runners under the stands. The space was safe from distraction of the small crowd in attendance. He needed the quiet to minimize the noise in his head. Nerves were a part of competition and by staying isolated, he remained in control. Today was no different except for this being his first competition in nearly a year.

A shrill whistle alerted the runners to the first race. "Finally," said Andy as he idly stretched his calves. "We get to race instead of bashing our heads against each other." Then giving D.J. a look., he retreated. "Except you. We haven't even been close to you yet."

He was sheepish. "It ain't like that. I'm just a little ahead of you. I ran a lot this winter."

Lee interjected, "D.J., don't bullshit us. You are the man and we know it." He slapped him on the shoulder and continued. "It's going to be a fun year. Just wait and see."

"Yo," D.J. replied, "and it starts today."

"Absolutely," said Andy. "And pretty soon your friend will be here. Mac. Coach Heck told us maybe he'll start next week."

He played it cool. Laying on his back, he clasped his hands behind his head. "Is that so?" Nodding his head, he smiled. "He knows his shit. I promise."

Lee responded. "He has to be better than Coach Heck. At least he knows *something* about distance running." He shrugged. "Heck said he'll be here when he passes all of the administrative crap." His eyes widened. "Then finally, we can get down to business!"

"Damn straight," said Andy. "Right now, we are running solo, so to have anybody help us is cool. Even some old guy from way back."

D.J. corrected him. "Mac is old but he gets it. He seriously gets it. Wait until you meet him. He's done running shit that you won't believe. Way more than me and you ever will." He sat up and crossed his arms over both knees. "Remember I told you he was in the Olympic Trials in '68? Damn near made the Olympics too."

"That's right, you did. 1968. Holy Christ, the dude is ancient," said Andy.

D.J. shook his head. "Just wait," he replied knowingly. "You will change your mind. Soon." With that he lay down and focused on the upcoming effort.

***

He was more nervous than expected. Last year he was under the radar, just a freshman with no expectation attached. When he performed well, he was hailed a young phenom. Now, among his teammates, his reputation built with each workout. As he had hoped, he was slated to run the sixteen hundred meters. The distance always felt right to him. A blend of speed and strength where only the toughest survived. Plus, it had a unique characteristic separating it from other events.

Extended pain.

Somehow that worked for him. The last six-hundred yards were a descent into a private hell runners either embraced or shunned. Those that avoided it were vanquished, those that absorbed it had a chance at victory. In every mile he had competed there was a finite moment of deciding whether to step off the cliff and suffer, or simply stride until the finish line. Most times he absorbed the body blows and even if defeated, accepted he had done his all. In the others, he internally scolded himself for competitive frailty.

He readied himself on the line of ten runners. He was Weston's sole entrant in the small triangular meet. Edging to the line, he placed himself in the middle of the pack. He was the tallest entrant in the race but that was erased by other physical traits. It was the eyes upon him that resonated. The others were locals that rarely interacted with those of color. He tried to chalk it up to hypersensitivity but when two runners whispered, his radar ramped. In response, his blood pumped faster and he was ready.

Then one of the competitors pointed to him and spoke. "Dude, your shoe is untied."

Just then the referee readied to start the race. D.J. slid back half a step and attacked the shoelace. Before he could reestablish, the whistle sounded.

"Damn!" he shouted as he pulled on the lace. He sprang from his crouch and played unexpected catch-up with the pack. Anger yielded adrenaline and he fought to relax. The trackside shouts from Lee and Andy reminded him it was a long race, which momentarily soothed him. Twenty-one and a half laps *was* a long time. But given the unsightly beginning, his margin for error had slimmed.

He set up behind the other nine as the race unfolded. The sharp turns were not conducive to a fast time so competition itself was the key. Given the awkward angles of the cones marking the track, when in full stride he concentrated on avoiding the others. The short indoor track also made passing opponents precarious. He cursed his pre-race error and focused on the task ahead. Absorbing the calls of encouragement from his teammates, he crept to the heels of the ninth-place runner. Willing patience, he shook his arms and settled into the pedestrian pace, content on biding his time.

His breathing stabilized and he waited. And waited some more. Then he saw it. The runner ahead of him drifted wide on the sharp turn. He immediately attacked and accelerated through the inside space. Nudging him with an elbow, the runner drifted wider and although irritated by the contact, provided no response.

"Good job, D.J.," hollered Lee. "Fifteen laps to go. Do it when you can!"

He accepted the challenge. The top five were tightly grouped and none appeared willing to press the tempo. D.J. estimated four minutes and forty second pace, glaringly slow but given the sharp turns it was all he could hope for. Still, he wanted more. This was his first race for Weston. For his friends. And even more so, for himself. He hit the halfway point and was increasingly impatient. At two twenty-two for the first half-mile, he was still fresh. Studying the competitors in front of him, he calculated they were all waiting for the usual put-the-hammer-down sprint to the finish.

He decided to take matters into his own hands. Storing emotional and physical strength, he let one more lap pass by. Then as they crossed the starting line, he drifted wide and set himself on the shoulder of the runner ahead. Waiting was hard. Aggression was calling. And he prepared to unleash his instinct.

The short backstretch beckoned and he exploded into another gear. It was too early to make a move but he had run out of patience. *Take that, bitches,* he wanted to shout. Passing the group took a matter of thirty yards and given the befuddled face of the leader, his tactic had been unexpected. Before reaching the far turn, he had a two-stride lead and settled into the top spot. He had no intention of slowing and an adrenaline rush spurred him on. The meager crowd was a blur, an inconsequential number eliminated from consciousness. Even the braying of team members was rendered impotent as he passed the starting line one more time.

Ten laps. Under two minutes of running left. He eliminated any thought of failure and focused on the trek ahead. Cone by cone, turn by turn, he drove on. The zone was unexplainable but like a fish in a bowl, he was captive to his surroundings. He lifted his knees and elongated his stride, releasing himself. Six laps, then five. His breathing escalated but he was still in control. Not worried but curious, he glanced over his inside shoulder at the runners behind. Nothing. No one there. This emboldened him and he hammered the final nail in place with a hard pace he could hold until the finish. Pacing was a crap shoot, but locked-in he was prepared to go the distance.

With three laps to go the effort reared its head. Racing was not about comfort and never would be. It was about who could absorb and deliver pain better than another. Each segment became harder but if estimations proved correct, he would cross the line just as his reservoir emptied. Two laps to go. Breathing was a course rasp and oxygen disappeared just when he needed it most. Today, his first race for Weston, he wanted to cement his status as a runner. And as a competitor. The thought spurred him on as he lifted and entered the last lap. The bell marking the final lap was shrill, like a fire engine of bygone days. But to him it meant something more tangible, something delicious.

It meant relief from the pain was not far away.

He tried to relax his arms but it was useless. He was tying up and no psychological ploy could erase the insult to his being. He simply had to hang on until crossing the finishing stripe. He stumbled around the last corner and fought to stay erect. Eyes blurring, he pumped his arms knowing his legs would grudgingly follow. When he crossed the line, there was no gushing of satisfaction or arrogance of winning. Rather, just a simple joy knowing he had done his best.

He stumbled, placed his hands on his knees, and fought to stay erect. When able, he walked a lap and slapped outstretched palms to those that beckoned. The race was the curious pleasure and pain mixture that running delivered. After the fact, the pain was quickly forgotten and rehashing of the effort began. Today was no different.

"Jesus, D.J." said Lee. "You ran a 4:39. Your last half-mile was 2:14."

Andy shook his head. "Coach Heck said you would have won the half-mile by two seconds." He paused. "Are you freaking kidding me?" he asked, rhetorically.

D.J. shrugged. "I felt okay, so I had to go. It was fun." He paused and corrected himself. "At least most of it."

The two teammates smiled and shook their heads in wonderment. Wiping the sweat from his forehead, nothing additional needed to be said. It was then for no other reason than curiosity, he glanced to the stands. He hoped Mac might be in attendance but he was nowhere to be found. But another attendee garnered his attention. Dalton Scarie. Their eyes locked and neither wavered.

D.J. simply nodded.

Chapter Twenty-Three

He was nervous. He could scarcely remember the last time he felt this way. Palms sweaty. Armpits flowing like a leaking faucet. Even worse was his stomach tossing as if on the high seas. He was already regretting having accepted the offer to coach the distance runners. Maybe the position was over his head. Beyond his abilities. And quite possibly, he was a tiny bit batshit crazy. But there he was. Standing in the gym, waiting for practice to begin. Having been approved as a coach had been a more laborious process than expected. Years ago, one could apply for the position and have the authoritative whistle dangling from the neck an hour later. But to be allowed to coach this group of athletes. he had survived a background check, references, and a course on ethics that nearly insulted his integrity. There was no turning back.

Standing next to Coach Heck, he waited for practice to start. He clasped and unclasped his hands as if preparing for a bare knuckles fight. The movement belied the placid face displayed to the team. *Never let them see you sweat,* he said to himself. To display weakness would illuminate a crack in the foundation diminishing his capacity to lead. And that he couldn't stand for. To properly coach, he was all in or it was a waste of time. Consciously, he clenched his hands and readied for the battle ahead.

Heck blew his whistle and the athletes in the stands quieted. The shrill sound echoed in the gym and when it dissipated, he spoke. "Good afternoon, all," he said. "First off, congratulations on a nice performance last Friday in the indoor meet. Some of you demonstrated your off-season work. Others…well, others showed they have a long way to go. Hopefully there will be enough time to get where you need to be." The murmurs from the crowd increased but stopped when he lifted his hand. "But today is a new day and the success or failure of last week is forgotten. Today we have an announcement of cavalry coming to help us." He nodded toward Mac. "This is Thomas McKinley. Because I have my hands full as head coach and specialize in certain events, Coach McKinley will help with the middle and long distance runners. He has quite a bit of experience in the field and I believe his wisdom will help bring out the best to those under his guidance. So, to cut to the chase, please welcome Coach McKinley."

A tiny smattering of applause filtered through the gym. Mac was nonplussed; he knew respect was earned, not granted. He had been there before. Running for a small high school and then walking on to a college team. Expectations were negligible but after countless miles and hard work, gradually respect was garnered from teammates. After that it was the coaches. Then the conference runners he left in arrears. When he reached the national stage, his threadbare uniform caused more second looks than fear. It was only when he defeated his competitors on the track that true respect was finally achieved. Then, just like now, action carried more weight than any manufactured introductory words. He opened his hands and relaxed his arms at his side. "Thank you, Coach Heck. I'm happy to be here." After those words, he quieted. It was almost like he was standing on the white line again, preparing for the contest.

He was more than ready.

***

The distance runners congregated in the far corner of the gym. Mac stood above them as they sat in varying stages of attentiveness. He had toiled in middle management for years but never held the top reins. That changed today. He was irrefutably in charge whether ready or not. He cleared his throat and began. "As Coach Heck said, my name is Thomas McKinley. But from now on, I will simply go by 'Mac'. Fair enough?" With no complaint, he moved on. "So, if you could, please introduce yourselves and tell me a bit about yourself and your running background." He pointed to the smallest of the group. "How about you, son?"

The small runner stiffened, clearly uncomfortable. Mac nodded as if to lighten the moment but didn't say anything more. Unexpectedly, the runner stood. "I'm Bill," he said. "But a lot of people call me 'Mini', 'cause I'm so small." He fidgeted but continued. "I'm a freshman and ran cross country in the fall. I wasn't very good but I like to run." He shrugged. "That's all."

Mac smiled. "And that's enough. But to all of us, you will be 'Bill'. You don't need to be big to be a great runner. In fact, it might even help you. But what you do need is a big heart. That's where the truth lies." He nodded. "Nice to meet you,

Bill." The boy smiled and Mac pointed at the boy next to him. "And you?"

He jumped to his feet as if lightning had entered his body. "I'm Ti, Ti, Till," he said in a stutter. "I, I ran cross country too. I didn't run much this winter but I walk three miles to school every day. I guess that's something." He then sat down as fast as he stood up.

Mac studied him before speaking. The boy was shy, living inside his own shell. But he had seen others like him burst forth from the cocoon and achieve greatness. They just needed a gentle push. "Did you know that many champion Kenyon runners ran six miles to school each day?" He paused for effect. "Six miles each way. Twelve total. In doing so they build an engine inside so bold it can scarcely be beaten on the track or the roads. The fact that you do what you do, you should be proud. Keep it up." He pointed to the third boy. "Next."

He stayed seated as if glued to the floor. Concentrating on the moment, his eyebrows merged as if they had become one. "I'm Ed," he said simply. "I'm here because my Mom says I have to. I'm better at video games but she says I play them too much." His eyebrows relaxed. "That's it."

Mac nearly laughed aloud at the display. He had never understood video games and never would. Yet, the boy was here and that was enough. "Well, Ed, your Mom is a smart woman. I don't know much about video games but I do know that girls like champions." He winked. "I guarantee if you win a race, you'll feel a whole lot better than winning something on the computer. Keep that in mind for future reference."

The others chuckled under their breath and the mood was lightened. With that, the next runner volunteered his information. "I'm Lee and I'm a junior. I mostly like to hunt and fish but running ain't half bad once you get the hang of it. I like running in the woods best. Ain't no one there to get in your face."

"Absolutely," Mac replied, "there's nothing better than the woods where it's only you and nature. There was a Fin named Lasse Viren who logged nearly all his miles in the forest. Because of that he has a whole drawer full of Olympic medals to keep him warm at night. If you keep that up, you just never know."

The next athlete didn't miss a beat as he stood and presented his case. "I'm Andy, Lee's brother. Twins," he said, unnecessarily. "I like running because it makes sense to me. The more you do, the better you get. It's like a business that you have to work hard at." He bit his lower lip before continuing. "I want to be in politics someday. Maybe change some things for the good."

Mac studied the sharp eyes of the runner. "Lofty goals. but I have no doubt you can obtain them. A runner named Jim Ryun was a member of the House of Representatives and he once held the world record in the mile. Not a bad life, wouldn't you say, Andy?"

"No, Sir," he replied.

"Mac."

"No sir, Mac," he reiterated.

Then he turned to the last runner. D.J. had been avoiding eye contact but stood and faced him. His jaw clenched and Mac wondered of his mood. He knew the boy, yet they had barely scratched the surface of each other's strengths and frailties. Then the runner spoke in a clear voice. "I'm D.J. I'm from

Chicago and sometimes I still miss it." He looked Mac in the eye as his chest rose and fell in an even swoon. "I don't hunt or fish. I run." He stopped, nearly embedding his feet into the floor before continuing. "And I want to go to State. This year."

Then he sat down. The others looked at each other and considered the gauntlet dropped. They were silent and switched their gaze from D.J. to Mac.

He slowly clenched and unclenched his fists before speaking. He looked to each athlete and studied them. Lastly, he settled on D.J. Then he spoke in an even tone. "A pearl starts as a single grain of sand. It accumulates layers. It is the same for us. The grain is the starting line. The layers are the miles. Miles not always easy. Nor pleasant. But miles that will make us the runners we will become." The words settled. "I think we have the makings of an interesting year," he said. "And it begins today."

***

The day held the blush of spring. Sunlight peaking through patches of clouds. A trickle of water dotted the streets as a thaw warmed the earth. With the temperatures approaching forty-five degrees, it was a nearly flawless day for distance running. Mac acknowledged the weather before sending the runners on his inaugural workout. "Today we will run a group effort called a 'fartlek'."

The group chuckled and Lee spoke. "Fart lick? You mean Andy's pastime?"

His brother rolled his eyes. "So stupid. Grow up, Lee."

"Too late. I'm three minutes older, remember?"

He sighed. "Yes. You remind me every day."

Mac regained control. "Boys. Brothers. I said 'fartlek'. A Swedish word that means 'speed play'. First you will do a mile warm-up together just to loosen the bones. Then the six of you will form a line and separate from each other by about five yards. Lee and Andy will keep it at a seven-thirty pace and the runner in the back will then accelerate to the front of the line. Not a full-out sprint but a strong move to the front. Each of you can determine what that means. Then that person will become the new leader." He looked to D.J. "It is not a race, but an exercise in both patience and learning to change pace. In races, the pace may vary and you have to learn to react. Even better, to alter the pace and destroy your opponent's will. That is racing 101."

D.J. spoke. "How long do we go?"

"The fartlek is five miles. Take Miller Road toward Thompson's Hardware store and use that as the turnaround. Take a one-mile cooldown after and that will total seven miles."

"Only seven?" asked D.J. "That's not very much."

The younger runners looked nervously toward each other. Mac responded. "As I said, it is about learning patience. Something that will come in handy at the most crucial of times."

D.J. stirred in his seat.

Chapter Twenty-Four

The weeks passed slowly. School then practice. Rinse and repeat. A rhythm settled in although partly satisfying, was also numbing. School was the least of D.J.'s worries. He maintained his coursework and ground through the monotony of the homework. It was after school that raised the hairs on the nape of his neck. The sport that drew him in and accelerated his heart.

At least it used to.

He was second-guessing Mac after only two weeks of guidance. They had performed a variety of workouts including overdistance peppered in with Mac's affection for fartlek. Although fatigued at the end of practice, D.J. wished to be unleashed on the track. The weather had been meek and as the indoor season closed, the team prepared for the real deal: the outdoor track season. D.J. had not been allowed to run the sixteen-hundred again indoors. Mac had him concentrate on double that and in an unexpected moment, entered him in the eight hundred meters. Specifically instructed to run "within" himself, he ran with the competition until turning on the jets in a successful attempt at winning. Times were said to be irrelevant. Rather, gaining experience was the requested goal. Mac asked him to feel out each race, live inside the pack and absorb the generated tension. If in a tricky situation where he was pinned in, the simple goal was to extricate himself from the mass of competitors. Mac likened it to a chess match, where moves and countermoves occurred until only a single winner remained.

So far, he had won all the events entered but his times were pedestrian. He scoured the internet for other runners' indoor times and scowled when his were well behind. One site even listed top performances by ranking results. Jimbo was third in the shot put but D.J.'s performances were nowhere to be found. He scanned the sixteen-hundred list where a recognizable name led the honor roll.

Dalton Scarie.

He memorized the other names and wondered of their abilities. Alternating between a desire to compete, there was also a trickle of doubt in the recesses of his mind. He flip-flopped between an unyielding belief he could beat all comers to the nagging uncertainty he was kidding himself. That maybe he was just a city-bred pretender who had no business even lining up with them. The internal struggle was constant and wearied him. It was only when he flew down the roads that the doubts eased.

"Dude, you okay?" asked Jimbo as he sat beside him. "You look like a zombie lost in the woods."

The remarks startled him. He *was* miles away but he did not reveal the dynamics. Among the group of Jimbo, Andy and Lee, they had become accustomed to eating lunch together and today was no different. The distance runners settled across from him with lunch trays in tow. Jimbo carried an oversized lunch bag filled with enough food to sustain a small family. "No," D.J. replied, "I'm good."

Both Lee and Andy chewed on fries piled on the ceramic tray. Between mouthfuls, Lee was the first to chime in. "You get that look in your eyes, D.J. Like you're in a different world. Sometimes in school but mostly when you run."

Andy wolfed down his food and nodded in agreement.

"Really?" D.J. asked rhetorically. But he knew exactly what they meant. When he ran it was like he was plunging deeper into his brain. Thoughts thrashed about like waves on a rocky beach. Some smooth and others so jangled they were simply shards that had no beginning nor end. When they bubbled forth, they were nearly uncontainable and oozed like sweat from his body. It was only when he stopped running that he recognized the trip his mind had taken; his body often simply along for the ride.

Jimbo tore into his second sandwich and between swallows offered his opinion. "You distance guys are whacked. So stuck inside your own heads you don't know what hole to shit out of. Not like us dudes throwin' the rock. Weights and 'Kates'. Now *that's* what it's all about."

"Kates?" asked D.J.

"It's what he calls 'girls'," Andy explained. "Like they are all interested in a big tool with ketchup on his face."

D.J. smiled. "Mac says a wise man once said 'women weaken legs'." He shrugged. "Just sayin'."

Jimbo wiped the condiment from his lips. "I seriously doubt that. At least not *my* legs. Just watch tomorrow at the meet where all the Kates are hanging out. I guarantee it's not near you guys' bony-ass legs."

Even the simple mention of tomorrow's outdoor meet caused D.J.'s gut to twist. He was ready, yet he wasn't. The training had not been at the level he expected and for that he blamed Mac's approach. He had come close to challenging him on the methods but so far held back. He pushed away the rest of his half-eaten lunch and thought of the increasingly uncomfortable Friday night dinner.

***

The dynamics had changed. From friendly mentor to becoming coach was a large step filled with peril. D.J. had underestimated the transition and for the first time since their initial dinner, he was hesitant. When the front door opened, he smiled but the greeting felt cellophane thin. "Hey, Mac," he said, casually.

Mac returned the greeting. Then leading the way, he focused on the highlight of the evening. "Mona outdid herself tonight and whipped up her secret lasagna recipe. It'll fill your gut but still leave you begging for more." He ushered him into the kitchen. "Mona," he said to his wife, "look what the cat brung in."

She turned from the counter where she was slicing bread. "D.J.! Welcome. I made lasagna for the big race tomorrow." She stopped her activity at the counter. "Carbohydrates are still good for you, right? I read about so many things bad for us, I barely know what to make anymore."

"Lasagna will be great," replied D.J. In fact, he barely remembered the last time he had eaten it. And undoubtedly it was a frozen variety direct from the grocery store. Homemade?

That had never happened. "I doubt I'll die from it. But I'll let you know if I do."

"Please do," said Mac. "Mona, are we almost ready?"

She nodded. "As a matter of fact, perfect timing. Have a seat, D.J."

He did and the lasagna followed. Steam rose from the dinner and nearly intoxicated him. A heaping forkful reached his lips and the flavors attacked his taste buds. Unintentionally, he rarely looked up as he absorbed the food. His mind wandered and couldn't help but wonder if his friends had meals like this every day. He had spent so many nights scavenging for whatever was left in the refrigerator, that a meal like this was a fantasy. It was something people ate on TV, at a table surrounded by loved ones. Love. The word was as foreign to him as lasagna. He wanted it, craved it, but was certain he would never obtain it. The love/hate with both mother and father created an emotional haze that had no name. It was a blankness that never left, never became more than a stream of muted sunlight that failed to warm his face. Yet in this kitchen, this ten by ten-foot room, he felt a glow warmer than the nearby oven. Love, or a close approximation, emanated within. He started to tear up and was embarrassed. Emotion was something to be avoided because it was worthless. It didn't change anything. Yet, at this moment he was helpless.

"D.J., are you alright?" asked Mona. "Is the lasagna too spicy?"

He wanted to come clean. To admit his true feelings. But he couldn't, not yet. "No, it's perfect. I think I just got a little something in my eye. I'll be fine."

Mac studied him and took a sip of coffee. The moment stretched. Then setting the cup down, he spoke. "Yes, it was probably some garlic, D.J.," he agreed. "Spices are a tricky thing. Too much and they ruin a dinner. Not enough and a dish is listless. Dead. But use just the right amount and a plate becomes alive. Worth its weight in gold." He lifted a piece of lasagna in the air. "Wouldn't you agree, D.J.?"

He stirred the remnants on his plate and stayed silent.

***

When the dinner ended, Mona immediately shooed them toward the living room. They ambled slowly and Mac made his way to the record player and without asking, placed an album on the turntable. The crackle of the record was followed by the strain of a single saxophone. Mac sat down, closed his eyes, then spoke.

"Charlie Parker, known as the 'Bird'. He was one of the great ones. Rare. Unencumbered. Always doing his own thing, no matter what. But sometimes his choices had a cost. It was lonely. Difficult. And full of complications."

D.J. studied him and dissected the words. They had meaning and were carefully chosen. But this puzzle was confusing. D.J. waited until he opened his eyes before responding. "His music is different than the others. I'm not sure I like it."

Mac smiled and replied. "He is an acquired taste. But given a chance, Parker displays a pulse all his own. Sometimes somber and sometimes out of control. Both have their place, but both carry inherent danger."

"Danger? In music?"

"Yes, in music. Just like in life."

D.J. wearied of the game. The old man liked to give lessons but he was not in the mood. Rather, he fast approached irritation. "Mac, I don't know what you are talking about."

Mac settled back into the armchair. As Parker's sounds filled the air, he began. "I'm talking about the cost of being impetuous."

"I don't know what that word means."

"Rash. Hasty. As in not having the patience to trust the process."

"The process?"

Mac nodded. "I think we both know what we are talking about. I see it on your face and in your attitude. And not so much in words but by their absence. You are not happy in your running and it shows."

It was as if a dam burst. "Well, why not? I waited all winter to finally get after it and now I feel like one of those horses penned in a barn. I just don't get it."

Mac's face was serene. He took a deep breath and countered. "You don't get my methods, I assume."

"No, I don't," he answered. "I thought a coach would want to work us hard. To bring out the best in us. Not fff…, not mess around like we can't handle anything."

Mac leaned forward and interlocked his fingers, then looked at D.J. "I understand what you are thinking. More is better. Harder equals faster. But do you know what that gets somebody right now?"

He nearly sputtered. "Umm, faster?"

Mac nodded and chuckled. "Maybe. But just as likely, injured. Even though you ran a lot this winter, your body is still adapting to the daily strain. The tearing down, then building of muscles and tendons among other structures. If you push too hard, the tissues will rebel and you'll get injured. Then you'll be on the sideline for days or even weeks. That I won't allow."

He scoffed. "I can handle it."

Mac sat back in the armchair as music filled the air. When a discordant note struck, he continued. "Even though you can't visualize this, I have been in your shoes. Feeling so strong and brash that you could run through a wall. That you can conquer anyone on the line by sheer will. Most times when I ran, I was self-trained. Just like now, the sprinters got the attention and glory. Back then I was just a skinny bird flying on his own. I was looked on as odd. A fringe lunatic." He remembered. "That motivated me even more and I beat myself up every day. I ran harder. Faster. Like I didn't deserve to lie on my pillow unless I had punished myself to the maximum. But after multiple setbacks. Injuries. I learned a truism."

He waited, expectant. "What was that?"

"That in distance running, less is often more. It's about building the engine. The heart. And then the brain to accept what the heart delivers. Even given that, the body needs rest in order to repair itself. And just as much, the mind too needs a shutoff valve. That to pummel oneself day after day leads to ruin." He paused. "Especially at your age. Your body is still coming into its own. Growing. Adapting. But the time will come it will take root and you will bloom." He leaned forward. "Trust me on that."

Growing? Adapting? Mac made it seem as if he was goddam flower. He was anything but that. He was coarse. Gritty. A piece of granite chiseled into human form. He remained unconvinced. He tensed within the chair and waited until the annoying stream of jazz ended. He prepared a reply in no uncertain words.

Then swallowing back bile, he stayed quiet and stewed.

Chapter Twenty-Five

The morning was crisp but not intolerable. Spring in Wisconsin was a sketchy affair, snow just as likely as was a pleasant day washed in sunshine. Watching a patch of dirty clouds drift past, Mac looked out his front window and wondered what the day would bring. He was preparing for his first meet as a coach; that in itself was more than enough stress. Worse than that was D.J.'s distancing himself from guidance. He knew that was part of the coaching game; the connection with each athlete. But D.J. was different. He was a rudderless talent needing cajoling to propel him to prodigious heights.

Yet, the boy was not convinced he was the man for the job.

"Honey, are you all set to go?" asked Mona from the kitchen. "I filled a thermos with coffee and packed you a lunch. Is a ham sandwich okay?"

He blinked at the passing clouds. He didn't deserve her. His preoccupation with his own missteps always rivaled her needs. He tended to the day's events but focus was never riveted on her but rather his own frailties and unfulfilled dreams. And now, after nearly fifty years, her decline was palpable. First it was inability to carry simple items; now even putting the cover on a tube of toothpaste was difficult. Leaving for a frivolous quest of coaching young runners left him full of guilt. Yet she was all-in, hook, line and sinker. "Yes," he finally replied, "ham is fine. And the coffee too." Then he worried. "Are you sure you'll be okay, Mona? I may be gone until supper. I really don't know how long this will take. I can always cancel, you know. It's just a little track meet."

Her exhale was audible from a room away. "Thomas McKinley, if you say something so silly again, I will have your head." A rustle of slippers followed. When she appeared, both thermos and brown bag were in hand. "You take this and go coach like you have never coached before."

"Mona, I never have coached before."

She nodded in agreement. "Well, Coach Mac, then no matter what happens this will be your finest day."

His smile was all the reply needed.

***

He drove his car to the meet. Sitting on a bus with the athletes held no charm, the time for that was nearly two generations in arrears. Pulling into the parking lot, a string of yellow school buses lined the asphalt. He had not attended a track meet since his last race, the day a blown achilles tendon spelled the end of his competitive career. Eyeing the track, a familiar churn in his gut followed despite his new capacity on the sideline. Taking a deep breath, he left the bag lunch in the car but carried the thermos. Caffeinated alertness was the least of his worries, but the warmth of the coffee would be welcomed as the day progressed. He walked slowly toward the front gate until reaching a small shack. Reading the sign of the entrance fees, he questioned how to proceed. A middle-aged attendant greeted him and added to his quandary. "Welcome, sir," she said cheerily, "senior citizen price?"

He studied her. Likely a mother of an athlete only volunteering time, he understood her question. He was an unlikely candidate for his current position. He too would have thought he was a grandparent hunkering down as a spectator for the afternoon event. Hesitating, he corrected her. "I'm...I'm a coach for Weston High School. Thomas McKinley."

He thought there may be a list of names to consult but she didn't even hesitate. "Oh, of course," she said. "By all means go right in. And good luck, coach!" she said happily.

Coach. The word was still surreal to him. The transition from a simple old man to being thrown back into competitive throes was sudden and alarming. Yet it flared a fire that had never been extinguished. "Thank you, ma'am," he replied.

Then with the crush of athletes on the infield of the track, it all became incredibly real.

***

He made his way toward a group of athletes bathed in kelly green. The "Panthers" school logo was unmistakable and the sight of the athletes in various poses quickened his heartbeat. He had rehearsed his greeting but words now escaped him. Instead, he sidled up to the head coach and tapped him on the shoulder. "Morning, Coach Heck," he said, "the boys ready for action?"

"Mac!" he replied. "Nice to see you. And yes, I guess they are as ready as they will ever be." He pointed to a group of runners twenty yards away. "Your runners are over there. I'll leave them to you so take it from here." Sensing nervousness, he reassured him. "You've been there, done that. Don't let a few years of being on the backburner get in the way. If you need anything, just let me know." He squeezed his arm. "Now if you'll excuse me, I have another headcase of a sprinter to attend to."

With that, he was gone.

There he stood. Alone. Sizing up the moment, he studied the boys. They were young. Eager. All with varying degrees of talent but with emotional maturity in need of guidance. It was Lee who spied him first.

"Coach Mac! C'mon over," he called. "Finally, an outdoor meet."

"It's about time," added Andy, "no more getting dizzy indoors."

The greetings gained the attention of the others. It was D.J. who was the last to acknowledge his presence. "Morning, Mac," he said, calmly.

He plastered a smile on his face. "Good morning, guys. And yes, we finally get to be outside. It is well past time." The three freshmen nodded their head. They wore the "deer in headlight" look so common to the inexperienced. Silently, they longed for words of wisdom that might lead them to salvation of the day. Mac measured their individual needs but decided to first speak in broader terms. The one-on-one coaching would come later. "This is a big day for all of us," he continued, "a new season finally underway. For Bill, Ed, and Till, their first outdoor meet. For D.J., his first meet in the Northwoods. And for Lee and Andy, their first meet as leaders of the pack. Captains." The two juniors beamed at the designation and whooped as they punched each other on the shoulder. "The freshman will all run the half-mile. Given it is only two laps, the race will be fast but in the same vein, it will be over quick. Consider it your baptism to high school track and field. Lee and Andy will grace the track by running the thirty-two hundred. And today D.J. will get a shot at the mile." He shook his head. "Ah, I mean the sixteen-hundred meters." He let the whispers die before continuing. "In today's race, like any other race, one must have a game plan. Given how early it is in the season, I have given thought as to how we will approach the day." He slowed in order to bolster the next words. "We have been working hard on pace and so today I want us to work on even splits. That means, each lap nearly a carbon copy of the lap before. Today will be testimony to both our emotional and mental strength. To resist the lure of other competitors and run our own race."

Andy interjected. "So how do we know what pace to run?"

He wagged a single index finger in the air. "Ah, there-in lies the rub. Each of you must develop an internal metronome. The simple tick-tick-tick that tells you what is right. Those doing the two-lap event must decide the pace they can sustain for both laps. A pace that will leave you totally spent just as you cross the line. D.J. will do the same for four laps and Lee and Andy for eight." He let the information settle. "A successful runner has to know his body. He is not a puppet a coach can program and simply push an automated button for the desired results. Acquiring the sense of pace is a learning curve and it starts today." He pointed to the starting line. "The runner that best achieves the desired goal will have the honor of this award." He brought out a yellowed ribbon with a gold medal swinging from its apex.

"Holy cow, Coach M...Mac," said Till. "Where is that from?"

He replied. "I won it in the Pan Am Games in 1967. It held a lot of honor and meaning to me. And maybe in its own way, to you too." He dangled the medal in mid-air. The group stayed quiet as the sway of the talisman held their attention. In many ways it was just a piece of metal. A trinket. But it was also history. Mac was sure the runners had no idea what the Pan Am games were, but discovery of that was for later. Mac doubted D.J. relished following his plan. Even splits were likely as interesting to him as toast without butter. Plain. Average. Borderline boring. But Mac was sure he had gotten his attention. "Any questions?" Mac asked.

The group shook their head. But it was D.J. who went against the grain. "What if the pace of the pack is too fast or too slow? What if it's all messed up?"

Mac smiled and shook his head from side to side. "D.J., you are missing the point. Today the pace of the pack is not your concern. *Your* pace is the key. Run your race at an equal pace. Demonstrate your strength. As an aside, look up Dave Wottle on the computer at the 1972 Olympics. You will see a perfect example of what I am describing." He paused and let the moment sink in. "Your speed will come later as the season progresses. I will make sure of that. Trust me."

Lee spoke up. "Coach Mac, we got this. It's gonna be fan-damntastic day."

Mac, among others in the group, was not totally convinced.

***

The sixteen-hundred meter run was the first of the distance events. D.J. warmed up with the ritual Mac had prescribed. He began thirty minutes prior to the start. A slow mile warm-up. Stretching. Another one-half mile. Then a progression of sixty-yard stride-outs at increasing intensity. When he hit eight, a slow trickle of sweat ran down his forehead, it was then he was ready. Mac watched and was satisfied he had followed instructions. At last call, nearly a dozen other runners milled in varying states of nervousness. Mac studied the group and assessed their chances. The youngest and physically immature were discounted. Those displaying more swagger caught his attention. They had obviously been there before and were prepared for the moment. Two runners from Montello and another from Dells High School caught his attention. Lean and rawboned, they had the look of the hunted. They had paid the price to be contenders. His heartbeat accelerated. He was sure D.J.'s was doing the same.

Moments later the runners were called to the line. D.J. had the third position and from there he caught Mac's glance and nodded slowly. More than that was not needed. Not with this athlete. They had not spoken after the pre-race talk and each had given space. Mac had made his point clear. D.J. had heard the words; the rest was up to him.

The gun sounded.

The burst of adrenaline was always a rush. The tingle coursing through a runner's legs was both disconcerting and expected. Mac wondered how D.J. would handle the intoxicating impulse. He expected the runner would desire to burst to the front but hoped his words held weight: *even pace.* He expected D.J.'s innate stubbornness to resist and he would yearn to run his own race. He was smart and talented yet needing direction; essentially a colt needing to be broken. As he hit the backstretch, he settled firmly in the middle of the pack. Mac calculated he was on sixty-seven second pace per lap, a four twenty-eight mile. The number was good, not great. But this early in the season, Mac estimated he could run even splits and carry out the plan.

His plan, not D.J.'s.

The expected threesome grouped at the front. As the first backstretch lengthened, they gapped the field. Three yards. Then five. Not insurmountable but enough to gain attention. When the group hit the end of the first lap, the timer called out the sixty-three second pace. Mac estimated it was too fast but wondered if the boy felt the same. "An even pace D.J.", he whispered. "Trust me."

The second lap mimicked the first. The threesome was the cream of the field, any doubt had been eliminated. They maintained their pace and the lead lengthened. Fifteen yards. And growing. When they rounded the far lap, Mac measured the lead over D.J. to be twenty yards. With over two laps to go, the distance would be made up by a sustained effort. D.J. rounded the far corner and approached where he was standing. He called to him. "Good job, D.J., they are too fast. Be patient and keep on pace!"

Then another call. A young voice exhorting the two lead runners from Montello. Then the person's attention turned toward the trailing pack. Particularly D.J. "Not so easy, is it, homeboy?!" he shouted.

D.J. gave a quick glance toward the boy and their eyes met. Smoldering. Thirty yards away Mac was helpless. He had long stopped considering D.J.'s skin color but knew he would never be in his shoes: the daily battle of blending into a primarily white world. All he could do was watch the moment play out. He whispered to himself. "Ignore him, D.J. Run your race." For a moment his plea appeared to be heard, but that impression dissipated immediately. D.J.'s cheeks hardened and he stared daggers at the threesome ahead. Mac watched as an impulsive decision was made. The increase in stride cadence was subtle. Then it ramped, step by step. Mac had watched a thousand distance races and the clues of attack were only a ripple on a radar but to a veteran observer they were unmistakable. First the arm cadence. Then the lengthening of the stride. D.J. was doing both and it was only a matter of time before competitors and spectators caught wind of his intention.

He was moving hard.

Mac studied his watch. Sixty-five seconds for the second lap. As D.J. continued to build momentum and regain contact, his stride incrementally elongated. Mac knew D.J. was all-in. Within one-hundred yards he was on their heels but was not content. After rounding the first turn of the third lap, he breasted the outside shoulders of the threesome and continued on. He was putting an early hammer down and the other runners were on notice. Gaining the lead before the far turn, he looked elegant; a superior athlete among the mere pedestrian. Yet the other three yielded nothing and gave chase to the new leader. Striding toward the end of the third lap, D.J. looked the part of an elite runner. Strong, upright and most of all, confident. Hitting the stopwatch, the numbers did not lie. Sixty-two.

Mac shook his head.

The bell sounded and the leading group snaked on. The string of four was well contained and the small crowd roared approval. Mac listened to the cajoling of supporters and the shouts from D.J.'s teammates. He knew the noise was lost on the runner; the pounding of his heart and the grip in his legs trumped any extraneous sounds. D.J. and the other runners were alone in their world.

Mac had been there before many times. A lap to go, seemingly a small task. But once fuel had been burned, there was a price to pay. The first clue was a subtle shift in form; driving forward was replaced by a shortening of the stride. First by an inch, then more. Shoulders clenched, then rounded as the upright stance shifted to a nearly imperceptible lean. The runners had gone out too fast and D.J. had taken the bait. He and the others existed in a vacuum where Darwin's theory would play out: survival of the fittest lie directly ahead. The resulting pain was both expected yet avoided if possible. The three early leaders were paying the price for their rashness, as was D.J. for his impatience. Approaching the backstretch, he looked to the trailing runners in a dead giveaway of his emotional and physical status. But those runners had their own concerns.

Survival.

D.J. trudged on as a death grimace overtook his face. His tortured journey continued as he furiously pumped his arms while his legs rebelled at the prodding. The three behind him were equally spent, maybe more. They had no response and were paying heavily for their early impudence. D.J. battled as Mac expected; rounding the final turn he continued to lumber down the track as no competitors could mount a serious challenge. As the runner stumbled past the line, Mac studied him as he neared the end. Crossing victoriously, he clicked the watch and reflected on the findings. Four twenty-seven. A seventy-three second plus final lap.

Even pace be damned.

***

Mac waited for the small collection of distance runners to quiet. Their excitement over completion of the first outdoor meet was difficult to contain. Patiently, he hovered until they silenced. He too had difficulty harnessing his thoughts. It had been decades since his last meet and even in his new role, he was engaged. His adrenaline had peaked multiple times and like he had run himself, the unexpected surges left him fatigued. He took a deep breath and studied the runners. Their eyes called out for him to bathe them in wisdom. Just like they all had stood on the starting line, he readied for the task ahead. "First off, congratulations on completing your first outdoor meet. To get that monkey off your back is no small task. Bill, Ed and Till, to be freshmen running on varsity is difficult but you competed. In fact, Till, you ran nearly exactly even splits and for that achievement, you are graced with an old trinket." He placed the medallion over his neck as the runner beamed. "It is yours to keep, so wear it with pride."

"Th...thanks, Coach Mac," he replied. "But I was so slow compared to the other guys."

He smiled. "Never diminish your accomplishments but rather build on them. Speed will come but only with diligence and patience." He paused and looked at each runner.

"Patience. Control. Keeping your head among any storm is a foundation of distance running." He looked to Lee and Andy. Then to D.J. They had not spoken after the race as D.J. had quickly disappeared. Mac had not sought him out as their time would come. "Each of us has our own obstacles. Size. Natural abilities. Internal battles." He held D.J.'s eyes for a moment. "The physical can be overcome. I ran against the scrawniest runner you will ever see, Gerry Lindgren, and he dominated me. Physical limitations can be improved but internal control is far harder. Battling self-doubt. Or lack of confidence. Of the emotion during a race because competitors get under your skin. Or from those in the stands or the sidelines." He waited and carefully chose his words. "There are those that get inside your head by finding your soft-spot. If you cannot absorb the blow and steel yourself, you will not be a champion at the highest of levels."

D.J. stirred and the inference stung. Still spiraling from the emotion of the race, he lashed out. "That ever happened to you?" he spat.

The question hung in the air. Angered him. But as coach, he was now the teacher, not student. He leveled his voice. "Yes, D.J. And if I am to do my duty here, I hope you will not repeat mistakes of my youth. Trust me, it is not pleasant."

D.J.'s jaw clenched once again. But this time he stayed silent.

Chapter Twenty-Six

Two weeks passed since the first meet. With the slow warming of the earth, the runners' training also accelerated. Instead of daily slogging on the roads, they held bi-weekly sessions on the track. D.J. still wasn't freed from Mac's constraints but he was able to burn stress and anxiety with the hard, anaerobic effort. Repeat miles, half-miles, quarters; all were performed in sequence as if progressive beads on a rosary. The plan was to complete them in Mac's prescribed times with D.J. typically given loftier goals than the others. For that simple fact, he was grateful. The last two meets he had run the half-mile and then the two. As icing on the cake, in both he was also lead-off runner in the mile relay. There he could blast the track, free from the constraints of pacing.

Those were wondrous moments.

Opening the refrigerator, he was startled by movement from behind. His relationship with his father had been ghostly; the road was his father's mistress and he was a distant second. The man appeared and disappeared randomly at any hour of the day. In some ways, D.J. liked the arrangement. Human relationships were complicated. Living inside his own head, although cluttered, held less concerns.

"Anything left in there?" his father asked. "I'll pick some things up tomorrow."

D.J. shrugged. "Bread. Cheese. Leftover pizza and some food from Mac and Mona."

He grunted. "Oh, your grandma and grandpa?"

D.J. chafed. As a boy he had spent a small amount of time with his grandparents. His father's parents were a distant memory. Old. Gray. He remembered smiles but little more than that. They had retired to Florida and he had rarely seen them since. Grandparents on his mother's side were more vibrant memories. Darker skinned with bigger smiles. And he remembered food. A table of delicacies poised to fill a barren stomach. The visits dwindled when they relocated to their natural home of Arkansas. When his mother struggled with addictions and her absences became routine, decreased contact with his grandparents followed. Soon enough they became faded memories of bloodlines passing him by. "They are not my grandparents," he said, bitterly. "I don't have any."

His father straightened. Holding the refrigerator door open, he waited for D.J. to back away. D.J. examined his face; an unkempt beard masked his features and crow's feet accented tired blue eyes. The comment vibrated and his father's eyes narrowed. "My father died a year ago and my mom is in assisted-living in Florida. I visit her from time to time. It's not often but I do the best I can." He blinked to regain composure. "I called her yesterday. She knows me, yet she doesn't. Dementia," he explained. "I have no idea how your mother's parents are doing anymore. I'm sorry."

D.J. had never heard him say he was sorry before. For that, he regretted his attack. "I...I didn't know."

He returned his gaze to inside the refrigerator. "How could you? You have barely seen them." Closing the door slowly, he crossed his arms. "Sometimes life sucks. You of all people know that."

He did. But what he did not expect was his father to understand. Of his longing for stability. His need for family. And his unrequited need for love. "I guess," was all he could muster.

His father then nodded. "I'm glad the old folks are around. At least when I'm gone there is someone to keep an eye on you. And it's nice the old guy is coaching you."

D.J. didn't disagree. Mona and Mac had helped. Even the complication of Mac coaching was tolerable. But with another race looming in a day, he suddenly jumped ahead. "I have a race tomorrow," he said, softly. "A big one. I race a guy who won state last year. Dalton Scarie." His body tensed. "He's fast. Really fast."

His dad observed him until it became uncomfortable. "I'm off tomorrow. I think I'll come and watch." He scratched his beard. "If that's okay with you."

D.J. swallowed hard. The request was unexpected. So far, he had run his races without any familial support. At first that harbored a lost feeling; a single sheep wandering far from the herd. Eventually he willed a transformation into becoming a lone wolf; unknown and untethered, ready to pounce when called to the line. But now, his father was asking to observe his singular passion.

Running.

He cleared his throat. "Umm, sure," he said. "But there are a lot of events so I don't know what time I will be running." The passive attempt to discourage his father from attending was dismissed.

"That's fine," he replied. "I don't have anything else to do. Just tell me where and when it starts."

There was no escape. He was to have a truly unexpected observer.

"The meet starts at ten at Wautoma High School."

With that, a baseball-sized knot in his gut suddenly appeared.

***

A blustery spring day arose. Even the school bus transporting the team was buffeted in gusts. High forties with swelling winds, it was far from ideal race day weather. He had competed in the notoriously brutal Chicago weather and the Northwoods were nearly a carbon copy. What the elements did was eliminate a race result yielding a preferable time. Mac's seeming love affair with pacing was no longer in play; the day would demand pure survival mode.

D.J. looked out the window and through silver slits of rain, studied the passing pine trees. The needles of the branches wavered in the breeze and created a mesmerizing summoning from the woods. A trance ensued and the gaggle of noise from his teammates disappeared; it was just him and the beckoning forests. Part of him wanted to escape into the solemn calmness of the lands. To run free and not look back. To leave behind memories and an unknown future. To start fresh and become reborn. He breathed deep and closed his eyes. The daydreaming felt good and calmed his impatient soul.

That disappeared in an instant.

"Wake up soldier boy," said Jimbo. "Time to go to war."

D.J. had not noticed the advancement of the weight man along with Andy and Lee. They filled nearby seats and waited for his reply.

"We there already?" he asked, looking out the window.

"Five minutes or so," replied Lee. "Pretty soon."

Andy nodded. "Are you ready for Scarie? He's been putting up some nice times."

The knot in his gut returned as did a bump in heartrate. He looked to the expectant faces and considered the words. Bluster was normally a part of the equation but today was different.

He was facing the king of the jungle.

"I haven't noticed," he lied. In fact, he scoured the internet for results even though a superior performance left him restless in the dark. His opponent had twice broken four minutes and twenty seconds and easily led the state honor roll. Given the runner's past, he expected the time to plummet even further. D.J. knew his own fitness was improving. The workouts had ramped up, but sharpness was far off. He felt like a dull machete that at best could hack through a dense jungle. Far from being razor-sharp, he only hoped he would be there when the time was right.

"Scarie is good," offered Jimbo. "But he's got nothing on our boy, right D.J.?"

He put on a brave smile. "I'll give what I got Jimbo, I always do."

He turned to the windows as the wind pounded the helpless pine needles.

***

Mac walked methodically and approached the small circle of distance runners. D.J. had noted his slow gait before but the mannerism was becoming more pronounced. Mac was old, no doubt of that, but his fixation on distance running never waned. Pre and post-practice talks held merit and encompassed a wide range of topics, yet it was pain and glory that stood front and center. Today was no different.

"Morning, gentlemen," Mac said. "It's a fine day, isn't it?"

Lee responded first. "Are you kidding us, Mac? It's blowing like crazy out here!"

Andy joined in. "The wind doesn't blow, it sucks!"

The group chuckled, especially the nervous freshman. D.J. remained quiet in the pre-race ritual. Race day was special to him, like attending a Sunday service. He recalled the scattered times he attended church as a child; the ominous arch of the cathedral and the eerie silence within. The priest in strange clothing and the echo of his voice as it boomed from the pulpit. He knew nothing of the message and had no memory of content, but the sanctity of the event never left him. The feeling arose again the first time he stepped on a track. That sensation had yet to wane, even on a day like this when the chill enveloped him like a threadbare blanket.

Mac didn't disagree. "The wind is just another obstacle to overcome. Or it can be viewed as a friend."

"Friend? How, Mac?" asked Lee.

He smiled as a ripple of wind rustled his thin hair. "I'm glad you asked," he replied. "What I mean is that every distance runner here is thinking the same thing: that this is awful, that it's cold. That it's raining. But do you know what I think?" The murmur confirmed they did not. "That weather is no barrier.

And to the toughest among you, the sound of raindrops is applause." He stood taller as if daring the wind to cross him. "Running can be a chess game. It is not about pounding as hard as you can and finding out who is standing at the end. It is about using your opponent and the conditions for your own best interest. I suggest today you let another lead the way and break the wind for you. Tuck behind a sturdy runner who will do the lion's share of the work. Let him be the early hero that he needs to be. In most cases, he will end up being the sacrificial lamb."

"Sacrificial lamb?" asked Till. "Like in S...S...Sunday school?"

"Yes, sort of," he answered. "But on the track, anything can happen. The pace will be slower and you will have to accept that. Vanity may call for you to quicken the pace on some preconceived notion of your goals. But today forget about the clock. Instead focus on the blood on the track left by those in front of you." He summarized. "In essence, run smart."

"And win." chimed in D.J.

Mac studied him and D.J. wished he had stayed silent. "Running smart and winning often go hand-in-hand. Other times reckless running may be necessary. My advice today is taking the conservative trek and see where it leads." He took a deep breath and narrowed his eyes before beginning again. "My goal is not to create running robots that only do as I say. A champion runner must blend his own instinct, talents, and desire to find the perfect combination. No coach is in your shoes and can guide you completely. In my opinion, fast runners are a dime a dozen, but it is the *thinking*, fast runner that is the one to be feared."

"The 'thinking' part rules out Lee," Andy said. "Just saying."

Mac ignored the jibe. "Run smart. Run hard. They can be separate things, or they can be in perfect harmony. Each race is a performance that needs to be played out." He took one final breath. "There is music to be made on the track. Just make it your own."

D.J. conjured the omnipresent jazz in Mac's home. When he looked up and saw Dalton walking in the distance, the music immediately disappeared.

***

He had completely forgotten that his father was coming to the meet. First preoccupied with the weather, then Mac's speech, lastly Dalton, the appearance of his father had taken him by surprise. When waved to from the stands, he dizzied as if in a trance. Although the possibility of attendance was discussed, D.J. thought it unlikely to occur. He expected his father to be called to work, oversleep, or flat out forget. When none happened, the stunned look on his face mirrored the unsteady walk toward the stands.

"I told you I would come, didn't I?" his father asked.

"Yes, umm, you did," he stammered, "but I thought maybe it would be too cold for you. Or you would be busy."

He shook his ballcap-covered head and smoothed his beard. "I'm not around much so I thought this would be a good day to see you run." He looked past him toward the infield. "I saw in the local paper about this other kid. I guess he's pretty good."

The comment unknowingly stung. He was good too. Better than his father knew. Better than most knew. He had yet to perform at his optimum and of that he worried. He trusted Mac until he didn't. Their relationship had become complicated, nearing that of him and his fathers. A shiver of stress set in that was impossible to ignore.

His father zipped his camouflaged hunting jacket tighter. "Yeah, it's cold," he agreed, "but you won't even notice when you get running. D.J.," he said with an intensity he had not seen before. "I'm proud of you. And good luck."

He scarcely knew what to say. Proud? The man barely knew him, yet what he said mattered. He nodded and was unable to formulate a response. Giving a half-hearted wave, he backstepped from the stands. Hearing the gun sound for another event, he jumped. He should have been hardened to the noise but something undefinable was happening. He boiled at the thought he was softening. That would not happen. Thawing, maybe. That he could stomach. But no weaknesses today. Today there was work to be done.

He turned and focused on the task ahead.

***

A sliver of guilt stewed as the meet commenced; he could not focus on his teammates because the distraction was too strong. He provided surface level attention to the other events but following the results was off limits. The endorphins generated watching competition only drained his finite supply.

Mac once talked about runners needing to be selfish. To absorb inwardly. To store juices for competition and expend them sparingly when called upon. Parcel them out drop by drop until reaching the finish line when the well was bone dry. D.J. had never thought of that before; he simply ran as fast and as hard as possible until crossing the finish line in a sodden heap. The purposefulness Mac suggested forced him to think, observe and reflect on the demands of becoming a champion. He closed his eyes and readied his body for the upcoming battle; there was no more time for excuses.

He spat a thick ball of phlegm onto the infield. Last season he never carried the weight of expectation. Then he was just a freshman blazing the track; if he won or even contended, he was viewed with admiration. He could afford to be reckless and any miscalculation would be chalked up to youth. But his intermittent sterling times and preponderance of success had registered in the small track community. Now he was a somebody. A runner on the radar. The position made him uncomfortable but he had no choice. He closed his eyes and willed away the thoughts colliding in his head.

***

A dozen runners toed the line. Each had their own peculiarities in the moments before the race. Some stood frozen and stared down the track as if awaiting an executioner's call. Others fidgeted with their shorts or shoelaces in a final attempt to eliminate equipment malfunction. D.J. had his own routine of rubbing his thighs as if readying them for the effort ahead. With each stroke he became more engaged, warmed, and closer to doing battle. When a voice sounded, the rhythm was disrupted.

"It's gonna be a windy one," Dalton said from his left, "kinda sucks."

"Yup," was all D.J. could muster. He was not one for small talk on the line. He absently rubbed his thighs again but stopped when he questioned if Dalton would view it as a sign of weakness. He then stood tall and shook out his arms while staring at his shoes. There he caught a glimpse of his main competitor's racing shoes; baby blue Nikes looking as if they were molded onto his feet. As Dalton ground the track, the tiny spikes on the soles were evident. D.J. had seen them before but in Chicago races they were a rarity. He surveyed the others and recognized most of the field was shod the same way. He studied his shoes: lightweight trainers that a months ago held promise of achievement. Now they only paled in comparison to the sleek trappings of his competitors.

The starter interrupted his thoughts and gathered the assortment of runners to give the usual instructions. D.J. heard the words but the message was garbled. He blinked, collected himself and followed the other runners to the line. Dalton was a lane away and as if given special dispensation, he was not encroached upon like the rest of the field. D.J. leaned into the runner next to him to provide a fraction more space. Then more words.

Runners on your mark...

The rest were a blur until the gun sounded. He reacted slowly and was instantly gobbled up by the pack. Preferring to be a near the lead, the deeper position was foreign to him. The splaying of feet and arms was unwieldy but he attempted to find a spot and settle into the run. The sound of footsteps and breathing ramped as they approached the first curve. Nearing the far end, the direction of the wind was evident. Buffeting his chest, the breeze chilled but the protection of the pack limited exposure. Mac's words echoed: *let them break the wind for you.* He was unaccustomed to letting others do the work but at the moment it massaged his fears. *Tuck in. Get your bearings. Do your damage later.*

The thought gave him solace and he settled into a rhythm. The pace seemed slow. He estimated sixty-five seconds plus but given the conditions it was prudent. Then he dissected the field. He didn't know the other runners but he did know one. Dalton Scarie. He was in second place behind a swarthy runner who literally ground up the track with each stride. Dalton was on his right shoulder, trancelike as his light steps barely graced the track. D.J. was five yards back but it felt like a chasm. He wanted to be there. In the mix. Letting his opponent know he was present and accounted for. He nudged his pace but with runners on all sides, there was nowhere to go. He simply had to wait.

He spied Mac on the far turn at his typical place. He rarely called out during a race but D.J. could read his thoughts. *Be patient. Let them do the work.* Mac had warned them he would not direct the runners during the race. He preached a true distance runner needed to be able to dissect a race and make their own tactical decisions. He explained each race was like a surgical procedure; expectation and expertise were tantamount, but instinct was a driving partner. *Feel,* he told them, *could not be taught, only learned.* D.J. listened and critiqued the words. He wanted a gospel that would specifically show the way. In those moments he felt distanced from the old man.

Fair or not, he had expected more.

The first lap split was sixty-seven. Substantially slower than he wished but there was still three quarters of a race yet to be run. Dalton held his position and did the same. He began to settle into the effort until an unexpected voice sounded from the stands.

"Go get 'em, D.J.!" the voice called. "You can beat those guys! C'mon!"

His father. He had forgotten he was there. Instinctively his pulse accelerated as did his pace. When he clipped another runner on the heel, he nearly created a domino-like tumble of the pack.

"Shit!" yelled the offended runner. "Watch it!"

"Sorry, man," he said between breaths.

The weight of his father's expectations reared and his own followed. He hated being trapped like a piece of cattle going off to slaughter. He was better than that. A whisper said to begin an attack and regain contact with the leaders. To take charge of the race and quit being such a pussy.

The die was cast.

The backstretch beckoned and when a gap opened, he bolted. The surge empowered him and the coursing adrenaline was intoxicating. The distance to the front disappeared and streaming past Dalton's shoulder, he was certain of his choice. *Be the hunter, not the hunted,* he told himself. The choice was made as he took the lead. Entering the far turn, he had a stride lead over the pack. Looking down the upcoming straightaway, Mac's pre-race advice was murmuring within his psyche. *Instinct. I'll show you instinct,* he thought.

The half-mile split was called at two-ten. His quick calculations meant he had ratcheted the pace to a sixty-three. It had felt easy and he did not doubt his decision. As he neared the turn, his father's voice bolstered his quest.

The backstretch sobered the moment. The gust of wind, all but ignored the previous lap, reared its head. He stiffened and leaned into it but it did not yield. He felt a runner behind him but that was the least of his worries. He was alone. Naked. And the bone-numbing wind was suddenly present and accounted for. He leaned further and summoned reserves. The far turn gave respite. It was there Mac stood stoically in the infield. He appeared like a trackside oracle as his nylon shell slapped in the wind. No words were spoken yet the connection was made. Five hundred yards left – a distance where hell could appear.

D.J. centered his gaze on the track and amped his resolve. He maintained pace and monitored his breathing. As expected, at this stage of the race the rate had increased. More important was the state of his legs. A subtle fatigue called. First like a whisper but then a voice warning of impending danger. But on the track, there was nowhere to hide. And more than once, the whispering voice might be a liar. A second wind might arise and an unexpected blast of adrenaline might rejuvenate neurons and muscle fibers nearing end point. A runner never truly knew. And even then, the best of them often ignored the red light flashing in the distance.

The third lap was called out at three-fifteen. An admirable time given the conditions. D.J. held firm and absorbed his father's plaudits. Pleasing the man warmed his soul more than he would have imagined. The simple rush fueled him as he neared the turn. He expected the runner behind him to be Scarie and a quick turn of his head indicated he was right. The state champ had been in that position before but D.J. didn't flinch. He would show them all. His teammates. His father. Mac. He was worthwhile. He was a survivor and nothing could keep him down.

Then another gust knocked him from his stride. He had not been prepared for the impact and he stumbled as a front toe caught the track. He steadied himself and reorganized his effort into the headwind. At the same time, he could both hear and feel his pursuer. Like a coiling cobra, the hiss was in his ear. The effort of leading had been building; his legs quivered and a sudden spasm appeared between his shoulder blades.

He wouldn't admit it, but the end was near.

The last turn beckoned and his stride shortened. Mac placidly watched the final two-hundred meters unfold. A silent acceptance of the situation arose and the ending was foretold. D.J. was spent and a superior runner would have the spoils. He pumped his arms but this time his legs failed to respond. In contrast, Dalton rose to his forefeet and like a conquering gladiator strode down the final stretch. The crowd roared its approval and the stands shook from stomping feet. Waving his right arm, the winner enjoyed the final steps of victory.

D.J. continued his death march as the proverbial lamb. His stride totally collapsed when the early leader passed him in the last ten meters. Stumbling past the finish line in third place, he nearly collapsed even with hands on bent knees. Sucking in the air, his defeat was numbing and inglorious.

He did not look up. Then he felt a hand on his shoulder. He knew who it was. Mac. The old man spoke slowly and distinctly. "Pressure comes from a place only you know about. It may come from competition. The fear of losing. The fear of winning. The fear of a competitor. Sometimes it will drive you and other times it will cause you to crash and burn. But controlled, it will fuel you to greater heights." He squeezed D.J.'s shoulder. "There will always be an opponent in your thoughts. In daydreams. Maybe even nightmares. Someone that seems unbeatable based on times or past performances. But there is something you need to consider." With that D.J. looked up. "He is also afraid. He has his own baggage. His own doubts and fears. He may cloak it in words, in a smile or a simple wave to the crowd. But fear lives in all of us. Be it just below the skin or hidden deep within the soul. The great ones layer it and bury it deep. The miles and work they have performed build a fortress around it. The more work, the stronger the mortar. But with execution of tactics, coupled with athletic excellence, a hairline crack in the foundation can be discovered. It is your job to expose it. It did not happen in this race. Maybe not even the next. But believe me, D.J., as God as my witness, it will."

Then he released his grasp and let him breathe.

Chapter Twenty-Seven

The days took on a clear pattern. He rose early, checked on his wife, then made a pot of coffee. After two cups, black, he nibbled on a hard roll until the gnaw in his gut quieted. Then he prepared for an early morning walk that had become routine since the season started. Much like fifty years ago, he needed the time to organize his thoughts and plan the day. He had remained lean and despite the cumulative years saw himself in a distant light – as an athlete. A creation built for movement. The years had shaved his abilities one layer at a time but they had done nothing to his mind. There he was still in training. For what there was no answer. He would never compete again. Not in any version including even a simple fundraising 5k where he would be praised for mere completion. His time on the white line was over.

Yet it wasn't.

He viewed motion as a simple exercise. From walking to the mailbox, to the simplest of chores. Pushing the lawnmower uphill was good for his quadriceps. Waxing the car worked his upper body. Vanity was never far away nor were murmuring dreams of the past; a place where the world called and his legs never wavered. But even though decades had passed, the present was still tethered to his time in the sun. Youth. The years he soared like a shooting star and bathed in brilliance that warmed his face. Reaching, straining, clawing at success, he strived to achieve all he could. When it was over, he was lost; caught in a crosswind that never receded. Buffeted from all angles, his bearing was never the same. As an athlete, he had purpose. Goals. But as years took their toll, he recognized his infatuation with past glories was misguided and borderline pathetic. Yet like an addiction, he could not stop.

He walked out the door intending to outpace the shadows lurking on all sides. He would do the best he could and accept the simplicity of the moment. He could do more than most his age, less than only a few. Looking down the road, he ignored the past and focused on the moment - his body striding to the best of its ability. He stood tall as the stiffness abated and the flow of blood warmed his joints. He was alive and began his morning quest.

He looked to the rising sun and charged ahead.

***

Mona was awake when he returned. She ambulated independently but the walker had become nearly an appendage. Her balance had worsened as had her capacity for anything physical. She had not left the house in weeks except for a fruitless doctor's appointment. The neurologist informed them there was nothing else he could do aside from attempting to stabilize the condition. His doctor-speak of her declines becoming the "new normal" was disheartening. Mona absorbed the information but he was embittered by the lack of options provided. He had requested the doctor do "something, anything" in more of a demand than request but was met with stony-faced silence. When the physician raised his palms in helplessness, Mac stewed silently.

"Mac?" she called in a thin voice. "Is that you?"

"Yes. You were expecting maybe that handsome mailman?" he replied. "The one with the dimples?"

"That would be nice but I'll settle for you," she said.

He followed her voice into the bedroom where she was working on a crossword puzzle. "Funny, Mona," he replied. He looked around the bedroom. "I assume you want your morning tea?"

"No," she said, "my stomach is upset. Maybe later."

He studied her. It was unlike her to pass up the beverage but her habits were changing. Her ailments were accumulating and her decline was ramping. Appetite. Energy. Activity. All diminished as winter ended and spring progressed. She never wanted to dwell on the changes and was angered when he probed. *I'm fine. Stop worrying,* she said. But she wasn't fine and his worrying intensified. Without her, he had nothing. A distant family and a smattering of obscure neighbors. If she passed, he would be lost. It was too much for him to consider.

"Juice, maybe?" he asked.

She shook her head. "Thomas McKinley," she said. "Just sit down and stop being a bother. Please." He complied. He was unable to provide remedy for her skid and it saddened hi. None of which was lost on her. "I'm fine, Thomas. I'll be better later."

He brightened at the thought. Even knowing it unlikely, he sighed and his shoulders dropped. "It's going to be a nice day, Mona. Perhaps later we can go on the deck and get some fresh air."

She nodded. "Perhaps. But for now, just fill me in on your doings." Her eyes twinkled despite her frailty. "Tell me about the boys and the running. Especially D.J."

His pulse quickened as she hit his sweet spot. The season was never far from his thoughts. D.J. even closer. His talent was special. Rare. But to tap into it and nurture to full heights was harder. "They are improving. The freshmen the most but that is to be expected. They have no background, so their bodies are becoming accustomed to the work. Andy and Lee, the twins, both set personal bests in the thirty-two hundred last week. They were pretty happy about it. As was Coach Heck, so I guess I won't be fired yet."

She set her eyes on his. "That much I assume, Thomas." She set the crossword puzzle on her lap. "And D.J.?"

He had no short answer. He was progressing but for each step forward, there was a slight slip back. A lesson learned was absorbed but then ignored a day later. D.J. had talent, but as an inexperienced prodigy, impulse reared its head at unexpected times. In the middle of a steady-state run, the first repetition of mile repeats, or even in a team cooldown where competitiveness reigned over the goal of running as a unit. "He is doing okay," he said, "but he doesn't like to listen to authority."

"Authority," she repeated. "Meaning you?"

He took a deep breath. He had been D.J. once. Questioning, knowing more than others, filled with an inextricable belief he was right. In some ways that was a gift, an impenetrable confidence beyond other mortals. But the blessing was also a curse because mistakes would be repeated. Mac wanted to spare him of that. To diminish downfalls and stumbles but at the same time allow the freedom to create an art form of his own. Ultimately, to become the runner he was destined to be. "Yes, me," he finally said. "He listens but resists. I think it may be his upbringing. He doesn't trust what adults say." He looked out the bedroom window into the morning light. "He has been hurt before. Nearly abandoned, so to trust others is close to an impossibility. He trusts only himself and in that he is bound to make youthful errors. I only hope I can help him achieve his goals."

"And yours too."

That blindsided him. "My goals?"

She nodded. "Yes, Thomas. To achieve like you believed you should have all those years ago." Her face softened. "To be a champion."

The words resonated in the still morning air.

***

Practice that afternoon took on the color of the day. Gray. Lifeless. Approaching borderline monotony. Mac had been there many times before. A day when motivation waned and each runner questioned his passion. He recognized the mood in both himself and his athletes. It was time for a break from the norm.

"Tuesday's are the worst," he said bluntly. "Three days until the next meet and four days from the last. No man's land." The runners looked at him quizzically but stayed silent. "We have officially one month to go until the conference championship, then the state qualifiers. A small amount of days but a lifetime in and of itself. Because of that, today is a free day."

Lee spoke up. "A free day? You mean no practice?" The others considered the question and waited.

He nearly growled. "No practice? After all this time you think I would have no practice?" Heads shook. "What I mean is that we need a break from structure. A break from rules. Pace. The clock." He paused. "A break from ourselves." He stood among them as the usual semi-circle surrounded him. "We need to remember what it is to be young. To play. To run because we can, not because we have to. What I am proposing is we take to the woods and simply run. We have the ability to cover great distances on our own two feet. Mostly because it is absolutely fun. In doing so, to remember why we are here: to leave our thoughts behind. There is no time like the moment to be free."

Till stuttered. "S…s…so, what do we do?"

He pointed north. "Just beyond the tree line is the Rock River. On this side of the riverbank is a narrow trail that goes on for miles. I want you to run as a group and enjoy the world you live in. The trail will take you far from school. Your jobs. From your parents." He paused. "It will even take you from yourself." He considered the sentiment of the words but pushed forward. "Running can bring balance. All the noise of the world can be nullified by the simple act of movement. Do not diminish the power of running. It can heal deep wounds within each of us." He avoided looking directly at D.J., but the connection was made. "After thirty-five minutes out, turn back. Stay as a group because if any of you never return, it will be the end of both of us."

The smiles on the faces needed no words.

Chapter Twenty-Eight

The bus ride home had been joyful. Winning had been unexpected and both the team and Coach Heck were buoyant. The school had not captured an invitational team victory in three years and its achievement brought a mist to the head coach's eyes. As the bus rumbled on, he stood and congratulated the athletes.

"An amazing day, men. An amazing day," he said. "So many good performances, it is hard to know where to start. Sprinters. Pete, Steve, and all of you. Individually and relay wins, simply incredible. Jimbo and the other weight men. Outstanding performances today."

"We got you, coach!" yelled Jimbo from the back. "Ain't no doubt 'bout nothin'!"

"Okay, Jimbo. Whatever you say." He then pointed to a group congregated in the back. "And the distance runners, what can I say. A freshman scoring? Till, congrats! Lee and Andy second and third with personal bests? Absolutely special." Then he waited for the commotion to fade. "Lastly, a shout out to the new school record holder in the sixteen-hundred meters, D.J. Johnson! D.J., stand up and take a bow!"

D.J. barely moved. He was unaccustomed to acclaim and although intoxicating, it was foreign at the same time. He wrestled in his seat until he found footing. Standing, he flushed in embarrassment.

"Four minutes and seventeen seconds," Coach Heck said. "I'll be moonstruck and hog-tied if I ever see that again. That was one amazing performance, D.J. You should be proud of your achievement." Then he turned his gaze to the team again. "Men, congratulations. Enjoy the day until we get back to work on Monday."

D.J. felt the blood escape from his cheeks. He looked out the window knowing he had only just begun.

***

He was anxious. It was a Friday night and in Chicago, that meant action. Whether it was simply walking the street or playing basketball on a corner lot, there was energy emitted. Here there was nothing but quiet unless one counted the croaks of bullfrogs. His father was gone again, on the road as usual. They had formed a tentative balance of staying out of each other's way and providing the space needed. So far it had worked and conflicts were few. But the boredom pervading the area was nearly numbing.

The buzz of his phone immediately remedied the malady. *Dude. Be there in ten minutes. Don't be a douche.*

It was from Jimbo. He smiled and had no intent of rejecting the invitation. He was starving for action and the timing was spot on. He replied immediately.

I feel you, bro. I'm in.

And the night instantaneously brightened.

***

He climbed into Jimbo's truck with the usual suspects. Lee and Andy held the backseats and D.J. was awarded the front. Unaware of their plans, he readied for the night. Jimbo was the first to chime in.

"Hey, man! Ready to kick it?"

He smiled. "I'm not sure what that means but, yeah, I'm ready."

Lee explained. "We could ride around but the rumor is a bonfire is happening at the ridge. Remember, D.J.?"

He did. The last time was in the fall when he was a newbie. Some of the turmoil of being the new kid in town had withered but he was still not completely comfortable in the environment. He still felt the glances and real or not, he was not one of the locals. Not born and bred on a farm or a wooded lot. Not comfortable with a rifle scope or bow, he was a definitive outsider. In that regard, he would never totally fit in. But he was with a threesome that didn't care about his background. For the first time since he had moved, he thought of them as friends. "I remember. In the backwoods. Lots of people there. Sounds good to me."

But it did and didn't. Social anxiety was not a measurable condition but he knew he possessed it. Even in a crowd, he often felt alone. He tried to blend in, but his tongue thickened and thoughts raced. Engaging in chitchat was a struggle and he stiffened at the thought. But he kept his uneasiness to himself.

"I heard there might be a barrel there too," said Jimbo. "Some guy from Montello."

"Jimbo, don't be stupid," said Andy. "If you get caught drinking, you'll get kicked off the team. Then going to state would be over." He leaned forward. "You wouldn't take a chance on that, would you?"

Despite the music, the question resonated in a vacuum. The foursome eyeballed each other and waited for his response. When seconds passed, he finally replied. "Shit! And I wanted to get my drink on," he said. "You skinny-ass distance runners suck, you know that?"

There was laughter from the back. "Maybe, Jimbo," said Lee. "But it's only because we love you like the dimwit brother we never had."

"Never had? You are dimwit twins for godsake."

Lee and Andy could only shake their heads.

***

The bonfire was in full force. D.J. estimated the crowd at thirty-plus. Having been there before, his comfort level had risen. Nodding at a few familiar faces, he blended in as best he could. The others meandered and he was essentially on his own. The quarter barrel was evident and the bulk of the noise came from its periphery. Shouts of *drink, drink, drink,* attested to the games accompanying the tap. He moved closer to watch the combatants but recognized none of them. Instead he found a cooler filled with other beverages and plucked a coke from the container. Popping the top, he studied the crowd. Nameless. Faceless. They were like him yet not. He believed he had a singular purpose of running. A calling. A place in the sun where his accomplishments would be recognized. He daydreamed of his future as he basked in the warmth of the nearby fire. He was ready to embrace destiny. A smile lit his face as he took a drink from the can.

Then a voice. Familiar, yet not. "Nice run today," it said. "It would have been good to go at it head to head."

He knew immediately. A thickening in his throat appeared. *Show them you don't give a damn*, said Mac from somewhere deep in his head. And so, he did. He methodically lowered the drink and turned to face his adversary. "I had a good day. The wind was at my back the whole way."

That garnered a laugh. "I guess. Even so, you are the closest runner to me in the area."

D.J. knew but he didn't let on. "Is that so? I don't keep track of everyone's times. I just run."

The dialog halted and eyes locked. A test of wills occurred and a stalemate was called. Dalton spoke first. "There is a lot of season to go, isn't there? Races to run."

He didn't waver. "Yes. Can't wait."

The comment was met by silence. Then a slow, measured smile. "I like your shit, dude. But that don't get it done on the track. Just saying."

D.J.'s heart ramped but he slowed it with a deep breath. He considered responses but chose the briefest. "Later, Dalton."

He turned and faced the fire head on.

Chapter Twenty-Nine

He was in a foul mood and did not want to be there. For the most part coaching had been fun but today other things were on his mind. He often spiraled into darkness but usually he could work himself out of it. When he was very young, it was pedaling fast on a banana seated bike; in high school and beyond, it was hammering a run at breakneck speed. No matter how pathetic and self-pitying he was, a full-throttled run cleansed his brain like running it through a car wash. In the later years, even a brisk walk elevated the endorphins enough so he presented to the world in an agreeable manner. But today was different.

Mona was changing.

Her breathing was becoming increasingly labored and she had taken to intermittently using portable oxygen. The doctor said her respiratory muscles were weakening and she was not getting enough airflow to sustain her needs. The portable unit would help but not eliminate the difficulties of daily activities. Her disease was worsening and there was not a damn thing anyone could do.

That afternoon his helplessness reached a boiling point when she shuffled toward the bathroom with an effort that broke his heart. Breath rasping and withered muscles trembling, she willed herself to manage the duty independently. *I refuse to be a burden,* she had said. *I can manage if you would just let me.*

So, he did. But standing close by, he avoided gaping at the image of what she had become: a woman struggling to perform the most basic tasks. They had promised if the time ever arose, they would not put the other in a nursing home. Better to die with dignity under their own roof than with a feeding tube strung into their arms. But now the promise seemed a long time ago and he wondered of the best course of action. He closed his eyes until a voice woke him from his trance.

"Coach Mac, are you okay?" asked Lee.

"Yeah," seconded Andy, "I…I thought you were asleep or something."

He collected himself. Thoughts of home life vanished as responsibility set in. He was here for a reason; to guide the runners toward becoming the best they could. He shelved his frustration and focused on the moment. Straightening to full height, he pointed to each runner in a silent count of attendance. "Thanks for worrying about me, but I'm fine. It's you that should be worried."

D.J. lifted his head in surprise. The edge in the voice gained his attention. Mac usually carried himself in a collected fashion but today his face was hard.

"We have two weeks until conference. Three until qualifiers for state, four until state itself." He paused and let the numbers settle. "Right now, you have all performed well in what you have been asked to do. And that was to develop the strength to carry you toward the finish in a strong pace. So far you have built the foundation - the masonry bricks and cement to support the house. Now it is time to build the next level. The place from where you will see the fruits of your labor." The freshmen looked confused but stayed silent. Lee whispered in Andy's ear but stopped when Mac stared him down. D.J. sat stock-still and did not utter a word until his name was called. "D.J., what is your goal this year?"

He was caught off guard. The question was direct but the answer was slow in coming. He cleared his throat and began. "I want to win conference." Then he stopped.

"Okay," Mac said. "And?"

"And?"

"Yes. And."

He stirred uncomfortably. His goals were his own. Personal. Close to his heart. He didn't respond.

"D.J.?" he repeated.

Eyes were upon him. He took a breath. "I want to get to state," he finally said.

Mac nodded. "Is that it? To simply be a competitor?"

He swallowed and looked into the old man's eyes. Eyes that had seen it all before. "No, more than that," he replied. "I...I want to win."

Mac nodded. With tight lips he didn't respond, yet simply acknowledged the words. Then a small smile appeared. "That wasn't so hard, was it?" When D.J. shook his head, he finished. "We'll get back to that in a moment." Then he went down the line and like sinners in a confessional, each runner recited their goals and dreams. When the group completed the assignment, Mac crossed his arms. "It's time, men. Time to begin to climb the mountain. To push to the summit that we have painstakingly been preparing for all season. Each of your goals are special, unique to yourselves more than anyone else in the world. But no one goal more important than the other." He paused. "In our training we have forged a blunt sword, worthy of battle. But it needs sharpening in order to achieve greatness. Sharpening that comes with pain. Pain that will occur on the track under my guidance. Pain in the form of intense speed work that will provide a razor's edge to your quests." He nodded at each of them "Too many runners want the 'secret'. That which is hidden from view. The truth is there is no goddam secret. Never has been. Never will be. The answer comes deep. Deeper than most men care to go." He stared them down. "Today we begin." He waited. "Any questions?"

When there were none, he turned and lurched toward the track.

***

The warm-up was as usual. As they lapped the track in a slow jog, the group remained silent. It was as if an undescribed torture lay dead ahead. Mac's mood dominated their thoughts and after a series of warm-up striders, they met at the starting line. His faraway look was still evident and none of them disturbed him. The freshmen fidgeted in place until Mac turned to face them.

"Quarter miles. The cornerstone of true champions," he said. "We'll start with six and build from there."

Lee looked to Andy. "Build from there?"

Mac didn't break from the moment. "We build from there," he repeated. "What will be next is a mystery. Like in a race. Planning and preparation can go sideways when the gun goes off. That is when great runners adapt to the unexpected. The best of them are drawn toward greatness like a moth to a flame." He paused. "It is then they either fly to heavenly heights or burn into oblivion."

D.J. studied him. He was the de facto leader of the group and they looked to him to speak. He did slowly and emotionless. "Mac, let's fly."

For the first time that afternoon, Mac smiled.

They lined up after instructions. Sixty seconds for D.J. Sixty-four for Lee and Andy. Sixty-nine for Till, Bill and Ed. Mac released them with a simple whistle. They exploded into action and their prescribed positions were taken. Rounding the last turn and heading to the finish line, the lap was completed as ordained. After stopping and placing hands on hips, one lap was done.

"Ninety seconds rest. Walk it off and I'll give you a ten second warning before the next lap."

The runners caught each other's eyes. Mac had not been distant like this before. Nor as callous. The unspoken consensus was to stay silent and absorb the blows as delivered.

"Ten seconds," he said.

They repeated the line-up and responded to the whistle. Hitting the prescribed pace, each runner was gaining rhythm of the effort. Gaining confidence, they lined up again. And again. The fifth repetition was harder. Fatigue reared its head and after crossing the line, hands reached their knees as each fought to catch their breath. With the whistle of the sixth lap, the effort was heightened as each runner battled to obtain the desired goal. Within a tick, D.J. had reached the sixty-second barrier for each repetition. The others had reached goal pace nearly the same. In doing so, they expected praise for the effort. That expectation was quickly extinguished.

"Running is hard work and not for the meek," Mac said as they caught their breath. He looked both toward and away from them. "What is even harder is life. Difficulty and pain come your way and you must manage it. Absorb it. Sometimes more than you think you can bear." His eyes glazed over. "When I was young, I loved to run. It was all I cared about. It was the only thing that meant anything to me. And there is absolutely nothing wrong with that. Passion is what the successful among us has in spades." He looked toward each of them, then continued. "But running and life need balance. A reason to be, a reason to push on." He looked to D.J. "Do not waste the years avoiding what can make you stronger. Faster. Maybe even a champion. Things like love. A wife. Family." He shook his head. Seconds passed before he continued. Then more. "Never mind," he said as his eyes misted. "I'm sorry, boys."

The group quieted and looked to each other, unsure of how to proceed. Then D.J. stepped forward. He walked toward Mac and placed a hand on his shoulder. "Coach Mac, it's all good. But I don't believe we are done with the workout yet. In fact, I think we are just getting started."

Mac straightened, blinked and composed himself. "D.J.," he said, "you are absolutely right." Walking down the track, he pointed at the stadium clock standing on the opposite end of the track. "You see that clock?" They nodded in unison. "That clock is both enemy and friend. It can provide comfort or deal in pain. Most times both. Our next effort will be to prepare one of us for greater heights. With that we will all share in the success gained." He turned and looked to D.J. "I never used to believe in the power of family. Or friends. But I do now. Together, we can achieve the seemingly impossible." He narrowed his eyes. "Are we in this together?"

The runners looked to each other and nodded. Then the unlikeliest of all spoke. "C...Coach Mac," said Till, "we are. Just tell us what we need to do."

Mac smiled and nodded to the group. Gathering himself, he took a deep breath. "Any runner worth their salt should be able to step to the line and perform. It cannot be only at prepared moments. But rather, at any instant a challenge arises." He pointed at D.J., purposefully. "Champions are always ready." He let seconds tick before continuing. "D.J., are you ready right now?"

He was surprised but did not hesitate. "Yes."

The singular word spoke volumes. Mac nodded. "In championships, like state competition, national competitions, there may be heats. In those you will have to learn to recover both mentally and physically in order to advance. A flash-in-the-pan will burn. Those that can handle the demands will survive. And ultimately win." He turned and faced the school. "Weston High School has never had a state champion in any sport. But this year, together, we will make history." He motioned toward the white line. "D.J., take your place. Lee, you will accompany him the first lap. Andy the second. Freshmen, the third." He reached toward his stopwatch. "Sixty-three seconds per lap on my whistle. Any questions?"

Till bobbed his head. "W...what about the l...last lap?" he asked.

Mac anticipated the question. "There was a marvelous runner named Derek Clayton who was all saliva and veins. He used to run his workouts as hard as possible so the pain would end sooner. It shall be the same for D.J. on the last lap." He looked to D.J. as if challenging. "Any other questions?"

D.J. looked to the others and licked his lips. "No, coach. None."

Lee sidled up to him as they readied for the countdown. "Yo, D.J., you got this."

The runner nodded and did not reply.

The whistle sounded and they exploded from their crouch. Lee led the way into the first turn and did as asked. The speed was not natural for him but he pumped his arms as the others cheered him on. Mac watched and evaluated the performance; Lee at near top-end speed with D.J. gliding behind. Rounding the last turn, Mac prepared the next.

"Andy, do your job."

The runner acknowledged the challenge and took off when his brother completed the first lap. Mac evaluated D.J.'s status and was pleased to see his comfort level. Calm, collected and proceeding on. Andy maintained the pace and separated from D.J. by three yards. Mac watched D.J. carefully for panic or impulsiveness. Neither reared its head and Mac looked to his watch. As they neared the mid-lap marker, he approached the freshmen.

"Relax, this is not a race. Steel the mind and the legs will follow. You can do this."

Smiles lit their faces as they prepared for the passing of the torch. Instinctively, their jawbones tightened as the oncoming runners approached the end of the second lap.

Andy reached the line first with D.J. in tow. "Dudes, go!" he shouted. "Do it!"

And they did. Bolting from the line, they led D.J. down the track. Mac noted the rasp of the trailing runner but stayed silent. He watched D.J. devour the track one step at a time. The youngest runners maximized their abilities while D.J. fought to keep pace. His stride maintained course but Mac knew the battle; keep calm while internally all hell was breaking loose.

He wanted to shout encouragement but as if reigned in, he remained silent. True champions needed no cheerleading. The ability was either within or it was not. From a distance, he watched D.J. to see if he had that which was required.

Till led into the first turn as the freshmen carried the pace. The leader had the most natural ability of the threesome as the others quickly approached maximum. Mac smiled as the freshmen remained glued together like the impromptu blood-brothers he willed them to become.

So far, they had passed the test.

Crossing the halfway mark of the third lap, the intensity ebbed. The freshmen strained at the same time D.J. revealed a new resolve. His carriage straightened and he melted the few yards between him and the group. He pushed to the threesome and settled behind. Finishing the straightaway, he moved wide and began to pass the trio. Then without prompting, the lead freshman accelerated and fought off the advance.

"Attaboy, Till!" shouted Lee. "That's what it's all about!"

Mac admired the pluck of the young runner and in an instant recognized a future. Distance runners came in all forms and this one had a chance. A smile crossed his face as the two frontrunners continued the battle and strode past the white line side-by-side.

Yet only one kept going. D.J. was alone now. Time to fade or stand up and be counted. The three-lap split was measured at three minutes and ten seconds, far faster than he had gone before. Mac knew D.J.'s body would rebel at the stress but that was the point of the exercise: to find out where the runner stood in the face of the extreme.

It was then an unexpected moment occurred. The periphery of the track held a smattering of athletes working on their own events; the sprinters on their starts, the hurdlers on technique, the throwers on the hoisting of implements. Yet they were drawn to the event on the track. A loud voice commandeered the arena. "Freaking go, D.J.!" yelled the baritone voice of Jimbo. "You got this, you beast!"

The call was met by others urging the runner on. The voices rose one by one as the runner hoisted a crucible of achievement. The distance runners were drawn in and did the same. Lee and Andy ran across the infield to meet D.J. at the halfway point of the last lap. "Go 'Deej'," shouted the twins in unison, "Goooo!"

The outside lanes of the track filled and a rhythmic clap commenced. Even Coach Heck joined in and the transformation was complete; the lone athlete strode down the track with the support of those that mattered. His stride devoured the yards as a harsh rasp of breath sought the oxygen needed. Mac watched carefully and analyzed his form; maintaining peak effort was a struggle many never attempted. Some never would. D.J. was not one of those; he was not afraid. In spite of the effort, he stayed erect and kept an efficient arm carriage. *One in a thousand,* Mac thought. His heart pounded as the athlete approached the last turn. It was then a tear welled in the corner of his eye. He had no idea why, aside from the fact he was getting old. Maybe even sentimental. His fists clenched as D.J. began the final drive toward the finish line. Seventy yards. Sixty. Given his fatigue, the distance seemed brutal but he did not waver. The cheers of onlookers heightened as Mac made his way to the finish line to meet the runner. When D.J. crossed the line and stumbled forward, he was there to catch him before collapse.

Painful groans echoed as D.J. fell into his arms. He held the boy as the warmth and sweat of the athlete flowed into him. D.J.'s heart jackhammered and Mac fought the impulse to tell the boy how proud he was, how much had been revealed. Instead he spoke runner's English. "Four minutes and eleven seconds." D.J. didn't respond. Maybe couldn't respond. "But you're not done yet, D.J."

The harsh breaths continued but broke for a moment. "Yes, coach."

Mac held him until he could stand on his own.

Chapter Thirty

The team was flying high after the conference championship. The bus ride home from the meet was a happy one and the noise peaked after Coach Heck finished his congratulatory remarks. "Three conference champions and overall team champions!" he said from the front of the bus. "An amazing day, men." He pointed one by one. "An unexpected champion in the thirty-two hundred running sub-ten minutes for the first time, Lee! And need I mention twin brother only one second back? Get him next time, Andy!" The twins exchanged fist bumps and he continued. "The big man in the shot, Jimbo! Beating the field by four feet, are you kidding me?"

"I would never kid you, coach!" shouted Jimbo as he stood and towered over his teammates. "I ain't that way."

"I would hope not," he replied. "Just keep on working because there is a lot more in store for you this season."

Flexing a bicep, Jimbo didn't hesitate. "I gotta lotta more," he nearly growled. "I promise."

"Ok, Jimbo, I'm sure you do. Now sit your big butt down so I can congratulate the last of our winners." The bus laughed as all heads turned toward D.J. "What a race, D.J., you should be proud. To overcome two stumbles, one on an illegal push I might add, and still do what you did is amazing. Four-fifteen with a lot left in the tank." He let the number sink in as the bus erupted. "Coach Mac and I are both very proud of you."

D.J. nodded but stayed seated. "Thanks, coach," was all he could muster as a wide smile lit his face.

"But bigger than the individual accomplishments is this." He bent over the seat and lifted an oversized trophy in the air. "Bringing home the conference championship to Weston High for the first time ever! Congratulations men, you have made an old man proud." With that, he misted but did not look away. "I will always remember this day."

Jimbo led the whoops and the energy hit peak. D.J. was connected to the moment but his mind still wandered. To his race. To the instant he was trapped in the pack and his foot nicked another. Pitching forward, he attached himself to another runner until disaster was diverted. One lap later when an opening arose, he made his move to escape the pack. Darting for the space, he had clear sailing until a hand hit the small of his back and pushed him ajar. He nearly crashed again but juked outside and was forced to take the race into his own hands. After spurting to the front, he briefly battled the leaders until he was alone. From there he didn't look back.

The last six-hundred yards he used his strength. Running from the front was liberating as well as risky. But the danger of the pack was left behind and on the last lap he caught a smile crossing Mac's face. This emboldened him and lightened his carriage. He would not falter. Not on this day.

After, Mac was pleased. "I wondered how you would take the jostling in the pack," he said. "I saw the stumbles and was worried. But you didn't panic. A sign of growth, D.J."

He warmed at the statement. "I was pissed at the first guy and wanted to elbow him but I didn't. The second push was worse but more than get even, I wanted to win. I figured that was the best way to get back."

Mac agreed. "Absolutely. And to use a long closing drive was the best tactic. Remember all the over-distance runs we did early in the season trying to gain strength?" D.J. nodded. "Races like you just ran are the reason why. You should be proud, D.J. You analyzed the situation and reacted like a veteran. Well done."

Hours later the praise still echoed.

He was startled when a trio of hands pummeled him from behind. "Conference champion, D.J.!" said Andy. "That was awesome."

Lee seconded the fact. "I thought you were going down in the pack. It got pretty rough."

Jimbo pitched in. "If that dude would have knocked you down, I would have drilled him with a discus. No one messes with our boy."

D.J. absorbed the praise. He never would have guessed he would bond with the group like he had. Eight months ago, he was tossed into a world unlike any he had known. A fish out of water didn't do it justice. More like a mangy puppy in a dark woods. He might never be looked upon as a local, but now that didn't matter. He studied the faces; Lee and Andy as identical as thin, pale reeds, Jimbo, swarthy with premature stubble lining his reddened skin. The threesome never said an unkind word and generated eternal optimism of events ahead. He had rarely encountered individuals of that ilk; most of his past had been posers and opportunists that could not be trusted. The city creed of *kill or be killed* was never far from his thoughts as he struggled for survival on the streets. Absent parenting forced him to manage responsibilities far ahead of the normal pace. Yet, he held on to a flickering belief that there was something out there for him. Something special he would be called upon to do. The tenuous belief bolstered him when he was offered illicit drugs or a chance at easy money. He didn't know what his purpose was then until his feet led the way. Embracing the challenges of sport, the choice became clearer.

He simply wanted to run.

Turning to the threesome, he shook off the praise. "I just got lucky. I mean, you guys kicked some serious ass out there. Lee and Andy, you guys beat your bests by over twenty seconds. Nobody does that." They flushed at the remark as he continued. "And Jimbo, when you walk into the shot circle the other guys just stop and watch. I swear one dude watching your winning throw almost pissed himself. He was that freaked out."

Jimbo nodded. "Actually, he *did* piss himself," he said. "Poor bastard." He shrugged his monstrous shoulders. "But what are you gonna do? I was born to search and destroy."

"And talk," countered Lee.

Andy agreed. "Mac said when Jimbo was born, he was given 'too much'."

"Too much what?" Jimbo asked.

Andy appeared puzzled. "Actually, he didn't say."

Jimbo roared. "And to think, I've only just begun. In fact, we've all just begun."

They all knew what he meant. State. The quest at the end of the rainbow. To get there was the dream of any athlete of merit.

The four of them each had a chance, some more than others. They had danced around the ultimate end-of-season experience for weeks. Afraid of jinxing the possibility, the topic had been purposefully avoided.

Until now.

Jimbo laid his right palm down. Nodding his head, he called for action. "Hands in, men." D.J. was the first and placed his hand on top. The two remaining runners paused until Jimbo urged them on. "Dudes, do it." First Lee, then Andy reached out and placed their hands on the others. Then Jimbo lowered his voice. "We've worked too hard to not finish the job. To go all the way." Their eyes met his. "You know what I mean. To get to State. Come hell or high water."

D.J. swallowed but didn't waiver. "To State."

Lee and Andy were the slowest. They looked at each other, hesitant to begin the pledge. Then almost as if practiced, their voices synchronized. "To State," they said in unison.

Jimbo placed his left hand on top of the others. "The evil deal is now sealed," he said in a snarl. He pressed the mass of hands together and the pressure welded the moment. When he released, a common goal had taken shape.

***

The others thought him strange for choosing to walk home. He said he wanted to stretch his legs but in truth he needed the quiet. He shrugged off their protests and they knew well enough when to quit. By now they had learned he would do as he wished. Saying their goodbyes, he promised to meet up with Lee and Andy for a shag run the following day.

But right now, he needed space.

The realization of battles ahead spiked his thoughts. The goals had always included State, but the pact magnified the races ahead. Regionals first. That didn't worry him. Sectionals was the place where dreams went to die. That race would be against those passing the early litmus test. He knew many local competitors by face, their names and abilities by time. He stacked up well and his personal results were on other runner's radars. But he knew there was only one big dog the others truly feared.

Dalton.

His pulse accelerated at the name. He didn't fear him but like any runner, those with faster times held superior sway. They possessed innate ability, that when coupled with magical training granted them special powers. Dalton's personal best was well beyond the others and he fully rattled opponents by his claim he would run under four minutes and four seconds at State. All other efforts paled in comparison to his resume.

At times like this, his mind was drawn to past conversation. Mac, always Mac. He presented pre and post-workout oration the likes D.J. had never encountered before. Most appeared extemporaneous and the ones that stood out were riveted to memory. Hypnotized, each runner gathered the nuggets laid out. D.J. still heard the words in his head.

Hopes and dreams drive us. Motivate us. They get us up for an early morning run and out the door on a sub-zero day. Dreams whip us to do things that others would never consider. But dreams can only take you so far. At some point a runner must harden. The dream still exists but it becomes more than that. It becomes tangible, no longer just a whisper in the night. It evolves into fibers of your being. Fibers

that take root and become flesh. When that happens, you will know.
No one will believe you, but I promise you, you will know.

After the words, D.J. stilled, mesmerized. He wanted more than anything to know. To have the knowledge that Mac promised. He wanted to ask what it felt like but held back. Some things cannot be explained. Love. Hate. Passion. None can truly be defined, only experienced. He expected this was the same.

He walked and worried about Mac. As happy as he was today with their performances, Mac was distant. His eyes hollow and face drained of color, D.J. worried about the old man's home life. He knew well the destruction of family and in that they shared a common bond. D.J.'s family disassembled nearly as it began; he never knew any other way. Mac had been blessed with Mona but her decline was leaving equally deep wounds. To be losing her and facing the world alone was terrifying. Mona was a part of him. All he ever had. To lose her would be to lose himself.

D.J. strode on and daydreamed of his own future. With his father. His new friends. School. And more importantly, the end of the season. The short hairs on his neck stood tall as he considered the upcoming races. Regionals. Sectionals. And if he survived that, State. His heart raced as chemicals streamed into his bloodstream. Palms and armpits moistened as his body reacted to the influx of elements preparing him for battle. In some ways, the competitive sensation had become the norm. Win or go home.

He itched to bolt down the road and despite the day's effort, run one more time. That would surely bleed the noxious thoughts from his being. Backpack or not, it was the only decision that made sense. Cinching up his bundle, he began a slow trot. Although dusk, a glimmer of sunshine lit the horizon. The straps chafed his shoulders but in discomfort there was pleasure. Pain in his life was a constant and in a bizarre twist, it grounded him. Spurred him to push forward. In that he had chosen the right endeavor.

He ran on.

Chapter Thirty-One

The days passed with gray skies only adding to his lethargy. He still fulfilled his duties as coach; all three upperclassmen had cruised through Regionals with little problem. Sectionals was the next day but that was the least of his worries. He was concerned he was not doing his job because his focus was elsewhere. Mona was worse. They had been to the doctor two days in a row when her difficulties with breathing intensified. Besides continuing home oxygen or admitting her to a facility, the doctor offered no further suggestions.

"No, Thomas," she said sternly, "I won't go to some strange place and be alone in a room. If my time is near, so be it."

He stiffened at the words and had no response. He understood stubbornness. He possessed the trait himself and between them, they had more than their fair share. Yet, he felt helpless. He could cook, he could clean, but those menial tasks held little consequence when weighed against the breathy rasp filling Mona's room. No longer getting proper neurological impulses, her lungs were struggling to provide what her body needed.

And there was not a damn thing he could do about it.

He puttered about her room and alternated opening and closing the window. Fresh air had to help, he told himself. Then he countered that the chill from the outside was a threat.

As he closed the window one more time, he was startled by a thin voice from behind.

"If you touch that window one more time, I'll scream."

He turned and forced a weak smile. "I'm sorry. I'm just trying to make it comfortable in here." He slid into the bedside chair. "Are you okay, Mona?"

She chuckled. "Just peachy." She patted the bed. "Sit here, Thomas." He complied. "You need to stop doting on me before you drive me fruitcakes. If you keep it up, I may go to that hospice center after all." She looked at him and smiled. "Then at least then I could croak in peace."

"Mona!" he nearly shouted. "Don't say that! That's horrible."

She did not disagree but continued. "Yes, I suppose it is. But this situation is real, Thomas. Unfortunately." Her eyes moistened and she reached for his hand. Fifty years ago, she had done the same but the texture was different then; smooth, moist, almost elastic in appearance. Now the coupling of hands revealed lined fingers with dark spots and purple veins. Enlarged knuckles where arthritis had taken an unabashed hold never to be relinquished. She placed an index finger on the back of his hand and gently stroked his skin. Her touch was soothing and he wished it would never end. Then she spoke. "Thomas Charles McKinley, you have given me a wonderful life."

He shook his head. "Mona, stop! Don't you do that. Don't you say goodbye."

She shushed him. "I am not saying goodbye. But soon enough we have to let go and let God. And when that time comes, we need to have spoken our peace, don't you think?"

His mind swirled and he had no immediate response. They had spent a life together. Filled it with ups and downs but had done it together. Even the brief trips when they were apart, their emotional closeness provided comfort. When they reunited, the mutual flame magically reignited. Now, a strong wind had appeared and the fragile nature of life was evident. "Yes. If you say so."

She grasped his hand harder. "Yes, I say so." Her eyes met his. "Thomas, I don't believe in being morbid, you know that. But I have been having dreams. Dreams of the past. And dreams of my future."

"Future?"

"Yes," she continued. "Dreams not of this earth." He shook his head but she ignored him. "In my dreams we are together. Walking in the light of a spring day. The sun gently bathing us with a glorious warmth." She paused. "Do you remember the cardinal tree?"

He did. "The one near Deer Creek. Yes, I remember."

"We discovered it so many years ago but could never explain it; why there were so many cardinals there. At least one, most times more. That one time six of them in all shapes and sizes. Do remember what you said about it?"

He did but denied it. "No," he said.

She nodded and smiled. "I think maybe you do. You called them the 'redbirds of hope'. You said the cardinals were spirits of the deceased coming back to visit their loved ones. That the deceased were happy and content in their new place. And that the beauty of the cardinals proved there was an afterlife. A place where happiness was eternal. Heaven." She closed her eyes and a small smile lit her face. "I've been dreaming of cardinals."

He struggled for air. Even harder were words. "Oh, Mona."

She let go of his hand. "You have given to me more than any girl can ask for. You have given me your heart. We have had our bumps in the road but we always survived."

He struggled to swallow. "Yes, we have. More than most."

"But I need you to promise me something."

He waited until he was able to exhale. "Promise?"

"Promise me that you won't stop living if I leave first." He started to speak but she quieted him. "You cannot turn off life just because another's might end. I know you, Thomas, and I know sometimes you act like you are in the midst of a thousand rainy days. And that you dwell on the past. What was and might have been. Sometimes that might drive one to greater heights, but sometimes it can stall a person like a frozen engine."

He looked to her. "I'm listening."

She touched his hand again. "Promise me you will wake up and take your walks like you always do. Promise that you will smile at a butterfly when it floats past your face. Promise me that you will see the beauty in the moment and let your heart open. That you will embrace the friendships you have and allow new ones to form. And if an obstacle comes your way, you meet it head on." Her eyes misted and her breathing accelerated. When she spoke again, her voice was threadlike. "Promise me, Thomas."

His breath caught in his chest. He could never lie to her. Even more, he could never say no. "I'll try, Mona. I'll do what I can." She looked at him, dissatisfied. "Okay, I promise."

She retook his hand and patted it. "I knew you would, Thomas." With the other she wiped moisture from her eyes. "Enough talk. A cup of tea would be nice, don't you think?"

He nodded. "Yes, m'lady."

With a beatific smile, she released his hand.

***

He placed the teapot on the stove and turned on the burner. At the same time the doorbell rang. Startled, he pivoted and made his way to the front door. Expecting no one, he hesitated as he turned the doorknob. His uncertainty turned to happiness.

"D.J.!" he said, smiling. "What a surprise."

"Well, I was in the neighborhood," he lied.

"Yes, I'm sure. Well, c'mon in."

He passed through the doorway and wiped his feet. "I hope I'm not interrupting…"

He waved the thought off. "No, not at all. I'm just making Mona some tea. I just put the kettle on."

"How is she doing?"

He knew the question well-intended but the answer was difficult in coming. "Fair, D.J. She is…she is slowing down." He had a difficulty continuing. "I try to do all I can."

D.J. looked troubled. He did not want to burden the boy but there was power in truth. Although their relationship had been short, they had bonded and subterfuge was unnecessary.

"Can I see her? I mean, it's okay if you don't think so." He took a slow breath. "I get it, Mac."

He waved his hand. Then smiled slowly. "No D.J., it's okay. She will be thrilled to see you. You can visit while I finish her tea."

"That sounds good." He paused, surveyed the surroundings, and spoke in a soft voice. "You have a nice place, Mac. A nice life. Someday, I hope I have what you have."

He chuckled. "We don't have much, D.J."

D.J. disagreed. "You have it all, Mac. A home. And a wife who loves you. I don't know what else you could ask for."

He stood stock still. Then blinked as if caught off-guard. He touched D.J. on the shoulder. "Go see, Mona. I'll meet you there in a minute."

He did as asked and Mac returned to the kitchen. He lifted the teapot and swirled it contents. A slim cloud of steam crested and he returned it to the burner. Reaching for her favorite cup, he rested a tea bag inside. He had performed the act so often, it was automatic. He knew her likes just as she did his. For him, chicken enchiladas and a cold Budweiser. For her, more simple tastes like fresh cut watermelon or a simple grilled hot dog, slightly burned. He smiled at the memories and anticipated the next time they took place. When the teapot finally whistled, he moved to lift it from the stove.

He halted at a cry from the bedroom.

"Mac, come quick! It's Mona!"

He pivoted and nearly fell as he rushed toward the bedroom. Seconds later, he entered the room and stopped cold at the sight. D.J., standing at the side of the bed, holding Mona's motionless hand. D.J. looked broken and stammered. "We were talking and... and then she just stopped... stopped talking. I waited for her but… but she just stopped." He looked to him. "Mac?"

He was numb but walked to the bedside. He released D.J.'s hand and placed hers on the bed. Touching D.J.'s shoulder, he guided him to the chair. Then he turned to face Mona. She appeared as if sleeping, but he knew the truth. He touched her hand. Still warm. Yet it was lifeless. The truth was in her face. He knew. He knew her better than he had ever known anyone in his life. And now he knew her in death. His Mona was gone. Her life force had vanished in the space of minutes. His eyes filled with tears and he picked up the phone on the small end table. Making the call, the emergency team would soon be on their way. He wished for more but knew the truth: Mona had gone the way she wanted. In her home. With her doilies and knickknacks surrounding her. With pictures of his athletic youth. With their adopted son, D.J., nearby.

And with him.

He tried to breathe but air was scarce. Then nearly falling, he braced and caught himself. He sat at the edge of the bead and reached for a curl of her gray hair. Pushing it from her face, the lack of rise and fall of her chest was encompassing. He started to speak, failed, but was able to whisper. "What happened, D.J.?"

The boy trembled. Mac reached and touched him on the shoulder. D.J. blew out a long stream of air. "We were talking. She seemed okay. I mean, not like she had been, but okay."

He nodded. "I know. She's been struggling." He trembled. A hundred questions and thoughts flooded his mind. "What did she say?"

D.J. looked to him. His eyes pleaded, unsure of how to proceed. Mac nodded and the boy began. "She said how wonderful it was to see me. We talked a minute of running. Of Sectionals tomorrow. Of how I thought I would do." He stopped.

"Anything else?"

He looked to him. "Then she asked me to take care of you. That you needed a friend. A family."

Mac blinked. Tried to make sense of it all. Then he turned to Mona and reached for her cheek. His fingertips touched her skin and he traced her cheekbones. Her jawline. It was there his fingers stayed as if frozen in place. He couldn't move. Couldn't breathe. Seconds passed. Then more.

The moment was lost in time as thoughts tumbled like an untamed river. Mona. His Mona. Gone. He dizzied and could not think. Then a pain appeared and he clutched his chest before pitching forward.

From somewhere far away, a shrill whistle of boiling water echoed in the air.

Chapter Thirty-Two

He had barely slept. After three hours in bed, his phone alarm jarred him from an unsettled slumber. Recalling the torrent of the past evening, he blinked to remember specifics. The emergency crew had made quick time and first tended to the living. Unexpectedly, they assessed a groaning Mac as he lay on the bedroom floor. He was responsive, yet bewildered as to time and place. A preliminary diagnosis of a heart attack complicated by a concussion from the fall was quickly applied. Backup was called as oxygen was administered. He would live, D.J. was told, but he needed immediate care. Mona was next. D.J.'s attention was broken between the two of them. Watching a helpless Mac broke his heart, but an unmoving Mona was far worse. Lacking any sign of life, a sheet was lifted over her inert body.

D.J. closed his eyes in a vain attempt to erase the tragedy. Failing miserably, he opened them and silenced his alarm. He sat up in bed and fought to steady his thoughts. Mac's coaching advice ran like a soundtrack in his head: *Don't unnecessarily burn mental fuel. Turn off the mind until it is needed. Control it and even in the worst of times, the body will follow.*

The irony of the words was painful. The worst of times, he had orated. Surely this was well beyond that. Death and near death. He closed his eyes again.

***

The bus arrived at the track and the excited chatter of his teammates intensified. Those qualifying for Sectionals had thinned the numbers, but energy peaked. Lee, Andy and Jimbo were wired and did not seem to notice the fatigue in his eyes. They chatted about the possibilities of the day. Specifically, of making it to State. D.J. was quiet but they let him be; he had been like that before. When they pulled into the parking lot, they slapped him on the back and barked out their expectations. He nodded and forced a smile. At that moment it was all he could call forth. He was the last to leave the bus and as he exited, he was met by Coach Heck. He looked tired. Drawn. He too was struggling with the series of events.

He laid a gentle hand on D.J.'s shoulder. Squeezing tight, he spoke. "I struggled with what to tell the team about Mac and Mona," he said. "In the end, I chose to keep it between us. I thought that competing with a heavy heart does no one any good." He paused, reconsidered. "But you'll be okay, D.J. You are strong. Mac has told me that many times."

He listened, then slowly responded. "It's fine, coach." He looked to the distant track. "Mac is going to be okay. I know that." He paused again. "He has to be."

Coach Heck nodded. "I am aware I don't have the way with words that Mac does, but I do know how he feels about running. And more importantly, how he feels about you." D.J. looked to the ground before their eyes again met. "He told me he has met countless runners but few have what you have. A natural gift for the sport. But he told me you have more than that. The ability to endure pain and summon something from

231

deep inside. He says you have that rare chance to be great. Even beyond great." He took a deep breath and finished. "To win it all. To be a champion."

D.J. swallowed. He thought of the last time he saw Mac. Pale. Aged. Clutching his chest with a slim stream of blood on his forehead. He winced at the memory. "I don't feel like a champion right now."

He understood. "The circumstances are horrible. But you can't let the hard work you have put in be wasted. Mac's too. You owe this to yourself, D.J."

He was right. He looked to the oval holding his destiny. Four hundred meters that seemed well beyond that. It was a path fraught with peril and disappointment as often as joy and exhilaration. But it was his to transform into whatever he could muster.

He shook off the thick fatigue and stepped toward the track.

***

They had arrived an hour before the meet as dark anvil-shaped clouds drifted overhead. The day was warm, with flickering raindrops polishing the fir trees surrounding the stadium. D.J. drank from his water bottle and studied the far corners of the track. The colors of each team created a human kaleidoscope. Red. Green. He continued searching until he zeroed in on one color. Dark blue. Almost approaching black. The colors of Dalton Scarie. His race was still two hours off but his pulse escalated. Scarie lounged on the side of a hill; fair haired, lean and from even a hundred yards away, oozing confidence. He didn't fear him but recognized until beaten, this singular competitor was the savant. The runner that no one could touch or even less likely, intimidate. He calculated his odds. He believed he could run with Dalton; the math even suggested it. But math and sweat were mismatched creatures living in conflict. The proof lay on the track. Four laps that left nothing in doubt. Until beaten, Dalton was the reigning king.

Until beaten, he thought to himself.

"Dude, what are you doing all by yourself?" asked Lee.

"Yeah, man," seconded Andy. "We thought you got lost." He pointed to the bleachers. "We found a place under the stands in case it rains. It looks like a storm coming."

"My phone says off and on showers all day," said Lee. "That sucks."

D.J. remained silent. A rainstorm seemed inconsequential given the tumult of the last hours. He weighed providing more information but decided against it. He finally responded. "We all have shit to deal with. Rain is not the worst."

The twins looked at each other. Then Lee spoke up. "D.J., is Mac coming today?"

The question hit hard. He hesitated and chose his words. "I'm not sure. I know Mona was having a hard time so he might stay back." The stress of lying weighed heavy. "He told me to tell you both to 'kick ass'." He smiled. "Well, he didn't quite say that but it was pretty close."

Andy beamed. "I wish he was here. He calms me. Like when I get on the track, my head is better, you know?"

D.J. knew exactly what he meant. He missed him too. Like a finely trued wheel, he was slightly errant without his mentor. "He is with us. He taught us to survive. To take the ugly and punch it in the mouth." He paused and looked in the distance.

"To finish in the top three and move on. That is all." He struggled with the rest of his words. "We do it today for him and ourselves." With that, he raised a hand in the air. Lee and Andy followed his lead. Touching hands, he said all he needed. "State."

They repeated his word and the promise was made.

***

Time passed slowly. D.J. commenced his warm-up and prepared as he had been trained. Jog. Stretch. Increase the intensity of strideouts until reaching race pace. Then calm the system and review the race plan.

Therein lie the rub. There was no race plan. Current events mandated he was on his own. The place was not unexpected nor unwelcomed. He trusted only himself. Not a long-gone mother. Nor a father on the road. But he missed Mac. A simple word of wisdom was all he wished for. Yet he was not there and was forced to conjure his voice from the depths: *You have prepared for this, D.J. Remember the miles in the fall. The winter. In the crushing heat. You have steeled yourself for this very moment. It is your time to shine. It is not about your family. Not your mother, nor father. It is not about me. It is about you being true to yourself and being who you were born to be. A champion.*

Then the voice disappeared and he was called to the start. He barely had time to toe the curved line before instructions were provided. He was in lane four. An advantageous position provided by pre-race seeding. He did not recognize the runner to his right but to the left he was unmistakable.

Dalton.

He had momentarily forgotten the rival who was the main stumbling block on the road to State. Bumping shoulders as they readied, their eyes met. Without words, they exchanged mute greetings. A nod. Scraping at the ground. Both prepared for the battle ahead.

The gun sounded an instant later. D.J. bolted forward and approaching the first turn, settled into second place. The scuffling of legs and arms calmed as each runner adjusted to their place. D.J. rounded the first corner and assessed his position. He recognized the lead runner for what he was: a fast starter who usually faded by the third lap. Dalton was perched in third place as he too settled into the effort. The reigning champ liked to hang with the field until the last lap when he typically exploded and imposed his will. Given Mac's consent, D.J. liked to do the same.

But today was different.

There was no script. It was the biggest race of his life and he lined up with no game plan. Zero. Nada. Mac was not there to impart wisdom and there was no roadmap for the laps ahead. He was undeniably on his own. Normally he was good with that but now the thought was disturbing. Striding through the backstretch of the first lap, he lowered his hands to relieve tension. Shaking the stress from his fingertips, he soldiered on as the race continued.

He was secure in his place, as was Dalton. He performed a check of his body. His legs were on auto-pilot, those he could count on. His arms and shoulders flowed in unison. It was his breathing that gained attention. Each breath was slightly escalated from what he expected. The pace was moderate but it seemed harder than what it should have. Sixty-five seconds at the quarter was brisk but nowhere near his maximum. Continuing to trail the front runner by a few yards, he tried to lock onto the challenge ahead. It was there the effort increased. Physically, he was fighting to maintain. Mentally, he was tired. Like a leaking faucet, the night had been a constant drip of resources, filled with thoughts he could not erase. Mac. Mona. Desperate eyes. Blood. The sound of a siren.

The hand in his back woke him.

"Dude! Watch it!"

He had drifted wide and then worked back to the inner line. By losing concentration, he also lost precious yards. He regrouped and focused on the runners ahead. The group behind maintained its rhythm, aside from the tail of the pack lengthening. Crossing the starting line a second time, a move revealed the race had truly begun. It was Dalton who began an earlier than usual long drive to the finish line. D.J. wasn't totally surprised, nor was the frontrunner. But his body's response was.

D.J. reached for a higher gear that was uncharacteristically resisted. By season end he had become accustomed to surging on demand whenever necessary. But this time his legs did not deliver. He nearly panicked until a voice echoed. *Never give in to the fear. Some races are touched by an evil God and you just won't have it. Maybe it's the devil rising from the earth placing manacles on your ankles. Maybe it is just a test from above. But don't lose faith. Refocus on the moment. Grind harder. Hang on like grim death and you may surprise yourself by the power within. A power you never thought possible.*

He looked to the infield for Mac. It took three strides before he realized the futility of the effort. Yet, even the thought of his spirit empowered him. *Grind,* he told himself. *All the way to the end.* He owed that much to himself. He owed just as much to Mac. His stride changed from long and flowing to a slightly shorter version. Less graceful but somehow more secure. The backstretch of the third lap broke the race apart as Dalton spread the field. Four, then five yards appeared between the trailing string of runners as they struggled to maintain pace. The leader was sailing and hopes of victory to the other runners lessened with each stride. D.J. was no different. Today was not the day he had envisioned. But his ultimate goal was to stay alive.

And make it to State.

He focused on the jersey of the runner in second place. Hang on to him and if he maintained third place, his ticket was punched. He used Mac's trick of tying an invisible tether to the runner and not allowing any more space to occur. Dalton was separating from the group but that was no matter. *Another day,* D.J. nearly said aloud. As he focused on the runner ahead, he made a rookie mistake and allowed a runner from behind to pass him on the inside. He cursed aloud and assessed the intruder. Slim, redhaired and freckled, the runner was less than imposing. But the wide-eyed focus of the runner was the only clue D.J. needed.

The runner was here to stay.

D.J. had seen the look before. Just as much, he had been that runner before. Under the radar, with nothing to lose and all to gain. The two feelings were a dangerous combination not to be underestimated. The tether to the second-place runner had been broken and he zeroed in on his newest rival. As the bell lap sounded, the roar of the crowd escalated. In the distance, there were calls from Lee and Andy and the baritone voice of Jimbo. They were there with him, tired legs and all. But this was no time for pity. No time for excuses. This was time for a cruel plunge into pain.

He dropped his arms and attached like a leach to the ginger runner. If he moved, he would cover the pace just as he had trained to do. He doubted few could match his closing speed and despite the hollowness in his legs, he believed. The backstretch sailed on and he gave a cursory look behind to ensure there were no surprises lurking. Seeing the space, the race was only ahead. Heading into the last turn, he forced his hoarse breathing to regulate and studied the markers ahead. Spying what he needed, he gathered himself for one final push. When the turn ended, the test of wills began. Lengthening his stride, he implored his weary legs to do his calling. Gaining inches with each stride, he breasted the third-place runner and expected his progress to continue. But he had not anticipated what was encountered.

The runner refused to fade.

They were chest to chest with under one hundred yards to go. The second-place runner was five yards ahead and he too was fighting for his life. D.J. dug deeper as the pounding of blood filled his ears. There was no crowd. No teammates. Only the gnashing of legs on a track where two of three runners would survive. His eyes bulged as he fought to maintain an efficient stride. The red-haired runner gave no quarter and with fifty meters remaining, the three drew abreast in the first two lanes. Each had their own deep-rooted reasons for competing. Each had their own strengths and frailties forging them into who they were. Each howled at the demons within and refused to wilt. D.J. churned and vowed he would die trying before giving in. As blackness cloaked his vision, Mac's voice reverberated in his head: *Run through the line, not just to it!*

His legs screamed toward the finish as he instinctively threw himself over the white line. Crashing to the track, the rough surface broke the skin on his cheek. Sensing the warm flow, it reaffirmed one thing.

He was still conscious.

Lee and Andy smothered him as their hands touched his back. His breathing spiked and he absorbed the available oxygen one rakish breath at a time. Sounds filtered in as seconds passed. Voices were gibberish and he struggled to make out the words.

"D.J., you did it! You got third! You got it by a chest. You're going to State!"

He didn't smile. Couldn't smile. *Third*, he thought. *That sucks!* But he didn't reply when the light dimmed again.

***

In a near photo finish, the three runners crossed the line within an eyelash. The officials sorted it out and designated D.J. as a survivor. It was not his best moment, yet it was. He had carried a heavy heart and a fragile frame to a place he had not been before. A place where pain was a simple barrier necessary to gain the ultimate prize. State. He had made it. He would gain no style points nor accolades from the press. To them he was just another number that would soon enough become fodder for the winner of the next race.

He watched Dalton talk to a reporter and soak up the acclaim. The runner exhibited natural charisma as the sunlight danced off his hair. He fit the part of the star; lean, sinewy, with a megawatt smile. A champion for the ages. D.J. bristled, knowing that under different circumstances, that could have been him. He stared down his opponent and spoke a simple promise aloud.

"Next week I bring it, Dalton. For Mac." He paused. "And for me."

The words warmed him as he picked at the crusted blood on his cheek. Reopening the flow, he refused to wince.

Chapter Thirty-Three

Mac was still groggy that afternoon. He had been told twice what day it was but he had to concentrate to remember. Saturday. It was Saturday. And he was in the hospital. He had a blinding headache but that was the least of his worries. He had been told he had suffered a heart attack, then fell and hit his head. A mild heart attack. A major concussion. Minimal solace. But neither would kill him, he was told. Unlike…

Mona.

He could not process the reality. Mona was dead. The memory of her lying motionless in bed was engrained. But someone else was there too. It took him a moment to recall. Then a face flashed. D.J. He had been visiting when she passed. He remembered them standing over his lifelong love. So frail. So terribly thin. Yet undeniably at peace. Somehow it was her time. But conversely it wasn't, because it was not *his* time to have her pass. Maybe that day would have never come but her death was too soon. His heartrate spiked and a machine on the wall beeped in warning. He ignored the noise and turned to look out the window. There a tree branch rippled in the spring breeze, green buds springing from its ends. A sign of life and rebirth. He stared at it, mesmerized. Wishing, dreaming, hoping. Of everything. And nothing at all.

Then a nurse startled him. "Mr. McKinley? Are you ok?"

A nurse entered the room in response to the accelerated heartbeat. To him she was just a child. A mere baby dressed in costume hospital scrubs. He blinked and collected himself. The words were slow in forming but when able, he responded. "Yes, I'm fine. Just fine." And yet he wasn't. His chest still ached and his head throbbed. Yet, more than that, he was lost.

"Well, that's good. Your vitals ramped and I just wanted to make sure you were okay. You took a nasty spill in addition to your heart attack. Your cardiologist says your heart should do well but the neurologist says the concussion is substantial. He can't even rule out a small bleed. And at your age..." She fidgeted and chose her words. "That the healing is hard to predict. Sometimes it can be very slow."

His mind jumbled but he replied methodically. "I don't care about me. What...what about Mona? She...she passed." He looked to her as his eyes swelled. "She needs a funeral. A wake. All those things."

The nurse's lips tightened. "I understand, Mr. McKinley. This is a very difficult situation. We put a call into a social worker to help you sort through all these difficulties. But...but she won't be back until Monday."

Monday. Two days. With Mona lying on a cold slab in some godforsaken place. He nearly exploded. "No goddam way! That will not do!" Spittle formed and the pressure in his head compounded. The warning of the machines began again and chaos accelerated.

Then his door opened slowly. A face peered in. The person looked bewildered and just as tired as Mac. The nurse moved toward him. "Can I help you, sir? We are in the middle of something."

Mac waved his hand in the air. "He is my friend. Let him in, for chrissake." He tried to say his name but he couldn't remember. He blinked. Then again. Finally, it came to him. *D.J.*

She appeared confused and struggled for composure. After seconds passed, she nodded. "That will be fine. But just for a short while because you need to rest." She looked to D.J. and nodded. "I'll come back soon."

He returned the greeting and faced Mac. He studied him, blinked, and almost lost his balance. Mac noted the teetering and warned him. "Careful, D.J. You don't want to split your melon like I did."

He smiled. Still silent, his eyes traced the various plastic lines leading to and from Mac's body. Then, tentatively, he made his way to the chair alongside the bed. Drawing a deep breath, he began. "Mac, are you okay? You look so...so---"

"Old? Pathetic? Both?"

"Yes. No." He sighed. "Seriously, Mac. How are you?"

He recognized the angst and softened his voice. "I've been better but they tell me I'll be okay in time." He touched his head. "Right now, the concussion seems the worst." He winced at the pressure of his fingertips. "I'm still not thinking quite right. Sort of confused."

"And the heart?"

He looked at the boy and felt for him. He looked afraid. Even small and vulnerable. He had not expected him to be so distraught at his condition. "They said something about coronary artery calcification leading to a heart attack. Maybe genetic. Then with, with all of the...the stress of Mona." He stopped talking at the mention of her name.

"Mac, I never told you how sorry I was. I mean, she was the best."

He returned a sad smile. "Yes, she was." He looked out the window at the approaching darkness. He blinked away moisture. "I miss her already." D.J. nodded in agreement. In silence Mac sensed his discomfort and took control. "But I'll be okay. So will you, D.J." He paused, realized the day and the events it contained. "Oh my goodness, I forgot! The meet! What happened?"

D.J. rubbed his lips and leaned forward in the chair. "Good and bad," he said.

"Good and bad?"

"Well, the bad is I ran like shit."

He was puzzled. "And the good?"

D.J. smiled. "I made it to State."

Mac blinked and swelled with excitement and pride. "You...you made it?"

He nodded as his face flushed. "I made it by a cheek." He turned his head and exhibited the scab on his face. "It took a faceplant to get there, but I freakin' made it, Mac. And I wouldn't have gotten there without you."

His heart raced and he looked to the monitors, afraid he would set off the alarm again. Absorbing the information, he wanted more. "Details, young man."

From there D.J. recounted the race. The uneasiness at the start. The unexpected battle with early fatigue. The self-doubt that nearly paralyzed. Then the resurrection on the last lap that squeezed all he had from his exhausted being. Lastly, the ultimate vindication as he crossed the line in the position he needed to be.

Mac absorbed the recap and relished the sensation coursing through his body. It was stronger than pride. Far better than that. Given his current state, it was unexpected. It was love. Love for a boy he had met only months ago. All the same it was real and unfettered by conditions and constraints. D.J. was part of him and in some strange and unexplainable way, they were joined by chemistry. Not DNA, but in a way no scientist could explain. They were joined by spirit. He couldn't tell him that now, maybe ever. But it was real and it bathed him in lightness and grace. He had few words in reply.

"Running is like life, a struggle. But you survived and moved on. You did it, D.J." He locked onto the boy. "Dalton has no goddam idea what is going to hit him at State."

The light in D.J.'s eyes said exactly the same thing.

***

The nurse interrupted their meeting to perform the duties of the day. She first checked vitals then followed with an uncomfortable sponge bath. Well beyond erotica, Mac complied with her demands and sulked at his predicament. Aging and well beyond his prime, he recognized the downward spiral. Leaving the hospital was goal number one. But to what? To an empty home? To absolute silence? Mona gone forever? His headache spiked as renegade thoughts ramped the effects of the concussion.

He closed his eyes and lay back in his bed. He envisioned D.J. battling his competitors. The grit and inner strength he had displayed was both admirable and remarkable. The boy had it. An "it" that could not be defined nor measured. An "it" that once upon a time he also possessed. But that was long ago and this was now. With night setting in, darkness filled him with memories. Of Mona lying in her bed. Gone. A body still there but her spirit elevated to a better place. No longer struggling to perform the simplest of activities, she was freed to walk in peace.

He spoke aloud. "I'll see you soon, Mona. I promise."

He opened his eyes and stared at the blackness beyond the window. He couldn't suppress a smile at D.J.'s news. The boy had survived the gauntlet and was moving on. More surprising, one of the twins, Lee, had edged out Andy for the last spot in the thirty-two hundred. D.J. relayed how Andy took the lead with six-hundred yards remaining in a blatant attempt to drain the kick from the front runner. Knowing Lee could mount a strong final two-hundred meters, the unplanned ploy worked magically. Missing State by seconds, Andy was nonplussed as he immediately hugged his brother at the race's conclusion. They had done it. Despite only one of them toeing it up at State, the blended heart had succeeded in their declared quest. One last piece of information was not unexpected. Jimbo had doubled down and dominated both the shot and discus. Or as D.J. had recounted: *The big sonofabitch crowed like an overfed Man Mountain after his throws. It was embarrassing and amazing at the same time.*

An unrestrained smile appeared despite the deep ache in his chest and head.

Chapter Thirty-Four

He was off kilter the rest of the weekend. Losing Mona and seeing Mac vulnerable hit hard. They weren't blood relatives but might as well be. His connection to them was instant and unlike anything he had experienced before. Even fleeting memories of his familial upbringing were marred by parental friction. Tension. Fights. A single bulb lighting a shabby room. Worst of all were anguished nights where his capacity to love clashed with abandonment. To deaden old memories, he tossed in bed and turned the music louder. Just like Mac, he was teetering on an unseen cliff and he couldn't escape the sensation of an impending fall into oblivion.

He would be on his own this week. He dared not ask Mac for any training advice. That imposition would be bordering on impudent. Yet, this was the biggest meet of his life and he needed advice on how to sharpen to a razor's edge. He thought of asking Coach Heck or Lee and Andy, but they each had their own gaps in knowledge or experience. There was no one else. He turned over and bumped the nightstand. Rustling on the edge was Mac's supply of donated running literature. A dog-ear of one source peaked from the bottom and gained his attention. He slipped it out and remembered the author. Lydiard. He paged through the book, remembering vaguely the contents it contained. Striking gold, he honed in on the training schedules prescribed from personal failure and success.

Reviewing, it all made sense.

In no uncertain terms, the old coach drew up the last week of taper for middle-distance runners: let the engine throttle up, then stow it to prepare for the culmination of the season. D.J. memorized the preparatory workouts of prior world champions and his mind settled. Mac related how past runners of eras ago were not so different. Ignoring the years, they were all merely men constructed of complicated layers of tissue well beyond understanding. Flesh. Bone. Blood. Mac recalled men that to D.J. were just names. Wolde. Bikila. Quax. Men whom D.J. had never heard of. Yet, Mac ensured him they were every bit as hardened as current champions, probably more. There were no subsidies then, no contracts, no six-figure bonuses for a win. Just passionate men engaging in a quest they could not explain nor control. Simply, to be the best.

D.J. ran down Lydiard's schedule one last time before succumbing to the day. He was tired but that was no matter. He had a roadmap to success garnered from the sweat and toil of those before him. He held no illusion he was special, at least no more than any other aspiring competitor. Yet, he vowed to commit each upcoming moment toward toeing the line against the best the state had to offer.

Closing tired eyes, the buzzing inside his head did not stop.

***

The Monday morning alarm went off far too quickly. He rarely remembered dreams but this one exhausted him. As was frequent, he was running. Sometimes he was nearly floating, covering ground like a cheetah in pursuit of a hapless prey. Those were the ones he relished. But that image was nowhere in sight when he needed it most. This time he was churning though ankle-high quagmire that drained his energy. He fought. Strained. His pulse raced and approached redline. Tossing in his sleep, his sheets were covered in sweat as if deep in competition. In that, he was.

This time it was with himself. He knew he could run; of that he had no doubt. He watched other competitors on the Internet. The best of the best. Those he was not afraid to compete against. But more than those runners, he battled the baggage in his head. It slowed him. Exhausted him. Caused him to question all he hoped for. He wasn't worthy because of who he was: a child created by an unholy alliance of two mismatched creatures. He tried to absolve himself a hundred times but the shadow of the past always loomed. Haunting. Echoing that his life was a mistake.

His thoughts were jarred by a voice from the doorway. "D.J., you up yet?"

His father. Their lives rarely intersected except for the proverbial two ships in the night. Yet, slowly, D.J. had come to a greater understanding of the man.

He was just that. A man. Full of enough flaws and contradictions to fill his truck. But he worked hard and provided what he could to his only offspring. A roof over his head and food on the table. While lacking in fatherly advice, he provided stability that had been absent. He returned the call. "Yes, my alarm for school just went off."

"Then if you have a second, c'mon out. I have a long week on the road and have to tell you a few things."

That worried him. Absence of news was safer and far less threatening. He made his way to the kitchen where his father was at the table. Sipping coffee, he motioned for him to sit down. "Have a seat." He complied and wordlessly waited. "I know we don't talk much, but I have to fill you in on something." He watched D.J.'s reaction and reassured him. "It's okay, D.J."

He remained silent and nodded at the grizzled man. Gray had crept into his stubble and the edges of his hair. He was no longer young and mileage had accumulated. The man's subdued goodness had been a revelation and deep-rooted anger had begun to thaw.

"Fine," he said, slowly. "What's up?"

D.J. watched him sip coffee. Then even more painstakingly, watched him return the cup to the table. The man studied him. Measured him. Then spoke. "I can't believe what you have been able to accomplish, D.J. It's amazing." He looked in his eyes. "To get to State is an incredible accomplishment. I only wish I could have been there."

He shook his head. "No, you don't. It was a train wreck. But thanks, anyways."

"Whatever. You made it. I'm completely proud of you." He stopped, swallowed, and then continued. "Your mom is proud too."

He froze as if an electrical charge had entered his body. Mom? He thought of her often but his anger relegated her to a dark, hidden space. She was gone and although not forgotten, she might as well have been. Now in a blink, she was back.   He nearly stuttered. "What do you mean?"

He let the moment settle before explaining. "We don't talk much, but she has my number. She called yesterday, D.J. Apparently she is in a detox center in Texas." He grasped his coffee cup and swirled the contents. "She said she is trying, D.J., really trying."

He struggled to respond. Trying. How big of her. To reclaim a life of abandonment. The mere words angered him. "That is so fucking special," he said.

His father nodded. "I understand. In many ways I feel the same." He took a sip of his drink and stroked his beard. "But it seemed different this time. Like maybe she has a chance." He looked at him, then beyond, as if he was looking into the past. "She was not always messed up. There was a time she was a good person, D.J. Be that as it may, she wanted to know about you. How you are doing. Anyways, I told her how well you run and that you made it to State." He looked him in the eye one last time. "She broke down, D.J. She cried. I know it was because of your accomplishment, and just as much, that she wasn't there. The situation sucks but she cares, D.J. She really does."

He balked at the words. And remembered. To days when he was young. To when she smoothed his hair in bed and whispered in his ear. *You can be anything, D.J. Anything you want. Don't be like me. Don't give up. Try and fly, little man. Fly high, to the stars.* Then another stroke of his head. *Promise me.*

And he did.

Yet now, he was too stunned to reply. To survive, staying silent was the best option. To open up revealed vulnerabilities.

That was not acceptable. When ready, he responded. "Is that all?"

His father nodded.

He did nothing but breathe.

***

The trauma of Mona and Mac coupled with the Sectional race left him drained. Then with his father's unexpected information, his stress levels rocketed. After his father left, he regrouped and concocted a smoothie laced with fruit. Gulping it down, he strove to fill even the deepest reservoirs of his inner core. A buzz began as nutrients circulated and attached themselves to hungry cells and neurons. Muscle fibers clamored for attention and soaked up the essentials provided. Fluid. Proteins. Carbohydrates. For the first time in his life, he concentrated on ingesting only those elements that would aid his effort.

Sitting down later at lunch, he carefully unwrapped a pair of peanut butter and jelly sandwiches. *A perfect food for the champion on a budget,* Mac once explained. Taking his first bite, he swallowed as a crowd of students milled about. He could still not completely escape his deep-rooted paranoia. He heard whispers about the kid from the city. The one who was really fast. *Probably to escape from the cops,* one kid snickered. It was times like those he angered and nearly rose in confrontation. Instead he seethed and vowed to unleash his bitterness on the track. He put his head down and chewed slowly and methodically. Each bite had a purpose.

This week he was all in.

"Dude, you okay? Something interesting written on the table?"

With that, Jimbo sat down beside him. Close behind were the bookends of Lee and Andy. They were his usual lunch partners and he enjoyed the company. They had a common bond of sports but it was more than that. They were just good people. He never felt color around them as he did with others. With them he was just D.J. With them, he let his guard down as best he was able.

He raised his head. "Naw, I was just hoping you wouldn't see me and I could eat in peace."

"Whoo! Nice D.J.!" said Lee. "Give it to the big guy."

Andy seconded. "He needs a little attitude adjustment. He struts around this place like a king."

Jimbo set down his loaded tray of food. "I am the king." He motioned toward his food. "See this heap here? That cute little lunch lady gives me an extra helping whenever I smile at her. My swag knocks her out cold."

Lee laughed. "Swag? She probably thinks you're on charity and feels guilty if she doesn't help feed the fat kid."

Jimbo instantly reached and put Lee in a headlock. "D.J., You see this little pimple of a head? If I squeeze hard enough, it will pop. Wanna see?"

He laughed and took another bite of sandwich. "Next week. After State. Then do what you want."

He released him from his grip. "Good idea. I forgot the little noodle has a race left yet. Who would have thought a one-hundred pound turd could get to State?"

"One twenty-one and a half," Lee countered.

Jimbo sniggered. "Holy crap, that's as much as my left testicle."

"Gross! But Mac says distance runners come in all shapes and sizes, right D.J.?" Andy asked.

He nodded. Although just another member in the group, it was as if his words held more weight. He guessed it was because he said less. Withheld more. Or maybe because he had done time in a big city. No matter, he kept close to the vest and revealed only what he wished. "It takes all kinds. Even scrawny."

"Scrawny?" Lee pouted. "Mac says I have a great power to weight ratio. A big engine on a small frame."

"The way a distance runner should be," echoed Andy. Then he slowed and softened his voice.

"Any word on Mac lately, D.J.? Coach Heck said we should hold off visiting him for a few days. Maybe tomorrow?"

D.J. understood their concern. He had visited daily and expected to do so again. Being Tuesday, he hoped for good news but had none to report. "I was there yesterday and he was still having headaches and pressure in his chest. They wanted to release him but his blood pressure was all over the place. Sometimes he still gets dizzy when he walks." He crumpled up his lunch bag and squeezed it in his hands. "He's pretty pissed because he wants to go home but they don't think he should yet." He shook his head. "But I wouldn't be surprised if he doesn't bolt soon. He told me they would never catch him, except for maybe the young nurse, he said she looks pretty fast."

"That's funny. Did he say anything about this week?" Lee asked.

D.J. knew what he meant. Preparation for the weekend. Advice for race day. Something. Anything. "Yes, he did. Andy, he talked about you first."

"Me?" He looked quizzical. "Really?"

"Yes, he said you are Lee's caretaker. That you need to minimize the stress and act as his coach. How you know him better than he does himself and you are in this together. That you are at State as much as him." Andy swallowed and nodded. "And Lee, he said you are as close to a human metronome as he has ever seen. That you can run even splits nearly all the way through. He said you can run seventy-twos in your sleep."

Lee calculated in his head and nearly choked. "That's four forty-eight a mile. A nine thirty-six two mile." He gulped. "I...I---"

D.J. interrupted. "He knew you would worry. He said don't. Trust yourself. To let the pack go and it will come back to you. To believe in yourself."

The moment extended until Jimbo broke the silence. "And me? Any advice for a beast of a thrower?"

"He did. He said tell Jimbo to get his big ass out there and bring back the gold. That you have worked for it and you deserve it. And now it is time to get it."

The table filled with smiles until Lee spoke in an even voice. "What did he tell you, D.J.?"

"He told me," he started, then stopped. He looked to each of them and considered his response. He balled up his lunch bag one last time and crushed it in his hands. When his knuckles blanched, he released it from his fingers. Letting it drop to the table, words were left hanging in the air.

Instead he only smiled.

Chapter Thirty-Five

He was an awful patient. Surly. Ornery. And at the worst of times, downright rude. Even acknowledging his shortcomings, he spewed out frustration on the unsuspecting staff. He rarely got sick and he let them know this simple fact. Even less, he informed them how rarely he sought out medical care. That was for people like Mona. Those with real problems. Not for people with a little flutter in their chest or a headache. He was healthy, dammit! He threatened to leave more than once until when standing, the dizziness returned and forced him back to bed. *It's going to take time*, the staff promised, *be patient.*

Ironically, it was that type of advice that left him more impatient. Time. He had none. Mona's earthly remains waited. The image of her flesh in a cooler broke his heart. He was failing her again. He painfully recounted that most of their lives had always been about him. His past. His failures and collection of long-gone successes. His disappointment toward unattained dreams. Rarely was it about her. Her hopes for family and a nurturing home. It was his fault they put off having children until it was too late. His fault they never adopted because timing or money wasn't right. It was his fault. All of it.

And now he was alone.

Lying in bed, he felt useless. He wished for nothing more than to be able to move again. Walk. And in his heart of hearts, to be able to run. But that was long ago. Never again would sweat run down his face while his heart pumped octane to every cell of his body. He closed his eyes and drifted back to the fateful day he quit on the track. The day he sealed himself off from the world and what it had to offer. Over fifty years later, he was still stuck in the past. He was old and could not erase the mistakes of his youth. Then he opened his eyes.

Maybe there was another way.

***

It was Thursday and as had been habit, D.J. stopped in after practice. The visits weren't long. Ten, maybe twenty minutes. Just enough time to update the boy on his lack of medical progress and to air grievances. When he was done, it was D.J.'s turn to fill him in on life, school and his preparedness for the race. The boy was leaving on the bus Saturday morning and his nervousness was palpable. He knew the sensation as he had been there many times before. Only this time he was armed with a lifetime of experience to throttle the boiling tension. "D.J., we both know you are ready," he told him. "You proved that at regionals and your toughness at sectionals confirmed it." The lack of any immediate response alerted him. "Right?"

The boy was noncommittal. "Yes. I guess."

"Wrong answer."

"Yes, I'm ready," he said, but when his eyes lowered, the truth was told.

Mac measured him. Confidence was a fleeting emotion. One bad race, one poor workout, one broken night's sleep could jar an athlete's momentum. When he was running, he could force himself into the proper mindset by blasting out a few quarters at race pace and regain the edge needed. Now as a coach, he had only motivational tactics on his side. He began slowly. "D.J., do you remember when we first met?" He nodded. "It was like I was struck by a thunderbolt. I had not seen a runner like you since I was young. Your feet barely touched the earth. I can still see you flashing by like a reel of film in my head." D.J. stiffened in the chair as if at attention. "And you remember the jazz records I put on?"

"Yes. Coltrane and the others."

He smiled. "Do you know why I played them for you?"

He shrugged. "Because you like them." Then he laughed. "And you hate what I like."

It was his turn to smile. "I do hate your music but that's not why. I wanted you to understand the excellence a man can obtain when he bares his soul. That perfection is possible here on earth. And if not perfection, if a man dedicates to do his best, at least the ability to touch an angel's wing." He misted, but continued. "D.J., many runners stand on the line but only a fraction leave their heart bleeding when they cross it. To do that is to be immortal." A single tear ran down his cheek. "I saw your stride and I saw a champion. Then when I met you, I knew I was right. Your fire burns deep. Be it from your trials on earth or from the grace of God, you have all you need. In two days, it is your chance to show the world."

D.J. was taken aback. His body quivered and it wouldn't stop. He reached tentatively then slowed. Gathering strength, he continued until he touched Mac's hand. "Mac, I wish you could be there. I'm…I'm nervous of the big crowd. I've seen pictures and it looks, well, it looks insane."

"I understand. But the crowd feeds you. Those that cheer for you, well, that's easy. They boost you. Those that doubt you, piss you off. From those people suck in their negativity like fuel and show those bastards who you are."

"And the others?"

"Those that have no idea who you are, you win over. When you spill guts on the track, they will stand and scream your name. It's time to show Dalton he's not the 'shit' he thinks he is." He paused. "Did I say that right?"

He laughed. "Yes, Mac. You absolutely did."

He nodded. "D.J. You are on the cusp." He squeezed the boy's hand. "I believe that."

The boy's pulse elevated as did his own. The symbiotic relationship was solidified and there was little left to be said except the obvious. "I still wish you were coming, Mac. We all do."

He let go of D.J.'s hand and wiped his face. "I do too. To be there for you. And Lee has a chance if he follows my advice. And that big galoot, Jimbo, he can't fail even if he tries." He paused. "I miss those guys, tell them that."

"I will. I promise."

He looked at the young runner. "D.J., you have come so far, everything else is gravy. Enjoy the moment, please. There are so few of them in our lives." He blinked before finishing. "I'll be with you in spirit, you know that. Every step of the way."

"I know that, Mac." Then he brightened and reached for his backpack. "Holy crap, I almost forgot!" Mac looked quizzical but he continued. "I checked out a school iPad so you can watch the race!"

He looked at the device. "Watch it on that thing? I have no idea how."

He shook his head. "It's easy. I talked to the nurse. I showed her how to log on and how to catch the live stream. But," he said as he slipped a small piece of paper into the bedside drawer, "I'll leave the password here just in case."

"I have no idea what you're talking about."

He smiled. "I expected that, but the nurse knows how it works. The bottom line is you can watch the race on the iPad. Like watching it on TV. I'm due to run at two o'clock Saturday but you can see the other guys compete too." His lips split in a smile. "Mac, it will be just like you are there."

He accepted the device and thumbed the casing. He had no idea how it worked but didn't care. He only had one final thought. "If that nurse screws this up, there will be hell to pay."

D.J. nodded. "Mac, I'd expect nothing less."

Chapter Thirty-Six

The ride to Madison was uneventful. The school van contained only those who had earned the privilege: Coach Heck, Lee, Jimbo and D.J. The rest of the team had to find their own way to the meet and given the hour proximity, the expectations were a good number of supporters would be there. The three contestants lobbied to have Andy be allowed aboard but the answer was steadfast. Only qualifiers were allowed the luxury. D.J. sensed Lee's disappointment and tried to sooth the situation.

"He'll be right behind us, Lee. Don't you worry about that. You guys have an internal GPS; he would hone in on you in minutes."

Lee didn't disagree and the words calmed him. He turned to the window and watched the passing landscape. D.J. did the same and hoped the scenery would ease his nervousness. He had only been a part of the Northwoods for eight months and Chicago was a fading memory. His old friends, the noise, congestion and even the scent of the city was a hard recall. It was like an interrupted dream; a fragment of dying thoughts. As much as he struggled with identity in a new terrain, he was becoming freed from a past that had hemmed him in.

Here, all he had to do was run.

The trees flying past mesmerized him. Given a lifetime of city dwelling, the picturesque view captivated. Cornfields and cow pastures may never become his norm, but they soothed an anxious spirit. He took a deep breath and reflected on past and present.

Images jarred, knotted, and turned into a mosaic of multiple emotions. Anger, happiness, contentment and disillusionment. Victory and defeat wrapped in a blanket of accomplishment and failure. He closed his eyes and let the moment pass. *Don't stress,* Mac's voice sounded. *Winners calm the soul when others panic. It is an art to be mastered, not one you are born with. Practice calm, then call on it when needed.* He remembered listening to him and mocking the Zen-like words. He talked like a running soothsayer from yesteryear. Yet, unknowingly, he filed the words for future reference.

The trip continued. The hum of the road comforted him and he set his head back. He was tired at the same time he was not. He had rested and filled his engine until it was bursting with energy. Yet, at the same time, life itself was drawing from concealed batteries. He missed Mac. Mourned Mona. He wished for a father presence that might never take shape. Unexpectedly, he couldn't shake the specter of an unseen mother, no matter how much he tried to forget. He stared straight ahead and blinked. He never expected to be in this position and the variables confused him. Glazing over, he scarcely noticed the person who had found a seat next to him.

"D.J., you okay? You look like you clubbed all night."

He turned and acknowledged the person. Jimbo. A rock within the madness. He gave a halfhearted smile and answered. "I'm okay. And no, electronic sucks."

"Yo," he said, "that's true. Sorry, 'bro." He paused and started again. "I mean you got that look on your face. The one that worries me."

He responded in one word. "Explain."

He did. "The look like the weight of the world is on your skinny shoulders. And you know exactly what I mean."

He did. But he refused to admit it. "No, I don't."

He nodded and took a deep breath. "Okay, make it difficult, D.J." Rubbing a hand over his lips, he began again. "I know it took a lot of balls to move up here. More than most of us have." He waited until D.J. gave a slight nod. "I don't know if I could have done what you did."

"You couldn't."

He laughed. "Maybe. But now that you are here, it doesn't matter anymore."

"What doesn't matter anymore?"

The pause was longer. He looked to D.J. and waited until the time was right. "Who you were. What matters is who you are now. And who you will be."

"I don't know what you are talking about."

He measured him. "What I'm talking about is that you came here and laid low in every way possible. In school. After school. You hardly said a word until you got on the track. Then you let your feet do the talking." Focusing on him, he continued. "I won't ever be a brain surgeon, but I know what I know. You have more talent than anyone I've ever seen." He smiled. "Even me. And that is damn hard to admit. But I watch you run and it is as close to perfection as my mom's pork chops. Anyways, I'm trying to say that I'm proud to know you.

Proud to be your friend. And I can't wait to see what you will do today."

He studied him and asked the question. "And just what is that?"

Jimbo shook his head as if it was obvious. "To run your ass off and win State. Do I have to spell it out?"

"You can't spell."

Jimbo laughed aloud. "I take back what I said. Maybe they never should have let you out of Chicago in the first place."

He responded slowly. Then smiled. "Jimbo, I'm glad they did."

***

As the van pulled into the parking lot, silence reigned. Each competitor took in the view of the stadium holding their fate. Jimbo had been there before; qualifying the previous year with results at State that bordered on failure. Finishing in the bottom third of each event, he returned to the venue that had been nothing short of cruel. For the others it was a chance at greatness that was both intoxicating as well as nerve-racking. The van circled near the gates and slowed when it reached its destination. When at full stop, the athletes stood in unison.

Coach Heck did the same. "Men, the end of a long season starts here. You should all be proud you have made it this far. Not many do." He pointed to the track. "Those grounds hold your future. It is time to impose your will on those you compete against. Reject any nerves you might feel, instead gather your inner strength and do what you do. Compete. Do it to your best ability and we will all go home satisfied." He smiled. "I'm proud of all of you. Mac is too." He paused. "Now let's get this done."

Jimbo whooped at the words. Lee smiled. D.J. simply lifted his gear and moved ahead. He was ready and words were merely unnecessary props. Slinging his equipment over his shoulder, he chose the moment to speak what was on his mind. "Guys, it's time to go to war."

Then he pushed past them and headed out the door.

***

The threesome set up camp near the south corner of the stands. Hiding from unwanted sunlight, they collected their thoughts and focused on their singular needs. Murmured wishes passed between them, but each athlete was now ultimately alone. When they lined up against opponents, there was no one to lessen their challenge; it was time to stand and deliver.

D.J. opened the backpack and studied his essentials. He spread them on a towel and organized them according to needs. Fluids. Energy bars. Spare socks. Cool weather gear. Then he hit on the most important of his belongings. His racing shoes. He had so far raced in shoes trimmed in weight and support. They had fared well but he wanted more. He wanted an edge.

He slipped out what he needed to see: Mac's spikes from yesteryear. The shoes that infatuated him since the first time he held them in his hands. His fingers smoothed the aged leather gracing the shoes. Next, the three iconic Adidas stripes decorating the exterior. Even the spikes on the bottom were still intact. In an act of courage, midseason he slipped them onto his feet. The moment was surreal as much as memorable; the fit was perfect. He wiggled his toes within and as if on cue, the shoes responded. His next move was the acid test. A trial run was in order where he would test them on the track under a setting sun. There with new shoelaces woven in, he secured them and admired the hug of the leather trappings. Standing tall and pivoting, the shoe held firm against the surface. Time would tell if he was only wishing or if instincts would hold true. He approached the track and like an impatient colt, pawed at the ground. Setting his watch, he readied to time each lap. He was nothing but astounded by the results when each lap surpassed the next. He estimated at the bare minimum a full second pared from his usual effort. After four single lap experiments, he was convinced of their merit.

The shoes were ready for a return to action.

Now, a month later, a simple stroke of the leather provided comfort; a grounded sensation not obtainable any other way. He scanned the nearby competitors and was secure his secret was intact. As a confident smile crossed his face, he tucked the spikes inside of his backpack.

In time, they would be unleashed.

***

Saturday was the second day of competition. Even with a portion of heats completed the night before, the excitement of the crowd was palpable. Given their mid-school status, the threesome had only one shot at their event. No heats or paring down of combatants, just entry into the finals. Jimbo had already begun his preparation and was ready to start throwing. Discus first, then shot later. D.J. next, then Lee. They had not conversed much; each was lost in their own thoughts.

D.J. caught site of Lee talking to Andy. The moment was surreal; identical faces, one in street clothes and the other in his gear. He smiled but at the same time a tinge of anguish arose. He would never have a brother to share moments like they did. Never a sibling to lift you when down or celebrate the joys. Those he was destined to experience on his own.

It was the way it was.

Then a voice. His name being called. He peered into the blinding sunshine. Then shielding his eyes, he made out a shape. A man. Bigger than the others around him. Somehow out of place even though a public event. He blinked until it registered. His father. He stood and walked toward him. The distance was under fifty yards but it might as well have been a mile. Each step was tentative as if on rocky soil filled with landmines. His heartbeat escalated and his mind swirled. When he reached the fence, he questioned. "Dad?"

The word just came out. One he had not used in years. Either accepted or unacknowledged, he wasn't sure. The figure nodded.

"D.J., I wasn't sure you could hear me."

Not hear a voice that echoed in his dreams? One he alternately missed and hated most of his life? He ignored the inner turmoil and approached the fence. "What are you doing here?" The smile on his face revealed the man was more than welcome. Even more than that, there was a sensation, a peculiar feeling he had not experienced in years. Unfamiliar, he questioned it until recognition. Happiness with a trace of love. His head churned.

His father didn't seem to notice his confusion. "C'mon D.J.," he replied, "don't ask a question like that. I came to see you run." He paused. "I should have been at all your races but..." The statement tailed off into oblivion.

D.J. shrugged. "It's okay. You're here now. That's what matters."

The man grasped the fence and white appeared in his knuckles. Then he released the pressure. "I'm here, D.J. And I can't wait to see you race." He looked to the track. "This place is amazing. I'm nervous just watching."

"No reason to be nervous," he said. "I got this."

He laughed. Then nodded. "D.J., just do me one favor."

"What is that?"

He narrowed his eyes. "Kick ass."

He laughed. "Any in particular?"

"All of them."

He smiled but did not reply.

***

The meet marched on. He alternated from small talk with Lee and Andy and kept a distant eye on Jimbo. Coach Heck stayed in the periphery but was there if needed. He added a calming influence but was aware D.J. was not his stallion to ride. He had purposely kept an arm's length from Mac's territory of the distance runners. What he did provide was a watchful monitoring on the timing of the meet and kept a running countdown until there was forty-five minutes before his race. It was only then the game ramped to greater heights. Coach Heck gave no racing advice. He didn't need to because Mac had provided a meaningful send-off: *A championship race is unlike all others. It is not about the time. Not about breaking records. It is solely about winning. But this race may be different. Dalton is the returning champion and he has talked about breaking the state record more than once. One does not obtain that by running in the pack. I suspect that due to nerves, a jittery runner or two will take it out hard. That may span the first lap. Dalton will let them lead and tuck in close behind. Another runner may then challenge the field and keep the pace alive. If this happens, it will play into Dalton's hands. He is clearly the fastest in the race, at least according to the newspapers. By lap three Dalton will feel the need to break free and begin his assault on the field. The intoxication of setting a record will draw him in. Seduce him like an irresistible temptress. Then the field will stretch. But you, D.J., you have the ability to respond and glue yourself to his heels. Put the rope around his torso and let him drag you with him. You will feel the effort but you can manage it. Absorb it. In turn you will get Dalton's attention. You will have a place in his head. But he may not worry. Not yet. Not until the bell lap when you attach yourself like a leach to his backside. Then it is no longer a test against a clock. Then time will be meaningless. It will be a test of wills. Yours and his. A test of who is willing to withstand more pain. To suck it in and embrace it. That is a lonely moment. But it is a moment to use all that has formed you. All that you are made of. It will be up to you to bare your soul.*

Bare your soul. The words reverberated as he began his warmup. He customarily jogged a slow mile to start the engine. Beginning his routine, he was calm. He had no reason to be otherwise. He was an unknown. He had won little. Against Dalton Scarie, the defending champion and odds-on favorite, he and the rest of the field were decided underdogs. The smart money was only on how fast Dalton would run. Whether he would break the state record. Not would he win. That was a given. The thoughts strengthened him. He bent down and laced his spikes. Mac's spikes. Like a streetcorner addict preparing his next shot, the methodical ritual was painstakingly completed. Standing tall, he took a deep breath and cleared the system.

He was nearing ready.

The warmup track was outside the stadium. A simple quarter mile designated more for gym class than competition. The rest of the field entertained the same needs and each kept to themselves. D.J. did the same. Focus turned inward. No thoughts of sunshine, clouds or wind. Rather it was self-check time. Bowel. Bladder. Thirst. Then muscles from high to low. Systems checked, he continued the obligatory laps and escalated the effort. He had traveled many miles to get here. Encountered hurdles and eclipsed them. Made friends, some transient, but others to span a lifetime. Most young, some surprisingly old. Mac. He wished he was here, but he wasn't. He sealed the negativity and redirected the thoughts.

He was at State.

"Dude, good luck."

He knew the voice. The peculiar blend of camaraderie layered with derision. Dalton. He looked up and acknowledged him. An obligatory response arose. "Same."

Dalton assessed him as expected. He wasn't done yet. "Nice day. I hope that breeze stays away though. The winds can be strong here."

Let the head games begin, he thought. "Yup." That was it. Less was more. Never let them in your head, Mac taught. Better you in theirs.

Dalton studied him. "Later, man." The non-committal tone pleased D.J. Landmines avoided, he hoped he had placed his own.

He shook out his arms and nodded.

Chapter Thirty-Seven

He fumed. Poking at the device he was getting nowhere. He had never been computer literate and the iPad confused him. "Damn technology!" he snorted. When he failed again, he admitted defeat. Time was short and he hit the call button to summon the nurse. When asked of his needs, he was decidedly brusque. "I shit myself. All over. Please hurry."

His efforts were rewarded when she appeared within a minute. With an accepting look, she pampered his ego. "Those things happen, Mr. McKinley."

He nodded. "I'm sure they do. But not today." Her confusion was obvious. "My undershorts are fine. It's this damn computer that I can't get to work." Again, the look. "D.J. said he showed you how to use it." She raised her eyebrows. "He's running at the state track meet right now and he said I could watch him!" he explained. He looked at her, pleadingly. "Please, can you help?"

She sat next to him and smiled. "Yes. Give me the iPad." He complied and she continued. "Mr. McKinley, do you remember the log-on? I think I have it at my desk." He was confused but then reached to the bedside dresser and gave her a slip of paper. She read it. "MacAttack?" He shrugged as she entered it. Then she clicked a few more times before handing the device back to him.

He was astounded. It was as if he was there. Commentary sounded and he watched a relay as it commenced. He looked to her with sincerity. "I can't thank you enough."

She stood and responded. "No, you can't. But please, Mr. McKinley, don't do this again. Just be honest and I'll be happy to help."

He was sheepish. "I'm sorry. I won't call you again." He dropped his head. "Unless I really do shit the bed. Then you'll be the first to know."

She sighed and left as quickly as she had arrived.

He was transfixed. The events unfolded before him as if he was there. The stands. The track. The athletes. The relay finished and the announcer informed of the upcoming events. The two-hundred meters was next. Then the mile. Three divisions, with D.J.'s the second to take place. His heartbeat quickened and he blew out a stream of air as he had done a thousand times in racing days. Slow the heart. Calm the mind. The mantra was repeated as if he was nearing competition. He wasn't, but he was. He was there.

The camera scanned the track. The stands were filled and the excitement transferred through the screen. A two-hundred meter heat was lining up as each competitor approached the starting blocks. Lining six wide with the inside and outside lane vacant, they were summoned to the blocks. The starting gun startled him as the sprinters exploded from their crouches. They crashed down their lanes and by the turn the previously smooth line of runners turned jagged. The sprinter in the third lane cruised to the lead and crossed the finish line comfortably ahead. Waving to the crowd, his place in the final had been secured.

Mac's heartbeat stabilized. This was the day. The day he should have been there guiding the runners. Alleviating their stress and concerns. But instead he was an old man confined to a hospital bed, a prisoner to his surroundings. The truth stung. He may have many years to live, but his decline was real. Thinking of Mona, his spirits dimmed. She was gone. Undoubtedly in a better place, but still gone from this world. He felt useless. Pathetic. He looked out the window and longed for the past. To a time he was young and powerful and the earth was simply a nuisance under his feet. He never knew it then, but all those years ago he had the world at his fingertips.

He looked out the window and longed to escape.

***

A shrill whistle sounded after the small school sixteen-hundred final. He stepped lightly within the parade of runners as the next division entered the stadium. They walked silently toward the starting line. All were lean. Whippet-thin. But in their sinew, there was no lack of strength. In fact, it was the opposite. The bodies were molded by countless miles and sweat. Power resonated from every pore, all of them just waiting to explode.

They were milers.

Each name was announced and a hand was raised in acknowledgement. Dalton's pronouncement received the loudest response from the crowd. D.J. ignored the acclaim and waited for his own to be called. When it was, he stepped forward. *DuJuan Johnson.* He rarely went by his full name but today he had no qualms. He was proud of who he was and deserved to be there as much as anyone else. Maybe even more.

He rolled his neck and a series of vertebrae popped in unison. Some of the runners he recognized by face. The red-haired runner, McGuire. The runner in the yellow jersey. And of course, Dalton Scarie. It seemed as if the sun shined brighter around him; as if his straw-colored hair absorbed the rays more than anyone else. Dalton's presence was impossible to avoid. But he was not afraid. Rather, he was alive. And ready.

***

Mac stiffened in bed and was glued to the screen. D.J. took a series of stride-outs down the track. He withheld coaching critique: too fast, too slow, too long. He swallowed and let the boy be free. It was his time, his turn at grasping the brass ring. He accepted he was only a distant observer. Yet, his breaths were shallow, sharp and ultimately unfulfilling. He was riveted on the event as it unfurled. Each runner approached the line as his name was recited, a hand raised in acknowledgment. Dalton stepped forward and reveled in the greeting; smiling and waving triumphantly to the adoring crowd. Mac trained his eyes on D.J.'s response. Hands on hips, he appeared unconcerned at the crowd's reaction. Mac followed his eyes and was pleased when a small sidelong glance was exhibited. "Yes, D.J.!" he said aloud. The boy was annoyed. Tired of the fuss and attention payed to his competitor. Yet, his look said more than that. *Just wait*, it said.

He couldn't have been more pleased.

The tickertape at the bottom of the screen announced his given name. *DuJuan.* Mac scarcely remembered the birthname and it took him a moment to recognize this version. "That's fine, D.J. Now you are under the radar even more." He smiled. "A fine place to be." Then he squinted harder at the screen. His right index finger reached and touched the object of interest.

The shoes on D.J.'s feet. Red. Leather. With three stripes. Showing age but bearing a sturdiness scarcely calculable. His shoes. The ones that carried him all those years ago. He watched the boy bend down and tug at the laces one last time, securing them for the ride. Touching the stripes, he said words that Mac could not decipher. He patted the shoes and stood upright.

Mac could hardly breathe.

***

D.J. took a deep breath but oxygen was suddenly scarce. He closed his eyes and willed his heartbeat to slow. When accomplished, he opened them and studied his spikes. Mac's spikes. Racing shoes filled with molecules of sweat and blood from a bygone era. He clenched and unclenched his hands as he readied for the start. He stepped forward to the curved line and stood statuesque, waiting for release.

The gun sounded.

The early tactics had been contemplated many times over. Top four. He wanted top four. He did not want to lead nor be rendered impotent deep within the pack. From his outside position, he accelerated into the amoeba-like creature and maneuvered within. Both accepting and delivering elbows and knees, he was able to land in the third-place position. *Perfect,* Mac's voice whispered in his ear. There he was able to stay out of harm's way and avoid the mass of legs gnashing in competitive confusion. He looked toward the leader as the red-haired runner towed the field. *Fool's gold,* Mac had called the thrill of leading this early. A position where vanity ruled over precedence. Leaders rarely survived in the long haul. *Except for Prefontaine,* Mac said, *but he was crazy. A pain in the ass too.* Frontrunners were mutations, runners to admire but not mimic. For now, the third position was more than comfortable.

***

Mac analyzed the hierarchy of the field. He broke down the twelve runners into three groups. The hangers-on, the bulldogs and the contenders. The four hangers-on had no chance; they had achieved more than expected by simply qualifying for the meet. For them the early effort was a strain; arms working and jaws clenched, they would do their best but fall short. He counted three runners in the bulldog group; runners that would battle to stay with the lead pack as long as they could. Yet, ultimately they simply lacked the firepower and the necessary body and mind carved from stone. That left five runners in the mix. Three of them he didn't know but calculated they had garnered the requisite miles to pare their bodies to elite status. More than that, they were not fazed by the surroundings. A victory might be an upset, but they were ready for the battle. D.J. and Dalton were the final two. Both used the oiled steel in their legs to glide through the backstretch of the first lap. It was subjective, but both passed the eye test; power and grace granted by heaven but sharpened on earth. "Stay focused, D.J." he implored. "Trust yourself."

Nothing else would do.

***

He rounded the far curve of the first lap. The effort was easy and he calculated he was running a few ticks over sixty seconds. Impulse demanded he soon take the lead but common sense won out. *Focus*, Mac whispered in his ear. *Trust your training.* He buried the desire and stayed secure in the third spot with Dalton firmly on his heels. He fought the craving to look back but did not. He was there. He could feel him. Hear him. Approaching the crowd, the call of Dalton's name insured he was close by. It was only a matter of when he would make his move. *Too early*, D.J. thought. *But be ready.*

"Sixty-two, sixty-three," called the timer as they crossed the lap marker. It was quick but he was comfortable. Strong. In control. Maintaining his position, his reserves had barely been tapped. McGuire continued to lead, followed closely behind by a shorter runner. They towed the field as they neared the turn. He could nearly hear Mac's voice. *Relax yet don't. The great ones let their body do the work while their mind rests. They use muscle memory while focusing on the moment. Take it all in. Play the chess game and expect the unexpected. Think like a surgeon, D.J. Be ready to cut when the time is right.* He barely knew what Mac meant the first time he heard it. But after visualizing the race a hundred times, now he did.

He was not afraid.

***

Mac could barely watch yet was glued to the screen. After one lap, D.J. had punched all the right buttons. He had avoided early physical contact and placed himself well. There was enough space to stride while proximity with the leaders was maintained. Dalton's nonchalance at the start had surprised him but he had seen the boy run before. His talent was indisputable and it was likely to surface at any time. Mac worried he had been too secure in his evaluation of Dalton's mindset and subsequent tactics. So far, he appeared unfazed and content to tuck in behind the others. He certainly had the speed to run a conservative race before exploding the last lap and win going away. Even D.J. would have a hard time matching his finishing speed. But Mac had seen ego before. He had been there himself. It could drive you or destroy you. Sometimes even both within the same race.

Then he gasped as a runner went down. Already on the backstretch of the second lap, the camera was far from the intimacy of the action. He strained to see the fallen runner. "Please God, no," he said aloud. The pack righted itself and Mac held his breath. The red-haired runner was still leading. In second was Dalton. A step behind was D.J. He had no idea what had occurred but disaster had been avoided. He was still in the race.

He grasped the iPad harder.

***

D.J. was both relieved and angry. As far as he could tell, the second-place runner had clipped the leader's heels and pitched forward. McGuire had stayed upright even as the trailing runner tumbled to the track. D.J. narrowly avoided the collision by swinging wide into the second lane. As the gap opened, Dalton preyed on the mishap and filled the open position. D.J. attempted to shoehorn himself into second but relinquished the battle when Dalton was having none of it.

"Shit," he said as he accepted his position. The fourth-place runner was right behind but he was not a primary concern. The mishap had given Dalton an unexpected opportunity to regain a gateway to the front. Entering the far turn of the second lap, D.J. willed the surge of stress-induced hormones from his system. The unexpected event increased his pulse but he was still far under his red-line. Better yet he was still standing. Still in contact. And far better than the fallen runner with dreams crushed by a single tangle of strides.

He focused on the runners ahead.

***

"Are you okay, Mr. McKinley? Your blood pressure and heart rate have been spiking."

He looked to the nurse before returning to the screen. "I'm fine. I'm watching a race. Now, please!"

She shook her head. "You need to calm down. If you can't, I'll have to take the computer away. Seriously."

He almost growled but thought better of it. "Fine. Yes. Now please, just let me finish this."

She clucked something but he didn't even hear it. He had more important things to do. He had missed a few strides but nothing had changed. The end of the second lap was one of maintenance. It was where runners took stock of their bodies and began to sense what lie ahead. That they were over their head or had a chance at greater glory. If the pace was too bold, some would pull back knowing they may not reach the finish line unless they slowed. In that, the pack lengthened to fifteen yards with those remaining in contact assessing their chances. Mac did the same. The redhaired runner was a pace machine and Mac estimated the second lap was only a tick more than the first. The first three runners appeared unfazed by the fall and Mac was proud of D.J. Understanding the rebound effect of wanting to attack, he had refrained and was content to tuck himself into contention. At two minutes and five seconds, the trio crossed the halfway point nearly in unison. That was the fastest D.J. had ever hit the two-lap marker but Mac liked what he saw. He was still strong. Relaxed. And thoroughly on his game.

Watching his old red spikes eat the track's surface, memories flooded. To the time he first saw them on a store wall rack. Then slipping them on as they cradled his feet. *Ostrich leather*, an uninformed clerk told him. Yet he believed him. They would lead him to greatness. Maybe even the Olympics. He paid for them with money intended for rent. But rent could wait.

Immortality beckoned.

***

The time surprised him. Two-oh-five. Sweat crawled down the back of his neck as a sliver of doubt entered. But this was no time to be meek. He had survived his whole life by living on the edge. By just getting by. No dreams. Only pain and anger. Rejection and abandonment. Many times more than he could bear. But now it was time. His time. No longer simply existing. No longer would he accept being overlooked. Being average. Being one of the crowd, milling on a city street. This time he would go for it. *Fuck it,* he thought.

The trio rounded the near turn of the third lap and he made a move. Catching the two runners in front of him unprepared, he flew down the backstretch and took a five-yard lead. Even from the distance, he heard a ripple from the crowd. The noise only bolstered his resolve as he hit the next turn. Less than six-hundred meters.

He could do that in his sleep.

***

His jaw dropped. Words choked in his throat. It was too early. D.J. had given into impulse for some godforsaken reason. He had gone all-in far too soon. Mac squeezed his hands together as D.J. rounded the turn and approached the end of the third lap. He had yards on the field and the crowd roared at his move. Mac shook his head, sure of the final fate.

Then he stopped, enraptured by the screen.

Dalton responded with a lightning bolt of his own. In a sum of ten strides, he passed D.J. The crowd roared approval at the reigning champion's statement and in unison rose to their feet. "Three oh-five, three oh-six", Mac recited breathlessly as the pair ran as if possessed. Mac blinked in disbelief as the red-haired runner was only steps behind, oblivious to the effort being expended.

One lap to go was more than he could bear to watch.

***

D.J. heard the roar of the crowd as Dalton flew by like he was standing still. It was clear he had stolen the favorite's thunder and it rankled him to his core. In an immediate reaction, the defending champion swooped in and reclaimed the lead. D.J. recognized that physically Dalton felt good. Jacked up. Omnipotent. He likely believed he would carry on and run away with the title. D.J. knew there was a chance he was exactly right. But he also knew he was not done yet. The surges tapped both runner's reserves but he remained calm. He had played pace games all spring and surges were now commonplace. He tucked in behind Dalton and worked to maintain. His breath came harder. Faster. A subtle rasp appeared in his trachea and he was nearing maximum. He approached the near turn and questioned his rash decision.

Then he heard it.

His name. "D.J., D.J.!" a small group chanted in unison. The boisterous crowd edged toward the fence and pounded on the links. "Gooooo, D.J.!" A quick glance revealed the faces. The freshman: Bill, Ed and Till. Lee. Andy. Jimbo. And another within the midst with both fists clenched and arms raised to the sky. His father. He had forgotten he was even there. But the visceral reaction to the sight was cellular. A shot of fresh adrenaline reached his bloodstream at the nick of time. The jolt refreshed him and he attached himself to Dalton. They entered the turn and shouts of the crowd echoed in the stadium. At this intensity, each runner's world was hardening. Oxygen was becoming difficult to find and thoughts turned inward. Legs quivered as lungs screamed for air. They were all feeling the pain of the race and no runner was left unscathed. It was only a matter of who was hurting worse and who could absorb even more.

D.J. prepared himself for impact. He bandied himself as a long closer. Dalton was an elite finisher. To have any chance he needed to take the sting out of his kick. And that began now. Just as the curve ended and the backstretch beckoned, he pounced. Elongating his stride, he let his talent loose. The accompanying pain was just a nuisance as he accomplished his task. Dalton had been caught off guard and from the second lane, D.J. sealed him off with his left shoulder. Rather than risk fouling or even worse, a dual collision, he backed off into the second position. D.J. edged ahead and was now the pursued. Dalton's hot breath was audible as they hit the midpoint of the final lap. Two hundred and twenty yards to go before the finish. Only a pittance in the distance world, but enough yardage to scar one's soul. But he wore a badge of scars. Life's pain darkening him; in some ways hardening his world but in other ways providing strength. He was callused and this pain could never equal what he had been through. He drove ahead and waited for Dalton's counterattack. He was sure it was coming. The final straightaway would be a test he had never experienced before.

In that he was wrong. In looking ahead, he lost sight of the events behind. Dalton had regrouped and unleashed an unexpected torrent. D.J. looked to his right as the runner steamrolled past him. Dalton was on the balls of his feet and his tan skin glistened in the sun. D.J.'s unpreparedness allowed his opponent to return the favor of forcing D.J. to chop his stride. Ungainly and losing momentum, he cursed under his breath. As his stride weakened, it was all he could do to hang on. A hidden part of him rose. A flicker of doubt entered his veins and flowed toward his heart. From there it was propelled through his body at a time he could ill afford. He squeezed his eyes and battled self-doubt. A thought jarred his consciousness, *not like this*, it said, *not again*.

He eyes widened.

***

Mac dizzied. The last lap had been a whirlwind. First, Dalton striking as the crowd roared approval. Then D.J. drawing blood as he surprised the leader with a move honed over months of training. But Dalton's resolve and response was just as enthralling. He attacked hard and true when his mettle was tested. The runner was skilled beyond his years and he deserved all he had achieved. With his counterattack, Mac's heart sank.

Runner's only have so many moves in their arsenal and D.J. had expended an inordinate amount of energy. The well was nearing dry and Mac expected the worst. Entering the last turn, the visible sag of D.J.'s body was evident. Mac closed his eyes and remembered. Of the hopelessness of being a beaten athlete. The loneliness of leaving blood on the track and knowing one would fall short. He remembered the ultimate failure.

Quitting.

Anger arose. A fire hidden for decades. It roared white hot and nipped at his face. He clenched his fists and mouthed words. "Not like this," he called. Then louder. "Not again." He focused on D.J. and growled a guttural demand. "Go." He had never been so enraptured in a moment and it was as if his body rose from the bed. The screen became a dreamworld of clouded dimensions.

Then in an instant, D.J.'s body lengthened and he maintained pace. He stayed on Dalton's heels as the antiquated Adidas kept pace. The crowd's spastic intensity bathed the action in insanity. They prepared for a finish of the ages, a scant one-hundred yards ahead.

Dalton knew it was coming. He refused to look back and pumped his arms furiously to propel forward. Lightheaded, Mac watched D.J. do the same. He couldn't speak, only whisper. "More, D.J.," he said. "It's time." D.J. did as he was told. Flailing his arms, he battled to keep form. Twelve inches behind, then six. In two more strides, he drew even. The runners were joined at the hips and neither relented. Neither will could be broken. D.J. dug harder as the finish line only taunted the combatants. "Run through the line," Mac intoned as a crescendo sounded. "Please, D.J."

With that D.J. threw his chest forward just as Dalton's toe stubbed the track. Both crashed toward the surface, as D.J.'s chest crested the unforgiving line. Heaving on the track, finish line attendants scurried to help the warriors. Arms waved as pandemonium ensued. Mac's vision clouded as results flashed on the screen. A dream had been obtained and a prayer answered.

He looked out the window at a tree branch swaying. As a

tiny redbird flew in to seek perch, the sight blinded him. With pounding heart, he smiled and embraced the unexpected brilliance of the light.

Chapter Thirty-Eight

He scarcely remembered the last two-hundred meters. They were a blur and it was only Lee, Andy and Jimbo's breathless recap that brought back the moment. He had no right to finish as he did. He didn't know how he had completed the race but instinct had won out. He was dead on his feet for the last half-lap but that was not uncommon. It was what milers did. Once they toe the line, the deal with the devil is made. He was no different than the others.

The gold medal around his neck said otherwise. The medallion and a new state record of four minutes and three seconds was his reward. Dalton had been gracious and the two embraced on the victory stand. D.J. drew him to the top of the podium where they raised arms and locked hands in a salute to the battle. The crowd gave a standing ovation and D.J. shivered at the attention. When it ended, he pointed to his dad who returned the salute.

Stepping down, he accepted the requisite congratulations and backslapping from supporters. Lee had achieved a personal best of just over nine minutes and forty seconds while Jimbo had garnered a gold and silver himself. Coach Heck was overcome by the results and tears filled his eyes. D.J. longed to talk to Mac, but given his disdain for the phone, he didn't even try. He hoped he had watched but tomorrow's visit would reconcile all. D.J. smiled at the thought.

But one thing remained.

The stadium had emptied and his van was waiting. He apologized but made an excuse that he had forgotten some clothing inside the track. He lobbied for a minute and promised he would be right back. The group didn't bat an eye as excited chatter filled the vehicle. He jogged to the entry gate and nodded to those milling about as he head toward his destination. Reaching it, he knelt as if at an altar.

The white line was silent. Then from inside his warm-up, he withdrew his parcel. The red spikes were still moist with sweat and blood. They had done what they were summoned for and deserved to rest. He placed the toe of the left shoe just behind the line. Then he did the same to the right. The laces were frayed but still intact and he tucked them inside. He ground each forefoot into the track as if preparing them for flight. Touching the three stripes, he said his goodbye. They had performed as intended and could do no more.

Standing over the shoes, he looked above to the reddened hue lining the approaching nightfall. Closing his eyes, his shadow loomed in the dying light of the day.

Paul C. Maurer is:
Husband. Father. Brother. Uncle. Chiropractor.
Chicken farmer. Horseman. Cyclist. Writer
Lifelong runner.

Enjoy *The Unforgiving Line*